THAT'S THE WAY IT GOES

**THE
GRINDA**

READ X RAP COLLECTION

THAT'S THE WAY IT GOES

ISBN 978-1-66787-729-7 (Print)
ISBN 978-1-66787-730-3 (eBook)

MIND-GRIND
PUBLISHING

DELUXE BONUS PAGE!!!

THAT'S THE WAY IT GOES
THE RAP ALBUM

FREE TO LISTEN ON SITE OR PURCHASE TO OWN!!!
SIMPLY SCAN THE QR CODE BELOW!!!

COURTESY OF ONE-WORLD RECORDS

READ X RAP

SCAN TO RAP ALBUM

ACKNOWLEDGEMENTS

My mind has always been a curious one. Needing to know the answers to the multitude of questions I seem to never have a shortage of is still present today. But when I was a child, my imagination and my curiosity were bosom buddies, aiding one another to help me understand myself and life in general. I would like to acknowledge my English Teacher Ellen O'Brien, who was a teacher at Shalom High School, the High School I graduated from. What makes Shalom High School such a blessing to me? It was funded by organizations and private donors to support troubled teens like me when I was young. In fact, it was my last chance to receive an education because I was kicked out of the Milwaukee Public School (MPS) system and the alternative school programs due to gang related activities and a yet to be opened young mind.

But my teacher Ellen saw something in me in the 9th grade. She had me do writing assignments and marveled at my ability to write very descriptive stories from either my life or my imaginings. She told me I could be a writer. No one had ever told me I could be anything remotely in my life before, so to have someone as esteemed as a teacher with a master's degree in English and Creative Writing tell me I could be something professional in the real world meant the world to me. This kindhearted White woman told me something no other Black person had ever expressed to me, and this is one of the many reasons why I could never be racist toward anyone. She dispelled any myths about all Whites being racist. I will always acknowledge you as my first muse and spark of inspiration that made it comfortable for me to create literature. I love your human being and I know many young poor Black boys and girls have also benefitted from you as well.

I will acknowledge other beneficial people in my life as I publish more books, but I would like to dedicate this one to Shalom High School—my English teacher Ellen O'Brien, and the other incredible staff who worked and still work there. Love Anthony Bradford aka Tony!

PROLOGUE

"Some hustle for success while others hustle to feed
their starving children. Either way, none of the things
you want will ever come to you if you don't get out there
and grind to get it. The only thing left to answer:
Is your hustle worth its consequence?"
—AJ THE GRINDA

When I was a kid growing up in the "53206" zip code of Milwaukee, nobody told me I lived in the poorest part of the city, all I knew was that my mama had to raise her three children there. Now don't get me wrong, I knew my neighborhood was raggedy, but I didn't know it was the worst one in the state of Wisconsin. More arrests happen in my zip code than in any other one in the state. Our city has around 2,100 police officers patrolling a population of almost 600,000 residents, and almost half reside in my zip code.

But why is it like that? Why is the area I live in so broke? I mean, as you grow older, these are the questions that start to form in your head. Then when you get old enough to fully understand the answers—it's a hard pill to swallow.

When you're young, you don't know that there are White people all around the world who hate you because you're a Black person. In your predominately Black neighborhood, you've never had to witness those things. The White people I'm familiar with who live in the hood are no different than anybody else there. In fact, almost every White person I ever met living in my hood was legit. I guess that's why the truth of why my part of town is so destitute makes it hard for me to stomach.

First off, you've got to understand more about politics. Most of us (Black folks in the hood) while watching a television show change the channel quick as hell when it's interrupted by politicians. Nobody I know (and I know a lot of people) watches political news channels like CNN or Fox News because it's boring and (yawn out loud) not very exciting. But to understand the truth—you've got to go to the source.

No, it's not necessary to remember politicians by their names (although knowing their name and views will benefit you), but you do have to understand why they're here. A politician is a person who is active in party politics—that means they strive for political positions in our United States Federal and State governments. They are voted into those positions by people who feel he/she will represent their political interests and views. In return for their paid placement somewhere on the political pyramid, the politician acts as a powerful voice (through legislation, by being on powerful boards and committees, and so forth ... to make bills for future laws or take part in other political acts to appease their backers) for the constituents who voted him/her into that position of power. And believe me, it is a position of power because they shape our entire society.

Currently, the two main political parties with the most campaign money in North America are: The Democratic Party and The

Republican Party. The Democratic Party was founded in Washington, DC, in 1828, and the Republican Party was founded in Ripon, WI, in 1854. Over the years, lower-income Black people have found one reason or another to join one of these parties in the hopes that doing so will make their lives better.

When I began to understand more of this, some of the truth began to expose itself enough to raise a few questions like: Could life be better than this? Whose life is better? And more importantly: How can I make my life better?

Over the years, I found out that a majority of the ethnic and White middle-class workers in America vote Democrat, and, adversely, a large majority of Whites who don't interact with ethnic groups vote Republican. Now, there are some Blacks—whose ancestors since the abolishment of slavery proudly voted as a member of the Republican Party (the party of Lincoln)—who believe firmly in the policies their party expresses as the best for the country, but a lot of Blacks who vote Democrat, look at which party White supremacists join (Republican) and consider the entire party possessed by satanic evil.

So, now one should be asking: Why is that so important? It's important because Blacks are and will always be a minority in this majority White country. Since the end of slavery, racist Whites have voiced their dismay and discontent of dissolving the practice by forming extremist factions of their political party, domestic terrorist hate groups, and race-based interactive social media forums to grow racist followings using cheap grassroot strategies and pricey media marketing tools to spread their bigoted propaganda. Their message is simple: WE ONLY WANT TO LIVE AROUND OUR OWN RACE—who cares if it violates the Federal Fair Housing Act (Title VIII of the Civil Rights Act of 1968).

To avoid the influx of poor Blacks (their destitution originating from the descendants of a large portion of slaves who weren't given proper education or reparations to jump-start their lives and break the poverty cycles) who were moving into their predominately White communities, many less racially tolerant Whites left the inner cities and fled to suburban areas and cities where they knew low-income Blacks couldn't afford to live. Hence, in the very beginning of the migration of poor Black people to find homes throughout the United States, they were given pocketed areas (government-created housing projects and low-valued real estate) by politicians to live in throughout designated (racially friendly) cities and towns.

As more financially suffering Blacks who were forced to survive off the meager supplements of their government to get by wound up turning to illegal activities in those tightly confined areas, the crime rate also rose. In its early stages, low-income Black sons/daughters of uneducated slaves who defined themselves as their ghetto's first hustlers did it to grow and prosper above their categorized and marginalized expectations.

The long, sought-after dream to achieve wealth by a hustler—whether by pimping and prostituting, selling bootleg liquor, running numbers, selling illegal drugs of that era, or anything else that created an underground black market—has always been met with the negative stigma of them (Black hustlers) being the perpetrators of the plight of their community. When in fact, the ghetto was a poor, plighted place way before any illegal markets ever arrived.

So, that's how I saw the truth of my zip code and why it's labeled the worst place to live in the state. The low-valued home and rental properties were remnants of a White middle-class society that migrated on to bigger and better things. How much better? Well, Wisconsin isn't considered one of the most segregated states in the country for nothing. Whites have utilized their groups and fortunes to create cities and suburbs that provide the best experiences and opportunities that life has to offer.

Early on, the luxuriousness and safety of most of these subdivisions were created by White sub-developers to be purchased and occupied by their own race. In the mind of a well-to-do White businessman, the best business comes from other well-to-do White people. And today too is no different, some of the most expensive places to live house hateful-minded racists who feel invaded and betrayed by the arrival of cultural and ethnic diversification there—and they show it! A Black man/woman will move to a wealthy community and be asked by a White person, "What do you do for a living?" before they'd even consider posing that same question to their White counterpart.

To make matters worse, some of those same posh communities house the negative hate groups that domestically terrorize other races of people. Who wants to put a $100,000 deposit down on a million-dollar home only to be harassed and even assaulted because they built up their wealth to live there? Who wants to deal with the negative actions of hateful-minded White people? Racism itself will always be nothing more than another profitable business product/ service within its own industry. What makes it unique is that it reaps its revenue from an industry specialized in hatemongering.

The cold truth is this: Whether you are college-educated or not, employed, self-employed, or unemployed, or went to the military or not, your Black desire to have the same advantages as Whites will always be met with adversity by "color haters" in this world. Who knows how many are out there? Millions? Billions? All I know is that oceans of blood were spilled all over this country by Black slaves, civil rights advocates, and activists of all races to have the federal and state laws that are currently in place to help make our dreams of a better life a reality.

Everybody all around the world is hustling and grinding to make it on a planet that interacts with one another. Some hold a higher sense of pride as a hustler than others, but a cop hustling a beat ain't no different than a homie hustling in the street—mainly because everybody's got to eat. I understand why I'm in the worst zip code and how comfortably people with more money than me are living. I also know if I break my poverty cycle (a cycle existing since slavery), there is going to be a higher presence of color haters running around spewing their vileness. And depending on how I hustle, I could set myself up for more run-ins with the law or encounters with haters from my own race.

I understand it all and truly recognize that there are crafty booby traps and perilous pitfalls associated with making money in America and I can wholeheartedly say as a Black man from the worst zip code in the entire state of Wisconsin (estimated population of Milwaukee at this time of writing is a little over 596,000): THAT'S THE WAY IT GOES....

Chapter One
MY GRIND

It was a late Friday night on the north side of Milwaukee, many of the city's bars, nightclubs, and taverns were closing for the night so there was more traffic in the streets than usual. They were filled with drunken partygoers doing whatever they felt like doing, from hanging out the windows of their vehicles with their sounds bumping, all the way to purposefully swerving side to side while they drove. One group of young Black males even stopped in the middle of a busy street to bounce around inside their customized car to their new music single and flash their wads of cash out the windows. The women were just as "turned up" as the men. They yelled, screamed, and paraded their sexiness out their vehicle's windows too, making it a fun time for the young and old alike.

Most definitely, Friday and Saturday nights are eagerly awaited after a long and tiresome workweek. A stressful week of work can be easily forgotten with a bar full of liquor and the opposite sex showing they're attracted to you. To many, it's their freedom after work. Unfortunately for a small dangerous few, it's their time to get to work.

"Nigga, all I'm sayin' is we always talkin' bout how White bitches can't handle Black dick—I think the shit flipped now," TRIGGAH G told his homie MEAN-MUG while he sat shotgun and puffed on a grape-flavored cigarillo of premium marijuana.

"Bullshit. Every White chick I fuck scream like they dyin'—then they start blowin' up my phone and cyber-stalkin' a nigga," MEAN-MUG bragged while he drove his silver 1992 Chevy Caprice Classic through the north side of Milwaukee, WI.

"Ain't no White bitches fuckin' you bro. You scare White people."

"Fuck you! Why do you think it flipped?"

"Because look what happened to the niggas who got some Kardashian pussy. Lamar Odom almost lost his mind, started smokin' crack, and almost died inside a hoe house. Then Kanye West lost his mind with the Trump shit, wanting to beat up everybody over his ex-wife, and now he bi-polar. And don't forget about the other ball player Tristan Thompson—he never had a jumper to begin with, but it ain't never gone happen now," TRIGGAH G fumed with disappointment.

"Why is that fam?" MEAN-MUG asked curiously as he grabbed the weed and took a few deep pulls.

"The nigga too busy jumpin' in drunk White pussy. Watch what I tell ya, his tall ass gone be on the bench in a minute. I'm serious bro—White pussy got a new gene in it that make Black men lose they fuckin' minds now."

They both laughed as they surveyed the different hoods they were driving through. Wearing fitted basketball caps, T-shirts, "skinny" jeans, and nice pairs of Air Jordan, both men felt like they were dressed to impress the sexiest catch. Bigger in ego than their size—with them being slightly over 5 ½ feet, they're the type who'd rather shoot you than fight. Both medium brown-skinned with facial hair, there wasn't much that made these early twenty-year-old men stand out much—except for their different haircuts. MEAN-MUG always wore a small, tapered fade with a few parts on the side and TRIGGAH G had a bald head with tattoos of two shooting AK-47's on the back of his head.

Unsuccessful in their attempt to find some action, they passed their time the best way they knew how—by talking shit.

"Oh yeah, I forgot to tell you yesterday I had to smack this crazy-ass bitch who disrespected me," MEAN-MUG told his homie.

"Fa real? What fa?" TRIGGAH G asked.

"I was in front of my crib with a couple of the little homies and the bitch just magically appeared from out a nowhere and started to cap about her havin' my baby."

"You bout to be a daddy?"

"Hell naw, I told that bitch she need to reboot 'Maury' and find that nigga—cause that baby don't look like me."

"What happened after you said that?"

"She started talkin' shit about how she wished she never fucked me, and she knew I wasn't shit and blah, blah, blah. I was yawning the whole time the bitch spoke."

"Damn, I bet that made her salty as hell."

"Hell yeah, it did—salty as fuck. That's when she got all up in my face and started to push me in my chest. She even called me out my name and shit. I ain't gone lie, she made me real mad fam."

"That's when you slapped her?" TRIGGAH G asked more curious than before.

"Naw, I just pushed her back off me and told her to take her stupid-ass home, but the bitch wouldn't leave. You know the little shorties in the hood look up to me and here goes this bitch cussin' at me and tryin' to push me," MEAN-MUG explained further.

"So, you slapped the shit out her ass."

"Naw."

"Damn nigga, so far, I think she deserved her ass beat and you still didn't slap her?"

"Nope. It wasn't until she disrespected me."

"Shit, when wasn't she disrespectful?"

"It wasn't until she shouted so everybody could hear I eat booty and got a little dick," MEAN-MUG muttered angrily as he recalled what happened.

"Damn, I bet she had the shorties on the floor with tears in their eyes laughin' after that shit!" TRIGGAH G exclaimed while he laughed uncontrollably at what he was being told.

"Yeah, they all thought it was funny as hell—especially the bitch. At first, I was gone knock her ass out, but I didn't want the po-po at my door. So instead of punchin' her ass, I reached back like a Major League Baseball pitcher and slapped that bitch with every-thing I had. At first, all you heard was muthafuckas laughin' and then everything went silent when I bitch-slapped her monkey ass."

"What happened after that bro? You crazy-as-fuck dog!"

"She put her hand on her face and then the bitch went in her purse and pulled out her thumper."

"What—she had a gun? What you do nigga?"

"What you think—I upped my nine," he further explained, then he reached under his seat and pulled out a black Beretta 9mm with an extended clip.

"What was she strapped with?" TRIGGAH G asked—amused by it all.

"A punk-ass 25 automatic."

"Damn, that's all."

"That's all I'm sayin'—she could've at least had a .380. That's why I stopped fuckin' with her because she think too small fa me fam. So, we standin' there cussin' with our guns pointed at each other and then we saw a squad car roll by. I told her she need to bounce before her baby end up born in prison," MEAN-MUG continued.

"Did she leave?" TRIGGAH G asked, wanting to know more.

"Yeah, she put her slingshot back in her purse and left rubbin' the shit out her face. She better be glad that's all I did to her dumb ass."

"That's fucked up bro. I only gotta know one more thing."

"What's that?"

"Do you eat booty?"

"Fuck you, nigga," MEAN-MUG retorted with a bitter look on his face.

"I'm just sayin', we smoke gas together. I don't want no booty crumbs on the blunt fam—that's all," TRIGGAH G laughed as he hit some more of the cigarillo.

MEAN-MUG was about to respond to his homie's wisecrack when he saw a new modeled black Dodge Charger ride by with a beautiful, light-skinned female driving it. Not wanting to let her get away, he quickly made a U-turn in the street and began to catch up to her. The whole time, his homie TRIGGAH G kept his eyes alert for reckless drivers. The last thing he wanted to do was get hit by some drunk fool leaving the club.

"I gotta have that bitch bro," MEAN-MUG said seriously.

"What about dude in the passenger seat?" TRIGGAH G wanted to know.

"Fuck him."

"Fuck him then."

13

Feeling like fate was on his side, MEAN-MUG noticed the car was going to have to stop at an approaching red light on 20th and Center Street. While they were still a couple of blocks away, he turned to his homie with a smile and told him, "She mine."

By the time they pulled up on the vehicle though, instead of pulling up on the side of her to talk, MEAN-MUG reacted too slow and ran into her rear bumper. The collision wasn't hard enough to knock it off, but it was forceful enough to make a large dent and lift everyone off their seats. Already knowing what was about to happen next, MEAN-MUG got out of his car first, while TRIGGAH G stayed inside and rubbed the pain in his neck from the crash.

And true to what he felt was going to happen, both the young lady and her male passenger angrily stepped out of her car to confront him. Feeling a little sore himself, MEAN-MUG didn't want to get into a fistfight with anyone, so he smiled as he approached them. Seeing they were already on their smartphones while they walked to the back of her car, he chose to speak first.

"I'm sorry y'all. MEAN-MUG expressed regretfully as they stood near her damaged bumper.

Calming his temper down some, the man asked, "Why didn't you see us? Was you on your phone or something?"

"Stop baby. He's upset because he almost hit his face on the dashboard. I told you to wear your seatbelt, but you think I be picking," the woman explained while she rubbed his back.

"Bro, you got every right to be mad. Is that 911?" MEAN-MUG asked curiously.

"Yeah, I'm trying to tell them where we are so they can help us out. Do you have insurance?"

"Hell naw. But check this out, I want both of y'all to hang up y'all phones and put 'em by y'all feet," MEAN-MUG demanded and then pulled out his gun.

Completely terrified, the woman cried out, "Oh my god! He's robbing us!"

"Grimy motherfucker!" the livid man exclaimed.

"I told you—you got every right to be mad at me bro. Now keep the phones on and die or hang 'em up and live—it's up to y'all."

Not wanting to be shot in cold blood in the middle of the street, they both chose the latter—and abruptly hung up their phones. Then with tears in her fearful eyes and murderous rage in his, they both waited for their next set of instructions from their robber.

"Cool. I really didn't want to kill nobody today. Now kick yo phones and car keys over here to me and y'all go sit over there on the curb. Once you get there, I want y'all to close yo eyes and count to a hundred. That's all y'all gotta do and this will be over quick as a bitch," MEAN-MUG promised.

"OK, please don't shoot us. I have a little son waiting for me at home," the distraught woman begged.

"Don't beg this sorry-ass nigga! He better be glad as hell he got a gun because I'd beat his ass if he didn't," her tall and slender dread-wearing boyfriend declared with confidence.

"See, every single time I gotta go through this shit. I get some stupid-ass fool who saw all the 'Marvel's Avengers' movies and think they dumb ass a superhero. You ain't the first nigga to think he 'BLACK PANTHER' and try to say some hard-ass superhero shit to me. So, all I wanna know is this: Do you wanna die today?"

"I won't be scared if it's my time!"

"I see you watched all they cartoons too!"

"Your type is why these racist White motherfuckers despise us! I hate niggas like you!" the man shouted at him vehemently.

"Good cause I'm the nigga you love to hate," MEAN-MUG stated coldly and shot him in the upper portion of his right leg.

Surprised he got shot, the attitude of the man switched from angry he was being robbed to afraid of being shot again. He quickly reached down and grabbed his injured leg. Letting out woeful cries from his burning pain, he tried to see how bad it was but there was too much blood seeping through the wound for him to do so. As he instinctively took his weight off it, he began to lose his footing.

Seeing her man get shot, the woman began to panic from the fear of them possibly losing their lives. At first, she screamed as loud as she could, but quickly covered her mouth with her trembling hands because MEAN-MUG signaled with his gun to shut up. When she saw her boyfriend about to stumble and fall, she rushed by his side to help hold him up. Then not wanting any further trouble, she slapped his phone out of his hand and let it fall on the ground; afterwards, she tossed her phone and car keys there too. When she was finished, she kicked everything over to the carjacker and walked her wounded boyfriend to sit down on the curb.

Hearing his car honk behind him, MEAN-MUG looked over at his victims and stated, "Remember, all the way to a hundred with y'all eyes closed."

Following his orders, they both closed their eyes and began to count. Not being able to see made them feel even more afraid than before and it showed as they counted. It was the pure fear of not knowing what would happen next and not being able to see it coming that made them compliant and obedient. Neither wanted to make matters worse than they already were.

Picking up the car keys and stomping on their phones until they were inoperable, MEAN-MUG hastily ran over to the Dodge Charger and jumped inside. He then put the key in the ignition and peeled off with TRIGGAH G right behind him. While he was checking inside it as he drove, he found a blunt in the ashtray that was partially smoked. Firing it up with his lighter, he pulled out his smartphone and called up his trailing homie.

"Yeah," TRIGGAH G answered.

"I told you I wanted this bitch," MEAN-MUG gloated.

"Fa sho'. What you shoot dude fa?"

"I had to remind that nigga he ain't in Wakanda—he in Milwaukee."

The next afternoon, in his $1.5 million-dollar new mansion in the "Country Meadows" Mequon suburb, Milwaukee recording artist "LOUIE-V" was midway into his interview with "LADY SHAY" from "GET WIT IT!" e-zine and vlog. Having been signed to a multi-year contract nine months ago to "BIG DOE RECORDS," the urban hip-hop rapper was busy promoting his new single release "DOLLAZ." Only being out for nine weeks, it's currently held its placement at #1 on the Billboard HOT 100 music chart for six weeks. Sitting in his living room, he coolly spoke to the lovely interviewer while he sipped a lemon-lime soda.

Relaxing in a chair facing him, LADY SHAY spoke bluntly about the issues her vlog watchers and blog readers cared about the most, even if some of her questions would bother him. Wearing a silk designer peach-colored skirt and matching silk sleeveless white and peach patterned top, her curvy legs sexily switched positions before she began to ask some of her tougher questions. Accompanying her were her two trusted cameramen Sam and George filming the entire exclusive interview with their video cameras, several fluorescent lights, and two boom arms.

"OK LOUIE-V, we talked about your family and your passion for Hip-Hop, but I think there're some things your fans are particularly curious about. For example, some people say you're still deep in the streets, even after gaining rapid traction in the top US music charts. What do you have to tell those people?" LADY SHAY asked politely.

"Well, I'll say this: My home is where my heart's at and my heart is the streets. Yeah, I got this decent crib in the burbs and the White people over here don't trip like that, but I'm still from the streets when it's all said and done. All my family and friends are there, so I'm there a lot. Now if you talkin' bout me still hustlin' that bag—I don't have to. This music pays me well fa now," LOUIE-V answered and took a sip of his favorite lemon-lime soda.

"But you would if you had to, wouldn't you?"

"My grind done took over my mind."

"I feel you—mine too."

"We do what we have to do to get through, you know what I'm talkin' bout?"

"Sure, I do. So, me and the rest of the world would love to know why you called out MACK DADDY? He's been in the game for over twenty-five years and has made a memorable name for himself. Are you sure you want to rattle that hornet's nest? I know his style and it's not about beefing. Are you sure this is the way you want to start your career?" LADY SHAY asked him with a look of uncertainty.

"Yo, this shit between me and him ain't got nothin' to do with no record labels or album sells. He's a part of the past and I'm the future. His lyrics' dusty and so is the flow style he uses to spit it," LOUIE-V told her disdainfully.

"But he's a vet in the game and still sells a lot of albums. Why go after him?"

"It's evolution. The old must die so the newly evolved can take over. Can you imagine how the world would look if dinosaurs still roamed it. The Flintstones is some bullshit—the dinosaurs wasn't all helpful and friendly."

"Now wait a minute, there's a lot of folks out there who don't agree with younger rappers trying to put an age cap on rap. I mean no one does it in any of the other genres—only Rap. Country, Pop, Rock and Roll, R&B, and even Gospel music support older artists."

"I didn't know that. But that's beside the point, niggas like MACK DADDY used up they message. Nobody is still talkin' bout how many hoes they pimp—it's all about money rap! Gangster rap is dead! Drill gone be too!"

"I don't know about that. The music from the harsher sides of the streets never dies. Now I'll admit, larger labels have been steering away from it, but independents will keep it alive. You don't think money rap is another fad that's here one day and gone the next?" she asked with a serious expression on her face.

"I don't think so. People like to hear about poor Black people from the streets livin' it up. It gives 'em a sense of hope that one day they'll make it big too. No one wants to feel like all their pain is for nothin' at all. They want to feel like there's a light at the end of the tunnel," he answered honestly, never looking bothered the whole time.

"OK, that's it. We'll edit in any commentary later, but we're all wrapped up here. Thank you for having us LOUIE-V, we really appreciate your open hospitality. Look for my email about previewing the article prior to print," LADY SHAY stated as she stood up and shook the recording artist's hand goodbye.

"Not a problem. Oh, I see we ended it right on schedule too. I thought we would have to end it prematurely because of my other meeting. I'm glad I didn't, it was nice. I think you're one of the best out there," LOUIE-V confided in her as he led her to the door.

While her cameramen disassembled their lighting kits and repackaged them back inside their protective cases, LADY SHAY and LOUIE-V continued to laugh and talk inside the front door of his eight-bedroom estate. By the time her crew had finished and were loading up everything inside her company SUV, he'd invited her to his upcoming album release party for another exclusive interview. Happily accepting his invitation, she gave him her personal number and urged him to call her to set it up before they left.

After showing a warm and friendly smile the entire time of LADY SHAY's visit, it vanished completely once he waved goodbye and closed the door. Now armed with a deadly frown on his face, he began to walk to the right wing of his estate where his game room was located. When he got there, several of his armed homies/security had two young men tied up with duck-tape and chains. From the looks of their bruised and battered faces, they appeared to have been there for hours and had endured some very painful beatings.

"These niggas still ain't talkin', huh? BIG DREW, hand me that pool stick over there," he commanded to one of his goons.

Doing what he was instructed, his large homie walked over to his custom white pool table and took a pool stick off the wall. After he gave it to LOUIE-V, he looked at their two bloody captives like they were going to get it now. Smacking the heavy brass handle in his hand while he spoke, every time it did, the two men's eyes widened in fear. They both knew it—they were screwed.

"Fifty pounds of gas don't just grow legs and walk out the trap. I put you two bitch-ass niggas in charge of it! Where's my weed?" he asked in a deadly tone and was not in the mood to play games.

"It was SQUEAK, he was fuckin' with these bitches on the 'gram' and had 'em come by and kick it! We smoked some bligs and drank some vodka—the next thing I know, it's the next day! I think we was drugged, and they stole it!" the distraught man told his employer, not wanting to make things worse than they already were.

"Fuck you BONE—you wanted to fuck 'em too! We both fucked up, but we can make shit right! Give us a chance to get it back! All we need is a few weeks!" SQUEAK exclaimed as his blood from his forehead began to trickle into is right eye, making him squinch his face and blink erratically.

"So, you mean to tell me, y'all invited some thirsty-ass thots to my trap? Then, on top of that, y'all dumb muthafuckas got drugged? Y'all lucky y'all ain't loopy fa life—even though it ain't shit they could give you to make you any dumber. You got three days."

SQUEAK panicked out loud and yelled, "Fuck! Three days!" and before a couple of LOUIE-V's henchmen came to rough him up for questioning him, BONE glanced over at his injured friend and shouted like he wanted to beat his ass himself, "Yeah nigga, you heard what the fuck LOUIE-V said! Three goddamn days! Now shut yo stupid ass up before shit get worse!"

After seeing he was about to catch a beat-down, SQUEAK humbled himself and remained silent. The last thing he wanted was his boss's 300-plus-pound goons to come over and punch on him some more. His jaw on the left side of his face already hurt and his lower lip was busted open. Just the mere thought of being hit again made him cringe with fear.

"I remember when both of y'all was nine or ten and y'all mamas used to keep y'all on the porch under them all the time. I'd be at the corner store and here y'all would come to buy some candy. Y'all niggas wanted to be down way back then, but I waited until y'all was old and wise enough to understand that y'all mamas *still* sit on those same porches," LOUIE-V reminded them while he pointed the pool stick at their faces.

SQUEAK, not wanting to end up on the other end of it, quickly added, "And my mama always says good things about you too LOUIE-V, she knew you was gone make it one day. Don't sweat it, three days is enough time to find they ass. We won't let you down again."

BONE, not wanting to rattle any cages either, remained silent. Instead, he shook his head to agree he wouldn't let him down again either.

Chapter Two
FA MY NIGGAZ

Green Bay Correctional Institution

Green Bay, WI

2 days later...

The cells are small, the guards have attitude problems, and the food barely keeps you sustained—no one said prison didn't come without a shitload of problems. Unlike the way they portray prisoners on television shows, most inmates (even lifers convicted of murder) try to be on their best behavior, so they don't ruin their chances of being paroled or granted an appeal. It takes a lot of patience and a strong will to do your time, and sometimes, it seems like the day to feel the free world again might not ever come, but like the night and day comes—so does your eventual release.

"So, how does it feel to get released today? FRICTION's back in the motherfucking streets! Aye family, I hope you still push that rap music when you get out. You're too good not to be heard," remarked a Puerto Rican inmate who stopped in front of his paroled homie's cell to say goodbye.

"I feel good, but all this green got to me though. Every single day fa three and half years, I saw a forest of dark green clothes and light green walls—I never seen so much green fa so long," FRICTION replied as he stopped packing up his legal paperwork, and other items he felt were important.

Possessing a medium height and strong build from daily work-outs in the prison gym, he looked athletic and agile. For a darker toned man with an average low haircut, he was still handsome with an inviting smile. He wore no tattoos and had no gang ties, but different gang members talked to him regularly and thought he was cool. The ones who heard him rap thought he had talent and didn't hesitate to remind him.

"Shit, you free now! And believe me, you want the green you see out there to be long as a bitch! Love bro, I'll see you in four! I got that info you gave me put up in my Bible!" the inmate exclaimed excitedly for him and began to leave.

"Hold up SLUG, this fa you. I would've given you my TV, but I told my celly he could get it. Ain't nobody sent little dog shit since he got here," FRICTION revealed and passed him his Walkman and half of his commissary—he left the other half for his seventeen-year-old cellmate.

"Real niggas do real things. I really appreciate the love bro. Don't forget about me when you get famous out there," SLUG expressed with respect and left to put his goodies in his footlocker.

While FRICTION's cellmate was in the dayroom playing dominoes, he took the time to let his freedom soak in. Like, for example, no more hearing the rantings of hostile inmates who should be in a mental institution yelling throughout the night or no more having to share a toilet and sink with someone you've never met before. While he was thinking of the things he wouldn't have to put up with anymore, he picked up a jail photo he took with his mom and younger sister.

To him, the photo showed a family trying to make the best out of a fucked-up situation. Yeah, there were smiles, but the picture didn't show the real emotions that were being felt—like the sadness from missing your loved ones, the regret of having to be locked up, and most importantly, him knowing every day he was in there, his family needed his assistance to maintain things and he wasn't around to help. The more he stared at the photo, the more he knew he'd let them down—but not any longer because he was finally coming home.

After sitting around in his cell an additional forty-five minutes since he packed up the last of what he was taking home with him, a correctional officer requested FRICTION by his government name (Malik Thompson) to come to the front desk on the pod's loudspeaker. Knowing it was the call he was waiting for, his heartbeat sped up as his anticipation of his freedom began to grow rapidly inside him. When he walked out his cell and headed to the correctional officer's workstation, a large amount of the inmates in the dayroom shouted out his name and sent their farewells with love and respect.

FRICTION's escort—once he left the pod—was a well-known and easy to get along with middle-aged White male correction officer whose last name was Carter. Since he was one of the more tolerable ones working there—all the inmates called him by his last name. Had he been one nobody cared for—he'd be simply addressed as "correction officer" or "CO."

"Yo Carter, I know you gone miss me man. If it wasn't fa me— you wouldn't have had shit to look forward to when you get here," FRICTION told him as they walked to the elevators.

"Yeah, you completed me. Now I'm lost in a void of emptiness and despair. Bye-bye bliss," the correction officer sarcastically replied while he held his broken heart.

"That was cold, even fa a White dude. But fa real Carter, I want you to know I respect you man. You come here and do yo job, that's it. I ain't never seen you judge or disrespect nobody. You a cool dude."

"I believe you should treat humans like humans—and animals like animals. Shit, I could've easily been in your shoes because that's how easy it is to wind up here. Hell, I got relatives locked up as we speak. All the shit some of these officers pull in here is done because they're afraid of you. So afraid, they figure they'll try to make you fear them too—that's all."

"Well, I appreciate you. I wish every prison had more good dudes like you. Man, I can't believe this day is finally here."

"Yeah, we only have to go through "Outtake" and then sign your release forms for your property. The whole process should take only a few minutes and then you're a free man. Do you have any parole to do?

"Yeah, I got a few years of papers to do. I wish I didn't though—I heard they set you up to fail. Violation/revocation after violation/ revocation—I don't know if I can do it," FRICTION stated doubtfully as they stopped in front of one of the facility elevators so the correction officer could push the button to call for it.

Sensing the young felon's apprehension, officer Carter looked at him with the maturity and wisdom of a man with ten or more extra years of living under his belt and told him, "Take it one day at a time. It's going to be an uphill battle, but you already know what you're up against. If I'm not mistaken, you were convicted of man-slaughter, right?"

"Yeah. The prosecutor wanted to charge me with murder in the first, but the attorney my mom bought fought hard fa me. I was only seventeen, so I got waived to adult court and had my first adult birthday in prison. The crazy part is me and my friends was the ones who got shot at first—all I did was try my best to survive and he died because of it."

"The self-defense law here sucks ass. Yeah, the game's rigged. So, what's your plan to stay free since you know that now?"

"Well, I wanna comply with all the rules I gotta sign. To do that, I need a steady job that pay good."

"You also must steer clear of the type of people who might lead you back into trouble again. Most people violate their probation/parole because they can't stop hanging out with their trouble-making friends. Take my advice: Keep to yourself and you'll be fine."

"Yeah, I got a few ideas. Who knows, you might brag about me one day," FRICTION said modestly as he intentionally changed the subject.

As soon as officer Carter was about to talk to him more about his release plans, the elevator in front of them opened and two correction officers with three inmates stepped off it. Officer Carter nodded to his fellow employees and spoke to them briefly before the five-man group headed to another pod. By the time they got on the elevator themselves, instead of speaking to FRICTION further, the correction officer chose to remain silent and let him focus on seeing the outside of the prison. Besides, the last thing he wanted to do was sound like an unwanted lecturer.

The process to be released from the correctional institution went without a hitch. FRICTION had heard inmates complain about not receiving their personal property in prison and even how it was either stolen (jewelry and watches) or misplaced while they were being housed, but none of that happened to him. Precisely the way officer Carter informed him, he got his belongings in about fifteen minutes. And when he went through his items, all his things were there from the time of his arrest: his black T-shirt, his pair of black denim jeans, his pair of Jordan basketball shoes, and an empty black leather wallet.

When he walked out of the maximum-security facility and could see everything around him unfenced, the reality of being free again began to truly sink in. No more officers telling him when to wake up and go to sleep or get up countless times to be counted; now, it was at his own choosing. He didn't have to unwillingly follow their orders anymore because he had his freedom back—finally.

When he walked down the stairs and headed to the public parking area, he noticed it was overfilled with different types of vehicles from people visiting their loved ones. Families of all sizes and colors (mainly Black) were coming and going as he stood amongst the vastness of his unfamiliarity. Not ever being a resident or even a traveling tourist of Green Bay, WI, everything seemed foreign to him. When he looked around, there was nothing but highways and a large factory.

But as soon as FRICTION was about to feel alone and lost in a community that had had him imprisoned there for over three years, he heard a voice call out his name. It wasn't close by, but it wasn't so far away that he couldn't make it out either. As he walked further into the parking lot and looked around for the person who was calling him, he knew they were somewhere near his current location because his name sounded much louder and clearer.

"What the fuck are you doing by my car, nigger!" someone crept up behind him and yelled while grabbing his shoulder.

"What the fuck!" FRICTION yelled out, startled by the sneaky approach and put up his fists to defend himself.

When he saw it was his longtime homie C-DOG, he felt a huge sense of relief come over him and gave his friend a hood hug and handshake. Knowing his buddy kept active warrants for his arrest, FRICTION never expected to see him while he was in prison. Actually, no one came to visit him—only his mother and sister. So, it came as quite a shock for FRICTION to see C-DOG there to pick him up—especially since he didn't even have a driver's license.

"It's ya boy C-DEEZY, bro! You should see how you look right now G! You look like you was finsta haul ass!" C-DOG laughed as he swung playful punches at his friend.

"Wrong, first I was gone bop a racist bitch on his head and then I was gone haul ass!" FRICTION chuckled back as he countered with playful blows of his own.

"What up, fam? I know you didn't expect to see me, did you?"

"Hell naw, you hate jails. Plus, I thought you had some warrants."

"I do, but that wasn't gone stop shit. You'd be there for me so don't trip."

"You mean to tell me you drove a car almost two hours up north—to the boondocks—just to greet me when I got out?"

"I ain't drive shit here! The homie MANIAC had his cousin GLOW bring us. He stayed in the car cause of the heat."

"MANIAC is here? I didn't even know you two hung out. Aye bro, you do know they say he kill people, don't you? Why the fuck did you bring him here?" FRICTION asked his good friend very seriously.

"It ain't like that—we got a business relationship and that's all. You know if I had to choose between my niggaz or him—I'm a put my life on the line fa my niggaz. Damn, FRICTION, all you gotta do is take the free ride home and listen to what the man gotta say," C-DOG advised his comrade of many years.

"Look man, they gotta bus that can drop me off in downtown Milwaukee if I wait around. MANIAC is one of those cats you don't wanna rub the wrong way. I think I'm good."

The shuttle's scheduled leave time to go to Milwaukee was still an hour away, but that didn't stop FRICTION from turning around and going to it. Conflicted by how he was feeling about the sudden surprises, he felt the best thing for him to do was to walk away from it all so he could process everything. His good friend popping up out of the blue and now hanging out with one of the deadliest heroin dealers in the city—who also just happens to be his ride home—was something he didn't see coming.

Seeing FRICTION wasn't going with him, C-DOG tried one last time to convince his skeptical friend everything was cool. Catching up to him and giving his left shoulder a hard shove to make him angry enough to make him stop walking away, he began to tell him why MANIAC wanted to speak to him.

"Look, I told him what you did, and he was impressed by your loyalty. Just think about it for a minute. MANIAC came to meet you in person bro. Do you know what that mean? This could be our one and only big chance to make some real money."

"Yeah, he got deep pockets, but he got one of those 'God complexes' that I can't roll with. Instead of seein' his hustle as a blessin' that can be gone at any moment, he chooses to be a demon. How we gone get rich with somebody like that?"

"We'll be plugged! We'll get rich because we'll have access! The weight will be at our disposal—that mean we can sell it in bulk or break it down! It won't matter either way because we'll be caked up regardless!" C-DOG proclaimed while he made money symbols with his hands.

Thoughts of all the things he could do with the type of money he could make being down with MANIAC began to take over FRICTION's rational thinking as C-DOG's words began to seep into his mind. Things like having enough money to help his mom, to pay the studio time for his rap album, and keeping himself dressed in designer clothes deeply enticed him. If temptation was the work of the Devil, then C-DOG took notes from him—the way his friend spoke of them living the good life.

"I could use some money to help moms out," FRICTION admitted to his homie while he weighed it all in.

"She'd be happy to get it," C-DOG agreed with him.

"Look man, I'll ride and hear what he has to say. I can't promise you anything more than that."

"That's cool. We parked over there."

The walk to where MANIAC and his cousin was parked went without any further conversation between the two friends—they were both too wrapped up in their own personal thoughts. C-DOG was hoping everything would work out and they'd make a lot of money very quickly. FRICTION, on the other hand, was thinking about the worst-case scenarios if he worked for MANIAC. Like, for example, him laying somewhere dead with a bullet in his head.

When they were close enough to their ride home, C-DOG showed his homie how they were rolling back to the city. FRICTION couldn't believe his eyes—it was an all-white Bentley Bentayga—an SUV that was easily worth $250,000. The top-of-the-line luxury vehicle made every other one in the lot pale in comparison to its elegance. Impressed by what he was seeing, FRICTION looked over at his grinning homie and proceeded onward to their waiting ride.

But what FRICTION didn't know was that officer Carter had been in one of the windows watching him since he had walked out. From his meeting with his playful friend to his walk to the expensive SUV, his eyes had been following FRICTION. With the look of a letdown parent, he let out a deep breath of regret for him and went back to his daily duties.

Back in Milwaukee, MEAN-MUG and TRIGGAH G were riding around in his (MEAN-MUG) car, trying to come up on another hustle to start the afternoon right. Having already sold the stolen vehicle to a frequented chop shop in the hood for several thousand dollars hours ago, most of the ill-gotten cash was spent on liquor, cocaine, and women. Now broke again, but sexually satisfied and high as research monkeys, they cruised around smoking on Newport 100's with only one thing on their minds: making some fast money—by any means necessary.

"I know where we could pop a lick?" TRIGGA G told his homie after he flicked his cigarette butt out the open window.

"Where?" MEAN-MUG asked like that was their next destination.

"We could jack that fuckboy Pedro fa givin' me that whacked-up ass powder last week. I bet he got some money and dope somewhere in his crib."

"Who else be there?"

"His baby mama and some little-ass kids. He had his cousin over there too when I went through there."

"He won't recognize you if we mask up, will he?"

"Don't trip. It's too many goons in the city that's my weight and height. His Mexican ass ain't gone try to recognize shit with a gun pointed at his face."

"Damn, he must've had some bogus-ass shit."

"You complained about it more than me. You said you think some bathroom cleaner was mixed in it."

"You talkin' bout that bullshit that burnt the insides of my nose and I *said* they used some Comet or Ajax to cut it?"

"Yep," TRIGGAH G answered as he turned up the music even more.

"Oh, hell yeah, that fuck nigga can get it. Where he be at?" MEAN-MUG asked, growing more hostile by the minute toward the corner-cutting cocaine dealer for putting him through such a painful experience.

"The fool stays on the south side—on Mitchell. We can be there in thirty if we get on the highway the fly way."

"We can jump on it, but you shoulda told me who gave you that bogus blow when I asked you last week. Why you wait till now?"

"Because then we had money. But he been on my stickup list after that. He usually be the last dude I know to run out."

"I get it, you didn't wanna burn a plug. You sure you wanna rob his ass?"

"Fuck his fake hustlin' ass! Real niggas don't use mystery mix in they work!" TRIGGAH G scoffed without any pity for their soon-to-be victim.

"We off to the south side then—fuck him and whoever else in there," MEAN-MUG expressed nonchalantly, then he sniffed hard and gently rubbed his nose while he had a painful flashback of tooting the bad dope.

The ride to the south side of the city took about twenty minutes. As soon they arrived, they began to see things that appealed to the Mexican culture. From restaurants to clothing stores, everything catered to the Hispanic community. Driving around and walking the streets were mainly brown people whose descendants immigrated across the Mexican border to start a better life for themselves in America.

When they made it to their destination on 18th and Mitchell, there weren't many people outside because of the excessive heat, but they didn't want to take any chances of being spotted by anybody, so they parked a block up from Pedro's house. Already prepared for such a thing because of their robbing lifestyle, MEAN-MUG went to his trunk and rummaged through his garbage bag full of costume masks. Smiling to himself after he found the ones he wanted to use, he quickly placed them inside a black shopping bag and joined TRIGGAH G, who was already crossing the street to cut through a neighbor's yard to go there from the alley.

Discussing their plan while they walked, by the time they reached where they were going, their roles and how they were going to do things was fully understood. And as luck would have it, there wasn't going to be a need to kick the door in like they had planned to because there were two young Hispanic girls—eight and five— playing with their unkempt dolls on their open backdoor's concrete steps. They also figured since they were young children, the screen door would be unlocked too; that way, the children would be able to go back inside the house when they wanted to.

When MEAN-MUG and TRIGGAH G entered the backyard, the two kids looked happy and content playing by themselves while Hispanic music grooved out the closed screen door. From the open backdoor that led into their kitchen, the smell of good Mexican food being cooked permeated the air. Concluding Pedro's girlfriend was in the middle of cooking a meal, they quickly put on their masks, bypassed the puzzled children, and, with TRIGGAH G leading the way, completely startled the woman in front of her stove with two 9mm semi-automatic handguns with extended magazines pointing at her head.

When the armed men came in, all she saw was President Barack Obama and President Donald Trump pointing handguns at her. With Donald standing in front, Barack stayed behind him and let him run things. While doing so, he quietly closed and locked the door on the kids as they were beginning to get up out of curiosity to see the masks again. With no time for playing games, President Trump spoke like a man who meant business.

"Where the fuck is Pedro?" he asked her angrily with his gun still aimed at her face.

"He went to make a run," she replied fearfully.

"When is he coming back?"

"I don't know—maybe twenty minutes. Please don't kill me."

"I won't if you do what I tell you."

"I will."

"Your food smells good and those kids outside look hungry so let's make this as quick and easy as we can. OK?" he asked her.

"OK," she answered him, too scared to move an inch.

"Who else is here?"

"No one, only me and my kids. Please don't hurt us."

"Don't give me a reason to."

"I won't, Mr. President."

"Good. First, you can turn off the stove before you burn up the kid's food; second, go get enough of Pedro's money and dope that'll make us leave. Now hurry up," he commanded calmly while motioning his gun for her to get it.

Without delay, she shook her head in terror and ran to their bedroom to do as she was instructed. As far as she was concerned, there was nothing in her home that was more valuable to her than her children—all she wanted was for the former presidents to leave her alone. When she came back, she handed him several rubber-banded knots of money and two knotted sandwich bags of cocaine.

"Do you think this is enough to make us leave?" President Trump asked her.

"It's all I could find. You could look if you want to, but you won't find nothing more than this. Please take it and go," the lady pleaded to him.

"If I find out you lied to me, I will come back, and it won't be pleasant. Do you understand?"

"I'm telling you the truth. I don't want any trouble."

"You know I'll deport you and your kids. Don't come to the door for five minutes and you all good," President Trump told the frightened woman.

"I'm an American citizen by birth. Please go. My babies are all I have," she begged, not wanting to be shot or wrongfully deported.

Accomplishing what they set out to do, MEAN-MUG and TRIGGAH G left with the stolen cash and drugs. Still wearing their masks, they stepped over her two children who returned to playing with their dolls. When President Obama (TRIGGAH G) looked back at the cute children, something about them touched him because he tapped his homie's shoulder and told him to give him one of the rubber-banded knots of money. He quickly peeled off a $100 and gave it to the oldest daughter and told her, "Don't tell nobody I gave this to you. Buy you and your sister some new dolls."

"Thank you," the older girl said politely with a huge smile.

While they walked back up the alley to go back to MEAN-MUG's car, they still had on their masks and held a brief conversation about what TRIGGAH G had done. Not happy at all, MEAN-MUG spoke first.

"Why did you give those kids our money? They not our responsibility!"

"Because the kids are innocent."

"Their dad is a criminal who makes a lot of illegal money! We can't afford to give money to help nobody! Don't waste no more money on kids when we do this shit again!"

"The kids are the future man."

"Fuck the kids!"

When they made it back to MEAN MUG's car, they took off their costume masks and placed them back in the trunk with the others. Wasting no time driving away, they headed back to the north side of Milwaukee with smiles on their faces from their successful robbery. TRIGGAH G, after counting the money and eyeballing the weight of the cocaine, looked happily at his homie driving for a job well done.

"Fam, we got about four racks and this look like a couple ounces! Hold on, let me check it!" he told him excitedly and opened one of the sandwich bags. With his pinkie fingernail, he scooped up some cocaine, sniffed it up his right nostril, and then stated with nasal congestion, "Damn, this shit pure!"

Glad to hear it, MEAN-MUG reached over and scooped some out with a key he took off his keyring since he didn't have long fingernails and sniffed it up both of his nostrils. The numbing rush from the potent cocaine was immediate and it perked up his mood even more. Turning up his music so the bass would knock louder, he then drove to the closest highway entrance to leave the south side of town.

Chapter Three
YOU BETTER CALL A CORONER

When LOUIE-V received a call from Arthur "STACKS" Moore, the CEO of BIG DOE RECORDS—the record label that signed him—requesting an emergency meeting at three o'clock regarding an urgent matter, he jumped into his Bianco Birdcage colored Maserati Gran Turismo convertible and sped off to their downtown office location. Not knowing the details of it deeply bothered him as he turned the curious heads of onlookers left and right while he drove through his beloved city. He wasn't worried about STACKS finding out about his private street dealings because the label wasn't concerned about those type of things. The only thing they're concerned with is the sales from music, not how he survived and took care of his affairs until then. The $250,000 advance he got from the deal did help him out a lot in the streets, but that wasn't STACKS's business.

No, LOUIE-V wasn't worried about that being an issue with him, but he did create some unauthorized beef with MACK

DADDY—a rap icon whose following was 31 million strong. The record label that signed him years ago, "PIMP HARD RECORDS," is a well-established veteran label that has sold millions of rap albums in target markets all over the world. In the ocean of rap music, PIMP HARD RECORDS is considered more than a big fish—they're the apex predator. For a meeting to be called out of the blue, he figured it was because of that.

Thirty minutes of driving later, but still fifteen minutes ahead of time for the meeting, LOUIE-V parked on 4th and Mason St. and walked inside a high-rise building that rented out business space. On the ninth floor, STACKS and his board of executives were patiently waiting for his arrival in their conference room. When he walked into the room full of head honchos, everyone there was dressed in formal business attire except him. He had on a designer T-shirt and matching jeans with a pair of expensive sneakers. Not to mention his jewelry, it blinded you with its precious gems every time he moved.

To show the seven executives he was aware of their serious attitudes, LOUIE-V didn't smile or appear jovial; instead, he sat down and looked oblivious as to why he was there. When the rapper looked around at everyone's stoic faces, deep down he knew their indifferent mood was because of him. Not wanting to give them a chance to berate or belittle him, he chose to deal with the matter from a position of power.

Looking like they were trying to withhold important funds from him, he frowned at the group and stated, "I hope you didn't call me all the way down here tell me the video budget I need wasn't approved. The director I want to use won't do it fa anything less."

"No, LOUIE-V, that's not why we called this meeting. We're all gathered here because it's come to our attention that you've singlehandedly caused a war between this company and one of our friendly rivals. You can't deny it because it's being covered in every hip-hop media outlet source around the world. I told you to create some hype for the PR firms, not create beef with one of the world's most respected recording artists. So, tell us, how do you plan on fixing this dilemma?" STACKS asked him from the head of the long conference table.

"To be straight up, I don't see a dilemma. Besides, I don't have any beef with anybody. The issue with MACK DADDY, I only used my freedom of speech to speak my mind about him. I wouldn't go so far as to call it beef though," LOUIE-V explained nonchalantly while he looked at his phone for missed messages.

"You don't have to—the media is doing it for you. They're creating a beef, so now, there is one. Listen, you only made it harder for yourself when you dissed MACK DADDY. He's positioned to headline any concert event—that means his sales and fan base is large enough for him to fill stadiums under his brand. You, on the other hand, are a new and upcoming artist who would be an opening or second show for an artist of his stature. Well, at least you could've been before this fiasco," STACKS tried to explain to him.

"I don't wanna open for that nigga anyway! If you provide me with the resources I need to properly compete with the dude, you wouldn't have to kiss his ass to book me as an opener! I'm the future of rap, and the world would know that if you fund my project to the fullest! You mean to tell me you signed me to open shows for bigger names? Why would you spend all those funds in radio promotion if you don't see me at this money as an international headliner?"

"We all agree that you can reach that level of success, but these types of antics won't make it an easy ascension. As for your total budget for this single release, aside from the video and its promotion, we've reached our projected cap for it—which is why you shouldn't have caused us a potential financial firestorm that we won't have the capital to extinguish. We're screwed if MACK DADDY takes your assault on his character personal and decides to dedicate a single dissing you."

"Why do I have to worry about that?"

"One release from him could seriously hurt your image because your album is already streaming. You can't create a new album with a track dissing MACK DADDY before we're done promoting the singles on this album. I won't even tell you what would happen if he decided to release two or three beef tracks against you—your career would be over."

"But how?" LOUIE-V asked confused.

"Because no one respects a person who talks shit and can't back it up! The whole point is this: Stay the hell out the fight if you can't fight fire with fire!" STACKS wisely shouted.

"Man, if he come at me, I'll go to social media on his ass! Cool, I ain't got no songs to use if he name-drop me. I'll figure it out if that time come."

"That's not how things work in this business—which is another reason why you're here today. To get a grip on things before they escalate any further, we've created some contingency plans to ensure this debacle you created dies down quickly."

"I own it guys, I messed up. So, how do we fix things?" the young rapper asked humbly after recognizing he still had a lot to learn about the different aspects of the music business.

"Ideas were pitched from everyone you see here today and from quite a few others you haven't. We know we want to get ahead of the negative publicity, so we're going to utilize some crisis management tactics. Also, we're going to do something new and different.

We were thinking a rap battle contest to curve your image a bit," STACKS stated with approving smiles from his board members.

"Damn STACKS, why mess with battle rap? I'm a beast at it, but I flow that money talk—you know how I get down."

"You're going to present yourself as an artist who battles any and everybody. Hopefully, the masses will see your comments about MACK DADDY as part of your rap battle way. You don't want to make MACK DADDY or anyone else in this music business an unnecessary enemy."

Not happy at all by what he was hearing, LOUIE-V knew there wasn't anything he could do about it. He signed a contract with BIG DOE RECORDS, and he didn't want to screw things up. With the advance he got and the million-plus they invested in his single's marketing and sales promotion worldwide, he knew he had to deliver, or risk being dropped. He concluded, at the end of the day, he was an independent contractor who was contracted to work for STACKS— not the other way around.

Uncomfortable with his image change, LOUIE-V shifted in his seat and asked, "What's the rest of it?"

"When asked publicly about MACK DADDY, speak only good things about him and refute anything the media will try to incite between you two. This isn't a request LOUIE-V," STACKS stated with authority while the other executives sat silently by and watched the recording artist for signals that he wouldn't go along with what they wanted him to do.

"Yeah cool, I got it. Anything else?"

"Yes, there is. I want you to oversee it. We've already named it the 'RAP or DIE' contest and sixteen of the best rappers around will square off for four rounds until there's only one man left standing. The almost three-hour event will be hosted by you at the Riverside

Theater, and you'll be the king to dethrone for the final fifth round. We'll give the winner of the fourth round $50,000 and a recording contract if they beat you in the final round. Instead of judges, we'll use a large state-of-the-art monitor with software that reads the volume of crowds' cheers—ultimately letting them choose the winner. We call it the 'CHEER-METER' and its colorful display will reach its peak capacity of '10' when it's insanely loud from cheers and '0' when it's at its lowest point."

"The CHEER-METER sounds cool. When?"

"Well, in a couple of days we're going to launch promos across several radio stations in six or seven nearby states to generate some buzz. Starting today, we have a team online spreading the info across a multitude of forums and we've already sent press releases to the PR firms we've hired. We're also expecting to finish our negotiations with the venue tomorrow—so we'll be ready to hold the contest in three weeks. We figure seven till ten o' clock will give people enough time to get home and change for the Saturday show. Everybody with kids will have more time find a babysitter," his CEO answered.

"Well, it sounds like everything is in motion already. My booking agent had a few things lined up for me around then, but I know how important this is to everyone so I'm in. Did you talk to my business manager yet?" LOUIE-V asked curiously while he wondered why he haven't heard from him.

"My secretary called Mr. Goldberg to arrange a meeting with him about any potential scheduling conflicts, but he didn't answer his phone or call back. She left a message on his smartphone and emailed him. Is he sick or something?"

"He's Jewish, rich and in his early thirties—he's probably somewhere passed out with a model."

"You should find out. Well, that's it, we're done here. Is there anything you want to discuss with us other than the video budget?" STACKS asked while he looked at his very expensive watch, hinting he was pressed with other business he needed to attend to.

"Nope. Call me or Freddie when things are set up and ready to go. You can count on me, STACKS. I'll be there for the show, and I'll make it epic," LOUIE-V assured his boss.

"Good, then this meeting is adjourned. We'll be in touch soon LOUIE-V," STACKS informed him as he and the other company executives rose out of their seats and began to exit the conference room.

When LOUIE-V got up to leave, his demeanor resembled a child whose father was making him do chores he didn't want to do. A part of him wanted to renege on the entire event, but he knew that was the emotional side of him thinking that way. He still couldn't believe all of this happened because of a social media rant he made when he was drunk off cognac and high as hell off weed. Not knowing intense interviews and chastisement from his label would follow, he'd take back calling MACK DADDY "a relic that should retire" if he could.

The walk out the building and back to his car was spent trying to reach Freddie. He was beyond upset for being blindsided by his CEO's project he was now in charge of. That was one of the main reasons why he hired someone to manage those type of affairs on his behalf. As far as he was concerned, Freddie was supposed to be notified first to let him know what the meeting was about. The "missing in action" manager made him wonder aloud, "What was the point in hiring him?"

After several fruitless calls to Freddie's phone, he got in his car and took off to his house near the lakefront in Shorewood. After almost twenty minutes of maneuvering through east-side traffic, he pulled into the driveway of the 1.8-million-dollar brick colonial-styled estate and parked next to his manager's black and chrome Tesla. Still calling his number as he walked up to the house without an answer, LOUIE-V rang the doorbell a few times until his manager's maid came to the door. After letting her know who he was and directing her to tell Freddie he's here to see him about some very important business, he impatiently stayed outside until his business manager groggily came to the door.

Wearing only his black and gold silk designer pajama pants, a matching silk robe, and a pair of expensive gold suede loafers, he looked as if he'd recently woken up from a long night of drinking and partying. Around the corners of his nostrils were still evidence of a white powdered substance he'd snorted, but it was difficult for LOUIE-V to tell if it was pain pills, molly, or cocaine; either way, it only infuriated him more about his lack of tact and poor professionalism.

Not fully snapped out of his haziness, Freddie yawned, "LOUIE-V, my man. What are you doing here? Please come in."

"Are you fa real right now, Freddie? I've hit you on yo phone nonstop since I found out—with no thanks to you—about a company meeting with STACKS. Why didn't you call me?" LOUIE-V asked him with an attitude while he stormed inside and walked directly to his manager's living room to sit down on his sofa.

When he gazed around after plopping down on his couch, he got a good idea of how much of a great time Freddie had. From the look of the empty liquor bottles and traces of white powder on his cocktail table, he'd been busy having himself a hell of a great time. Deciding to press him further about it, he looked at him seriously and remarked, "Look man, I hired you to manage all my business.

That also means notifying me ahead of time about meetings with the label."

"Look, I'm sorry. Do you want something to drink? Maria, come here and bring my friend something to drink. What's your poison?" Freddie asked him while he tried to shake off his wooziness.

"Lemon-Lime soda please. I wouldn't be so thirsty if I didn't have to ask so many questions about a damn contest I'm now obligated to participate in! Didn't you get their messages? They told me they even emailed yo ass!"

"No way! Fuck! Where's my phone? I bet it's dead and under my bed or something. What time is it anyway?"

"Really? Freddie, it's 4:34 pm and you dressed like Hugh Hefner in this bitch. What the hell did you do last night? I see all the bottles and shit."

"I was at the casino and there were these two beautiful Black goddesses eyeballing the hell out of me. I mean, I couldn't blame them, I was wearing Tom Ford from head-to-toe. I'm talking drop-dead gorgeous, and they looked bored, so we had drinks and talked for a bit. The next thing I know, they were following me home in their Corvette and they had ecstasy and blow to go with the ton of booze I keep here."

"I hope your threesome was lit," LOUIE-V told him sarcastically, shaking his head in disappointment.

"Honestly, I was so fucked up, I don't remember. I don't even know what time they left. Hell, I thought when you were at the door it was nine or ten in the morning," Freddie replied still quite out of it.

While his manager tried to clear his head, LOUIE-V's phone began to ring. After a few minutes of conversing with someone on the other end, he abruptly hung up and began to get up to leave.

"On second thought, I'll pass on that soda, Freddie. Some business came up I gotta deal with," LOUIE-V stated without explaining any further and stood up to leave.

"No problem, no problem. Hey, I am sorry about everything. I hope you haven't lost trust in me," Freddie spoke worriedly as he walked his client back to his door.

"I trust you enough to know that I can't trust yo ass at all when pussy around. But don't trip, pussy's caused distrust between men since cavemen carried clubs," LOUIE-V stopped at the door and joked.

"I get it. That's a good one. I'll call you later. And don't forget you have a show to do in London. The promoters are sending half tomorrow and we get the other half before showtime. Ching-Ching bitches!" Freddie exclaimed, hoping the reminder would cheer up his upset client.

Being told he was going to make some money usually lightened up LOUIE-V's angry mood. That was how Freddie stayed on the rapper's good side when he'd upset him. But after this screwup, he wished he could tell LOUIE-V the funds were already transferred into his account. Freddie knew he needed to say something to keep things kosher between them. He was relieved when he reached out to fist bump his now smiling client, LOUIE-V coolly returned the love.

"Now that's what I wanna to hear, dammit; let me know what's up tomorrow! Hey, don't worry, Freddie—we cool, but you're fired if you leave me stuck again," LOUIE-V made it clear and left without saying anything else.

Freddie silently waved bye and watched his client get in his car and drive off his property. He still couldn't believe he slept through his business calls and emails mainly because that sort of thing doesn't happen to him. The alcohol he drank wasn't nearly as much as he consumes at parties, and he'd never overslept before. The thought of him losing such a talented artist and his commissions over a blurry night of liquor, drugs, and sex made him look at LOUIE-V's car as it left and yell, "Fuck!" before he closed his door.

While FRICTION lay on the full-sized bed inside his room, he replayed the earlier events of his encounter with MANIAC in his head. The way the man looked confidently and majestically at him with a glass of cognac in his hand intimidated him some when he sat in the backseat next to him. He was already a mean-looking and ugly-faced man, making it easy to understand why he was feared so much, but if you coupled that with his muscular strength and dominant character—the man was absolutely frightening.

When he sat down, MANIAC was staring at the road ahead of them and casually stated, "Most niggas step out a prison and have to go back home to a reality that's a lot worse than the prison they were incarcerated in. No money to buy shit and no decent crib to chill in is all they got to look forward to. Fa some, they broke fa the rest of their life. But a select few step out to much bigger and better things. You, my friend, are fortunate enough to be one of those select few."

"I guess that's what I've been tryin' to understand. Why am I so fortunate?" he remembered asking him.

"Because you possess certain qualities that make you the type of man I want to have in my circle."

"Qualities?"

"I peeped several strong ones that make me believe you cut out fa the line of work I'm in. I only hire grown-ass men to work fa me—no children or fools. And those men I bring into my circle, they all live and die by the code because of those qualities. Do you live and die by the code?"

"Yeah, I do."

"I know you do. C-DOG told me that too, but I go by vouches from multiple sources. You should know there was several trusted homies locked up in there who also vouched fa you too. These are niggas you don't need to concern yourself with, but I wanted you to know that good things were mentioned about you," MANIAC assured him as he continued to stare ahead and sip some of his cognac.

"I'm glad your associates told you positive things about me. I believe, no matter what, we should always keep it real," FRICTION recalled himself saying.

"We should and that's why we're together today. I'm gone keep it real with you right now and tell you I hate snitches."

"I hate 'em too."

"I don't know if you fully understand the depth of my hatred. I hate snitches so much that I don't consider 'em human anymore. To me, they're worse than flesh-eating parasites."

"They are the worst."

"In my life, I have met enough men to recognize certain qualities that snitches don't have. For example, a snitch doesn't possess the quality of loyalty. Sure, he can pretend he does, but at some point, his true disloyal nature will emerge and reveal itself," MANIAC explained and then moistened his mouth with another sip.

"Without loyalty, you can't grow and develop the trust you need in the men around you. Loyalty is one of the foundations that's used make unity possible," FRICTION told him honestly.

"I knew I wanted to meet you for a reason. Good men are hard to find, but real niggas are a rarity. I need the realest niggas created."

"I feel you."

"The shit you did fa C-DOG, that was a real nigga move. It showed me that you feel fa others more than yourself—those are the two qualities of care and unselfishness. You took the murder rap for your friend because he was a felon on probation. Do you know how many people would do that?"

"Not a whole lot, I guess."

"Not enough."

And that was it. MANIAC instructed his cousin to play some music and he refilled his glass with some more liquor. No more discussions or talking of any sort. FRICTION felt like he didn't even exist to the man any longer. So, not wanting to say or do anything offensive to him, he sat quietly and stared out the passenger window at the acres of farmland and commercial properties they were regularly passing by on their way back to Milwaukee.

The only other thing FRICTION recalled happening was MANIAC telling him he'd be in touch before he got out. That's when C-DOG handed him a burnout smartphone, but there wasn't any pressure to join him. He figured MANIAC only wanted to meet him and feel him out personally. When he got dropped off though, he had to admit there was some enjoyment in the attention everyone gave him when he got out the luxury vehicle—everyone looked at him like he was an A-list celebrity.

But when he knocked on the door where he lived, the feeling of being a celebrity went away as soon as his mom opened the door and shouted, "Boy, don't be knocking on my door like you lost your damn mind! Come on in if you gone come in! I don't want you letting all those flies and gnats in my house!"

While he lay in his bed thinking about his mother's first words to him after being released from prison, she knocked on his door and asked, "Are you dressed?"

"Yeah Mama. What's up?" FRICTION asked respectfully.

"I want you to walk with 'Ki-Ki' to the corner store. Make sure she only gets some chips and a pop. I still need to go shopping later today and that EBT card don't have much on it.

"Man, the last time I saw Lakisha, she was just a little squirt. Now look how big she's grown."

"Yeah, she's almost ten and thinks she's twenty."

"I missed her a lot. I missed you too, Mama."

"We missed you too. I hope you looking at those job leads I left for you on your dresser. Did you see the paper?" his mother asked him while she stood in his doorway.

"I got it right here next to me. I promise I'll check 'em out tomorrow," he told her, hoping it would ease her mind about it some.

"Alright, but make sure you do because I can't afford to take care of you and your sister. I need you to help out around here."

"Don't worry, Mama, I'm gone call everybody on this list. I just hope they don't trip about my felony conviction."

"Well, you won't know unless you try. Nobody ever achieved anything by thinking negatively. Stay positive and good things will gravitate your way. One thing I know for sure is that our gracious God takes care of his people. Don't let the laws that are aimed at you and names like 'felon' or 'convict' that these White folks use stop you from being who you are."

"Whatever you say, Mama. Is she ready to go?"

"Give her a minute and she'll knock on your door," his mother responded dismissively and left to wash the dishes in the kitchen.

Sensing she was still upset about the choice he made when he was seventeen, he began to lay back and recap what happened that ill-fated night in his mind like it was a true confession:

"C-DOG and our other homie MOOCH was with me. We just left this girl's house who stayed a few neighborhoods away from where we lived and had to cut through a park to take the bus home. Since it was only seven in the evening, the park still had a lot of people there. We didn't know anybody from those neck of the woods so we chose not to make any eye contact with any of the groups there—everyone hoped we could make it back without any trouble. Unfortunately for us though, things don't always go the way you want it to sometimes.

'Hey, what hood y'all from?' I remembered one of the curious young gang members ask us while he and several of his partners sat on a park bench smokin' weed and drinkin' beer.

I sensed some drama was about to go down, so I motioned for C-DOG and MOOCH not to speak, even when C-DOG wanted to rep our hood. But as soon as we passed by, the small group of bullies jumped off the bench and began to follow us. Still tryin' to question us, one of the fools started to act like he'd had enough of the silent treatment and flung an empty 40-ounce bottle over our heads. It shattered into pieces only a few feet ahead of us.

To let 'em know our mamas didn't raise no punks, we turned around and C-DOG shouted, 'What the fuck is wrong with y'all? We ain't from here and we headed to our hood!'

'What the fuck is y'all over here fo'?' another one asked us with a frown on his face.

'It really ain't none of yo business, but we was at a bitch house who stay over here. Y'all be cool.' I told the gang members and motioned for C-DOG to end the chit-chat and step.

But they wouldn't back off, as far as they were concerned, there was some off-brand-ass niggas about to trespass in their hood. So, one decided he'd had enough of the pleasantries and disrespected us. Out of the blue, he yelled, 'Get y'all bitch asses out my park before we beat the shit out y'all!'

You only got two choices when you're placed in that kind of predicament: you either run and hope you can all get away unharmed or you stand your ground and fight. Choosing to fight, we turned back around and began to disrespect them back.

'Fuck you bitch-ass niggas! Ain't none of y'all gone do shit to us! Don't get fucked up in this park!' MOOCH turned around and shouted at the gang members with his mind made up to fight.

I was just as heated as everyone else and added, 'Fuck you hoe-ass niggas and this hood!'

After that, things went from bad to worse. The gang members could handle personal verbal attacks against them, but having strangers talk down on their neighborhood sent the group into a primal rage. So much so, one ran up on MOOCH and tried to hit him in his face. Luckily, he ducked and shoved the dude hard in his chest—it made his drunk ass fall on the ground and hit his head on the concrete walkway. When the other three ran up on us—the fight of all fights began. Punches and kicks were followed by body slams and foot stomps on fallen bodies.

We were about to win until someone upped a gun and shot at us. I didn't even know C-DOG was strapped. He thought we was about to die so he pulled out his .380 and shot dude twice in his chest. When their friend fell to the ground lifeless, the rest of his homies ran off to avoid being next.

'You better call a coroner!' C-DOG yelled at them while they bolted off in the wind.

Completely shocked by what happened and afraid of what might come next, I looked at my friends and shouted, 'Yo, let's go!'

But what we didn't know was that there were four cops on bicycle patrol on the opposite side of the park. They heard the gunshots and immediately used their police radios to request assistance from mobile units in the area. Before we had a chance to make it out the park, the police on bikes began to chase us through a wide-open area of grass and police cars had the entire place surrounded.

Fearing he was about to go away fa the rest of his life, C-DOG took his gun out, wiped his prints off it and yelled to us while we ran, 'I'm on papers and the police got a warrant out fa me! They gone give me life fa this shit! Ain't no place to throw it! I'm fucked when they find it!'

Since I just turned seventeen and didn't have a juvenile record, I shouted back to my homie as the cops got closer, 'I ain't got no record! I'll say the gun was mine and I shot it to protect us if they do!'

The next thing I know—they caught us, found the gun, I told 'em it was mine and shot to protect us, C-DOG and MOOCH was released that night, and I got released today."

Being able to tell the truth to himself about what happened made it easier for FRICTION to accept his new reality. He'd never been in any real trouble with the police before, so he didn't know he had any rights—especially one to remain silent. The only reason he took the case for C-DOG was because he thought he'd either beat the case because it was self-defense or get probation in children's court. He never imagined he would get charged as an adult and be sentenced to prison. With a long sigh of regret, he wished none of it ever happened while he waited on his bed for his little sister to finish getting ready.

Chapter Four
AIN'T NO HOE
IN ME

Back in the hood, BONE and SQUEAK had issues of their own. They tried to contact the thieving women, but their social media accounts were no longer active. It was as if they vanished off the face of the Earth. Fearing they would be shot or worse by LOUIE-V for letting his bale of premium marijuana get stolen, they sat over SQUEAK's mama house and talked about how they were going to fix things. Playing an NBA video game to entertain themselves while they brainstormed ideas around, SQUEAK rolled up a fat blunt with some Backwoods cigar wraps. After taking a few pulls, he hacked back out the smoke and passed the blunt to BONE.

Coughing loudly as he hit the potent marijuana, BONE leaned back on the leather sectional sofa and spoke as if there wasn't any hope left, "I blame you. We got robbed by some beautiful-ass bitches because of you. Why couldn't it be by some ugly-ass niggas? No, not

BONE and SQUEAK—it had to be by some beautiful-ass bitches. Now bro don't think we can handle our business."

"You still on that?" SQUEAK paused the game and asked while he sat a seat over from his homie on the same couch.

"You had to "accept" they snake-ass friend request. I swear these broke bitches is worse than these thirsty-ass niggas out here."

"You right, I fucked up, but you need to own up to what you did too, fam. Shit, we both let the hoes in the trap."

"Well, it won't matter anyway because we both dead if we don't get it back."

"We need better ideas."

"We can search everywhere in the Mil and still not come up on shit—they might not even live here. That's the problem, we don't have a way to find they ass," BONE bitterly replied and then took a deep pull from the blunt.

"Maybe we should figure out how to make things right even if we don't get it back," SQUEAK suggested before going off into his own thoughts.

He knew they needed a way to get back in good standing with LOUIE-V and the only way to do that was to give him the money he would've made off his package. To SQUEAK, looking for those women was a waste of time because they were already long gone if they were smart. After judging their intelligence by the way they played him and BONE, he felt they were smart—real smart. So, instead of focusing on the females who robbed them, he decided to think about other ways to get the money. After several minutes of brainstorming, he came up with an idea, but he needed to know for certain how much they needed to have.

"Hey BONE, how much money did fam want to see off that anyway?" SQUEAK asked curiously, knowing his homie was privy to those matters and he was in the weed house more as his backup.

"One-twenty-five. Why?" BONE replied like it was a question not worth asking or answering.

"I think I know where we can get the bread to pay him bro, but things might get messy."

"Wait a minute, you mean to tell me you know where we can get our hands on that kind a scratch and you decide to wait until we have to give it up before you tell me this shit."

"That's because we gone do some shit that's only done when you run out of options. Bro expects his bag back in three days—it's the only Ace I can pull out my sleeve."

"SQUEAK, spit it out!"

"We kidnap CASPER," SQUEAK murmured like the name carried an omen of death attached to it.

"Aw hell naw! Bro. Fa real?" BONE sat up on the couch and asked with a dreadful look on his face.

"As real as it gets—fuck CASPER! I don't care about his homies, his guns, or his money. I'm sick of fake-ass goons like dude."

"You just mad because he punched yo sister in her eye. I don't condone domestic violence, but yo sister be talkin' a lot of shit bro."

"She only talk shit to you and that's because you irk the hell out of her. But that fool CASPER, he beat up every female he sleeps with. I bet my sister is just one on a long list."

"Wasn't he over here a few days ago?" BONE asked as he put out the last of the blunt in an ashtray.

"Yeah, he still come by and see her a couple times a week. That's what I've been tryin' to tell you—it doesn't get any easier. When he pulls up on his late-night rendezvous with her, we come out the shadows with them choppers and lock shit down," SQUEAK spoke with an expression of accomplishment for coming up with his brilliant, but dangerous plan.

BONE sat back and let the effects of the premium marijuana aid him in weighing out the pros and cons of SQUEAK's idea. They needed to square things with LOUIE-V, but his homie wanted to kidnap someone who was known for having a violent reputation in the streets. The cost could be great if things didn't go right. And thinking back, he could remember a few times when SQUEAK's plans failed miserably.

Valuing their lives more than their potential victim, BONE glued his eyes on SQUEAK with a contemplative stare and asked, "How much and how we gone get it?"

Happy to see BONE was on board with him, SQUEAK replied coolly, "Dude got the weight on the boy, girl, X, and syrup. I bet we can get two hundred easy fa his ass if we let the muthafucka call somebody who care about his life."

"I like the plan so far. Where we gone have 'em drop off the money?"

"We'll have 'em drop it off at the gas station by the 35th Street bridge that takes you to the south side. We got open traffic on both sides of the street if we need to dip out a there and we can't be ambushed because of the bridge. We'll be able to see any trouble before we feel any."

"What about straps?"

"I got throwaways. You ask a whole lot of questions fa somebody who only need to know how much and how we gone get it."

"Only a fool don't ask questions. So far, your idea sound good. You know I'm the type that'll tell you if yo shit fucked up. More homies need to let they bros know when they idea is a bad one," BONE spoke like a man who'd never follow anyone blindly.

"I feel you. Look, I got everything we need covered. I even know a place where we gone house his ass until we get paid. So, you need to let me know if you in or out because I'm doin' it tonight," SQUEAK told him and meant it.

"Damn, tonight? I see you determined. Are you sure you wanna kidnap CASPER?"

"Bro, fuck CASPER and any nigga who roll with his bitch ass! Is you down?"

"I heard CASPER made a nigga eat his own shit before. The shit out of his own ass, SQUEAK."

"I don't give a fuck."

"I heard he knocked a nigga's teeth out with the back end of a hammer."

"I don't care, BONE!"

"I heard he broke this dude—"

"Is you down or not bro?"

BONE sat back and continued to weigh out the pros and cons of SQUEAK's plan, but one question seemed more prevalent than any other one he thought: Are we prepared to kill CASPER if our lives depend on it? He knew his answer was "yes," so he had to be certain his homie fully understood the risk.

"Ain't no goin' back once we start this. I want to know all the details and don't leave nothin' out. For CASPER's sake, he better cooperate, or he gone be CASPER The Unfriendly Ghost," BONE uttered in a deadly tone while he reached over and showed his homie love with a hood handshake.

"You had me worried fa a minute, especially when you made the nigga sound all supernatural and shit. I don't know—I thought he spooked you," SQUEAK spoke in a way that suggested BONE might be.

"Nigga, ain't no hoe in me! CASPER can get it too! To me, he's a solution to a major problem—it ain't personal."

"I'll be straight up with you, it's personal as fuck fa me bro."

"Is she good?"

"Who?"

"Naomi."

"Sis good, she still got on shades everywhere she goes though. I wish she didn't mess with these trash-ass bums, but she likes who she likes."

"Fucking with CASPER, I see she likes 'em over forty. Ain't she almost thirty?"

"She twenty-six. You know age ain't nothin' but a number. She attracted to OGs with money."

"I'm just sayin'," BONE replied as if he had more to say but decided to leave the subject alone and started the video game to finish hooping.

"Sayin' what?" SQUEAK paused the game again and asked defensively.

"She could a had a pimp like me—play nigga!" BONE yelled with a smile and restarted the game.

"Fuck you!" SQUEAK yelled back, and they continued to play their game as if they hadn't plotted to kidnap someone for a hefty ransom later that night.

As for MEAN-MUG and TRIGGAH G, they decided to take the cocaine and money they stole from Pedro's house and treat themselves to a VIP room at one of the strip clubs in the city. Choosing

"Hickey's" on 37th and Hopkins Avenue to hang out, they bought a private room and requested girl after girl to entertain them while they snorted coke and tried to figure out their next score. With cocaine dust on his nostrils, MEAN-MUG turned to TRIGGAH G and shouted, "You see this shit right here, we should have beautiful naked bitches around us whenever we want! This blow—we should have it anytime we want bro!"

Nodding to the music and feeling the strong effects of the alcohol and cocaine he heavily indulged in, TRIGGAH G could only say, "Facts."

"I know why we can't come up. When we think of a lick, it's not big enough to make us rich. That's why we need a move that'll have us set fa life."

"Facts."

"We put in work."

"Facts."

"Damn, this stripper got some big-ass titties!"

"Facts!"

Taking a minute to gaze at the heavenly body of the Black stripper giving them lap dances, MEAN-MUG almost broke the house rules by touching her large, natural breasts. The sexually stimulating moves she made enticed him the more she rubbed her body against his. When he touched her swaying thighs, she gently removed his hands from her body and shook her head in disapproval. Smiling and respecting the sexy young stripper's wishes, he didn't touch her again. Instead, he took a rolled up hundred-dollar bill and snorted up a half a gram of cocaine. When she was finished, he tipped her and told her to send a new girl to their private room.

"The whole point is: *We're* better than this shit! Every single day we out here and fa what? I wanna fancy car or a tricked-out truck to floss! Why do we have to settle fa crumbs?" MEAN-MUG asked with agitation while he took swigs from his bottle of beer.

Deciding to finally say more than one word, TRIGGAH G took a toot of blow first and stated, "We need to rob a fool who got bricks of dope. If there's bricks, you can bet there's plenty paper too. You know what, I heard Pedro brag about his older cousin Carlos to his younger cousin the last time I went through there to catch. Now Carlos is supposed to be the man out here. Let Pedro tell it, dude gotta storage room full of dope."

"He gotta storage room full of kilos?"

"That's what I heard."

While in the middle of feeling his giddiness about stealing multiple kilos of cocaine intensify within him, MEAN-MUG's attention to his homie was diverted to another shapely stripper walking in their room. With tattoos covering most of her baby-oiled-up body, she twerked her large, round butt rapidly and erotically to the music she chose to dance to. Liking everything he saw about her, he quickly threw a few singles and placed one inside her red laced G-string panties. When he moved it over to expose her vagina, she didn't stop him or disapprove of his actions.

Sensing he had a stripper with them who'd be more receptive to their sexual mood, MEAN-MUG offered her some cocaine to toot, and she eagerly accepted. While she did, he began to massage her naked breasts. To show he wasn't the type to skimp, he pulled loose a crisp C-note from his wad of cash and placed it in front of her. Saying nothing, she took the money, pulled out a condom from her purse and began to give him mind-blowing fellatio. While he leaned back and enjoyed her expertise, MEAN-MUG began to rant under his coke-induced high.

"This the shit I'm talkin' bout, fine-ass bitches should give us head whenever we want! If this is really the concrete jungle, then we the lions in this bitch! It should snow cocaine every damn day fa niggas like us!" he exclaimed and snorted some more blow.

TRIGGAH G, very high and enjoying himself, interrupted him by saying, "We just robbed Pedro's crib. How we gone get him to tell us where Carlos stay?"

"We gone make Pedro call dude and then we gone snatch Carlos when they meet up. Then we off to his stash. Simple."

"So, you wanna go back to Pedro's crib? I don't think his bitch can take another home invasion, but it is what it is."

"Nope, we gone catch his ass in the street."

"So, we gone camp outside his crib until he leaves?

Then with a devilish smirk on his face, MEAN-MUG answered, "Not right in front, but we'll be on the block."

Not wanting to sit outside their mark's house all night long, especially when he wanted to party more, TRIGGAH G leaned his head back unhappily and asked, "When?"

"Tomorrow morning."

Pulsating multi-colored strobe lights and Black urban street music altered their senses while the intensity of their euphoric state was magnified even further with more cocaine and liquor. The dizziness of the liquor coupled with the anxiousness of the blow made strange, yet familiar bedfellows as TRIGGAH G began to succumb to his erotic surroundings. Pulling a hundred-dollar bill out of his share of the money they pilfered and slamming it down where the busy stripper/prostitute could see it, he got up and started unbuckling his black denim jeans while he danced behind her.

A true hustler herself, the lovely woman briefly stopped her sexual performance long enough to purse her cash and retrieve another condom for her erected dance partner. As soon as she gave it to TRIGGAH G for him to put on, she turned back to MEAN-MUG—who was on the verge of climaxing before she stopped. To make up for her abrupt hiatus, she used sexual maneuvers on him that she saved for her best clients. With his toes clenched and his free left hand frantically feeling around the small table beside him for his bottle of beer, he had absolutely nothing to complain about.

An hour later, they were back in MEAN-MUG's car and cruising the streets for something else to get into. Still energized from their sexual activities, they were riding high on the moment—as well as the drugs and alcohol they heavily used. Opting to play a heartless game of "I Dare Yo Ass..." with his revved-up homie, MEAN-MUG pointed to a bus stop with a man sitting alone and told TRIGGAH G, "I dare yo ass to walk over to that man on that bus stop and bust him in his shit."

More than willing to play the coldblooded game with him, TRIGGAH G shouted excitedly, "Pull this bitch over!"

When MEAN-MUG parked across the busy street from the man sitting on the bus stop bench, TRIGGAH G got out the car and ran across the street pretending to catch the bus too. But instead of sitting on the metal bench with him, he walked over and stood directly in front of the clueless pedestrian. Then without warning, TRIGGAH G drew back his right arm and punched the unsuspecting victim in his face as hard as he could. The back of the older man's head slammed into a section of glass from the metal and glass bus stop shelter around the bench and cracked it.

Fearing he was going to die, the man tried to get up and run but TRIGGAH G had him boxed in. Now riding the adrenaline high that comes from making someone else feel afraid, he gave the injured man a right—left—then another powerful right jab in his face and made the visibly shaken man fall back into the bench. Completely confused about why he was being viciously attacked, the now bleeding man desperately tried to ball up in the corner of the bench and protect his head from any further abuse with his arms. Pleading for his assailant to leave him alone the entire time, a new flurry of punches and kicks began to slowly overpower him.

TRIGGAH G wouldn't let up. He wanted each punch and kick he threw to hurt the man badly. With a sick sense of enjoyment from seeing him cower in fearful pain, his ruthless attacks continued until the man was unconscious. Acting like he won a mixed martial arts fight against a top competitor, he hurried back across the street and jumped back inside the car.

"Boom! Did you see how I faded that fool!" TRIGGAH G exclaimed after he slammed the door shut.

After MEAN-MUG passed his homie a blunt to hit; he was beyond amused by the spectacle he put on. So much, he laughed uncontrollably and cried out, "Fam, I recorded it so the whole world can see it—you gone go viral!"

Not wanting to let the weed slow down the rush he was feeling, TRIGGAH G was hesitant to take the blunt from him, but MEAN-MUG sensed his apprehensiveness and remarked, "Don't worry G, I put at least a half a grit in that bitch—you ain't gone come down no time soon."

"My nigga," TRIGGAH G replied coolly as he hit the cocaine-laced blunt.

"You do know the dare was to only hit him one time," MEAN-MUG chuckled as he steered through traffic.

"He tried to get up."

"He ain't now."

"No sir."

Chapter Five
LA DI DA DI DA

By the time FRICTION and his little sister Ki-Ki finally left the house to walk to the store a couple blocks away, he'd lost some of his excitement to go. He was happy to be free and back on the block, but so many things he remembered had changed since his incarceration. He recognized only a few people from the many that lived in his hood. To make matters worse, he was just as broke as the day he got locked up. The walk to him was more a "walk of shame" for his current financial shortcomings than a simple walk to the store with his younger sister.

Ki-Ki wasn't doing anything to make him feel any better about his situation either. Wearing her favorite lavender-colored leggings under her new purple short set outfit with her matching gym shoes and hair barrettes, she looked at her big brother while they walked together and told him, "You look mad."

Not wanting to share his innermost thoughts with a child, he looked at her with the frustration that comes with being penniless and sighed, "I'm not mad."

"Mama said you was stupid for going to jail."

"She right—it was stupid."

"She said you fucked up your life."

"Don't cuss."

"That's what she said. She also said you gotta move out if you don't get a job," she divulged innocently enough, but the blow from her remark killed what was left of his optimistic spirit.

"Mama said that?" FRICTION asked her with a serious expression on his face.

"You look mad."

"I'm not mad."

"Don't be mad, we still love you."

"I love y'all too."

"All you have to do is get a job and you can stay."

Choosing not to talk anymore, he silently walked with his little sister, looking at all the changes around him. Where there used to be a duplex he hung out at, an empty grassy lot was there now because it was bulldozed. He also didn't see a lot of people he grew up with. Honestly, he was beginning to feel more and more like an outsider.

The rest of the way to the corner store was uneventful and rather peaceful. FRICTION did get jealous when he saw a couple of large-rimmed, newer modeled cars he'd never seen before drive by him having a great time with their lives; but other than that, he was busy enjoying the fresh air. Breathing in deeply and exhaling out slowly so he could appreciate it more, he was relieved to be back home—even if home had changed quite a bit. The one place he knew hadn't changed was the corner store. It was Arab-owned and had been around for many years before he got locked up.

He couldn't remember when or if the store was ever Black- or White-owned, but Ali, the owner of Friendly Foods, was someone he saw his whole life. Ali had a long and gray beard and wore a cultural turban every day; he and his son Abdul were both known as good people who always tried their best to look out for folks in the neighborhood. Seeing a few new faces standing around when they made it there, FRICTION ignored them and walked in with his little sister. Once inside, he was surprised to see how packed the small store was with customers.

There were people standing in two long lines. Before he'd left to do his time, there had been only one, and it was for the front counter. The second line he saw led to a small deli shop they'd added that sold various hot and cold foods to eat. He took a whiff of what they were serving and was pleased by the smell. The sub sandwich he saw a coworker making for a customer was stuffed with so much deli meat, vegetables, and cheese—his stomach growled just looking at it. When he glanced down and saw Ki-Ki staring impatiently at him, he stopped gazing hungrily at the food and began to maneuver his way with her through the waiting crowd of shoppers.

"They sell the best beef nachos—they use a lot of everything and it's really delicious. You should try it," Ki-Ki suggested to her big brother, completely unaware that he didn't have any money.

"Maybe later. What did you come to get?" FRICTION asked her while they moved slowly to the back of the line.

"I want my favorite candy bar, a bag of hot chips, and a grape soda."

"Mama told me chips and a soda. She didn't say a candy bar."

"But she knows I get the same thing every time I come here!"

"OK, don't snap. Hey, I'm sorry Ki-Ki. I should a been around to know yo favorite stuff."

"You're here now."

"Yes, I am."

While they were approaching the refrigeration unit to get her grape soda, FRICTION inadvertently stepped on the expensive basketball sneakers of a duck-footed teenage boy who was already in line. Immediately upset because someone he didn't know scuffed up his new shoes, the teenager frowned at FRICTION and shouted, "Watch yo feet bitch-ass nigga!"

Embarrassed and angered by the teen's disrespectful outburst, FRICTION's first thought was to punch him in his eye; but instead, he chose to try a less violent approach since his release from prison wasn't even a full day yet. So, after looking at the teen like he wanted to put his hands on him, FRICTION switched to a smile and politely told him, "I ain't no bitch-ass nigga, but I do apologize fa the marks I made on yo kicks."

"La Di Da Di Da! That's what yo chirpin' sound like to me bitch-ass nigga!" he rudely replied as he stood in line and continued with his blatant disrespect.

"Fuck yo shoes then if you gone be a little pussy about it! I hope they get stole little bitch!" FRICTION yelled back and proceeded to get his sister's soda with her right behind him.

When they got to the refrigerator, Ki-Ki nervously grabbed her brother's arm and told him, "He's here all the time."

"Who—that punk?"

"Yes. He's here every time I come here."

"Forget that little wannabe. Is this the soda?"

"Yes, that's my favorite grape soda."

"Here you go. I want you to run over there and grab yo chips while I get in line, OK?" FRICTION asked his young sister, hoping it would move things faster.

"OK. Don't let nobody jump in front of you," Ki-Ki instructed and skipped over to the area where the convenient store's various kinds of snack chips were located.

While he waited in line, FRICTION began to think more about his current financial circumstance, and it bothered him greatly. He wanted his own money to buy his little sister the things she liked to have, and he didn't. The whole ordeal made him feel less than a man and even worse—less than a big brother. Feeling tempted to take MANIAC up on his offer to work for him, he convinced himself to wait and see how his job hunting goes.

As the line slowly moved, he imagined what he'd do if he had a lot of cash and thought, *I'd buy my mama a house so she wouldn't have to rent from anyone else. I'd also buy me a house to live in because I don't wanna stay with my mama forever. I'd have one of the coolest cars in the city to flaunt my swag in.* Of course, there were a lot more things he wanted, but those were the "top three" on his list.

Just as FRICTION was about to feel uncomfortable standing around so many people he didn't know, Ki-Ki came skipping back to him with her favorite bag of chips swinging in her hands. When he saw her smiling face, his subtle anxiety went away.

"Me and my friends always eat these. Mama don't let me eat them all the time because they the hot kind, but they taste good," she insisted with a warm grin while she opened the bag of chips and began to eat some next to him.

"Don't they burn your mouth?" he asked to keep her talking to him.

"Yeah! That's why you got me a grape soda! Everybody knows grape soda makes the burn go away!"

"Oh yeah, I forgot."

"You look mad."

"Why do you think I'm mad?"

"Because that boy called you names."

"No, he didn't.

"Uh-huh, he said La Di Da Di Da and then he called you a bitch-ass nigga two times," Ki-Ki vividly reminded him.

Hearing snickers from a few people who witnessed the verbal exchange he had with the teenage boy, FRICTION tried to make light of it by saying, "His moms didn't home train little dude."

"I think the home where he needs his training is close because he's always here when me and mama come to the store," Ki-Ki added for good measure.

When they finally made it to the front of the line, FRICTION was surprised to see only Abdul working the cash register behind the counter. Dressed in regular American clothes and not wearing anything on his head, he was busy chatting with customers, directing his coworkers, and ringing up items for sale. By the time he noticed FRICTION, he was standing in front of him. Remembering him right away, Abdul smiled and reached out for a handshake.

After FRICTION warmly shook it, he smiled at Abdul and joked, "Gimme all yo money."

"Shit—take it! Here, you can have the whole damn store! I want to see you deal with this angry mob day in and day out! I bet after one day of this madness you'd beg me to take it back! You'd beg me to take it back and you'd leave all the money in the register! Shit, you'd beg me to take back, leave all the money in the register and add several more hundred to it because you pity me! My man, FRICTION! It's good to see you!" Abdul joked loudly as he greeted him like a close friend.

"It's good to see you too, man. I dig what you and your dad did to the place. Where's Ali?"

"Aw, you didn't know, but my dad passed away almost two years ago. Yeah, he was the greatest Ali I ever knew—not taking nothing away from the boxer."

"I'm sorry bro, I didn't know. Yeah, he was one of the great ones. I remember when he used to let me get some meat, bread, and cheese on credit until moms got paid whenever we ran out of food. Yeah, I'll miss him."

"I miss him too. But hey, look at you! You used to be a scrawny kid and now you a grown-ass man! I see you've been working out!"

"I keep myself busy," FRICTION replied as he flashed back to all the workouts from boredom over the last three and a half years.

"As you can see my friend, I keep myself busy here too! You know what, I might have a security/deli/janitor job for you if you're looking for work. I need some dependable employees here who show up on time!" Abdul shouted loud enough to make sure his two workers in the deli heard him.

"I got some things in the mix, but I'll be here to see you if they don't pan out. I came with Ki-Ki to get her favorite zoo-zoos and wham-whams. Can I get that candy bar right there please?"

"That's her favorite. How are you doing today, Ki-Ki?" Abdul asked her with a smile while he took her folded closed bag of chips and put it in a black shopping bag with her candy bar.

"I'm fine. You don't have to put my soda in the bag because I want to open it," she told him maturely and then looked at her brother like she wanted him to do it for her.

After he opened and gave it to her, FRICTION let Ki-Ki give Abdul the EBT card to pay for her snacks and then he gave Abdul one last friendly handshake goodbye before he left the store and headed back home with her. They were only a block and a half into their walk when a new modeled red Nissan Maxima with extremely dark-tinted windows slowly rode by bumping their music. Then FRICTION observed the suspicious looking car stop in the middle of the street only a few houses from where they were and turn down its loud music. He wasn't alarmed until the car suddenly reversed and stopped next to them.

Thinking it might be some lost females or something, FRICTION was caught completely off guard when the back window rolled down revealing the barrel of a black AK-47 assault rifle pointing at him. The only thing that came to his mind was to protect his little sister, so he grabbed her by her arm and swung her behind him to shield her from any gunfire. As far as he was concerned, he'd die before he'd let any harm come to his family. He could hear her yelling for him to let her go and could feel her trying to yank her arm free from him to show she didn't appreciate what he was doing to her, but his focus was truly on one thing: the assault rifle aimed at them.

"What up now, La Di Da Di Da ass nigga! You dirtied up my kicks and then you tried to treat me like a hoe-ass nigga! I should chop yo bitch ass!" the scorned young thug yelled at FRICTION while he kept his firearm pointed at him.

Not able to think of what he could say in time to pacify things, FRICTION could only look at the armed teen like he wasn't afraid to die. With his sister gripped tightly in his right hand, he remained alert to run with her in front of him if they had to dash through a yard to get away. He knew it really didn't matter what came out of his mouth anyway because the young hoodlum wanted FRICTION to fear him and that was something he wasn't going to give the little punk the satisfaction of having.

"You scared to speak bitch-ass nigga!" the young gunman yelled at him, but it was FRICTION's young sister who replied.

"He's not a bitch-ass nigga! Leave my big brother alone! He's been in jail a long time and now he's home!" Ki-Ki shouted back fearlessly at the car full of goons after she broke free of FRICTION's grip and stood in front of him.

Still looking brave enough to fight every single one of them to the death, FRICTION remained silent and tried unsuccessfully to pull his little sister back behind him. As much as he tried, she defiantly resisted his efforts to restrain her. The reason she was doing it touched the deepest depths of his soul because he knew she loved him enough to help. Regardless though, he understood her actions were coming from a child's mindset. His frustration with her increased the more she wouldn't let him shield her when he tried to.

Seeing he wasn't getting the reaction he wanted, the young gunman and FRICTION remained in their standoff of wills for two heart pounding minutes before the armed teen leaned halfway out the window so his face would be remembered and stated, "Yo sister saved yo ass! Drive G."

Then the car sped off and was gone.

After taking in a deep sigh of relief and shaking his head about how crazy his first day free had been, FRICTION didn't bother reaching for his little sister's arm. Instead, he began to walk home and waved his hand for her to follow him. From what Ki-Ki had shown him today, there wasn't any need to hold hands anymore. He was just glad she was too young to realize they were about to be shot at by a weapon that leaves very few survivors.

The entire situation silently bothered him so much he didn't want to talk. He only kept replaying the dangerous event repeatedly in his mind. He couldn't believe it all started over a stupid shoe being stepped on. Wanting to see how the armed teen's pipes would hold up under the same kind of pressure, he made sure he remembered his face and the kind of car he was being drove in.

His sister did as she was signaled to do and began to skip beside him singing, "La Di Da Di Da!"

FRICTION turned to her and told her flatly, "Stop Ki-Ki."

Not understanding what was wrong with singing the catchy melody, Ki-Ki looked over at her big brother and asked, "Why?"

"Because I said so."

"But I like it."

"Stop it, please."

"You look mad. Are you mad?" Ki-Ki asked as she grabbed her brother's arm and began to swing it playfully.

"A little," FRICTION replied stone-faced and continued to walk her home.

Later that night, BONE and SQUEAK hid behind some over-size bushes beside SQUEAK mom's garage and waited for CASPER to pull up. To protect their identities, they both wore all-black clothing, camouflage skull-printed face masks, and baseball caps. While they sat on plastic crates, their impatience started to show from waiting so long and from constantly being bitten by bloodthirsty mosquitoes. They hoped CASPER would show up soon to his erotic escapade with Naomi because they didn't know how much more they could take.

"Damn, these mosquitoes eatin' my ass up!" SQUEAK complained as he tried to swat the small swarm away from him.

"They *is* deep as hell," BONE responded equally frustrated.

"We need to pick another place to lay low if he don't bring his ass on cause I'm a die in this bush if I stay here! I feel sick—I think I got the West Nile Virus!"

"Calm yo ass down, he'll be here. We both heard yo sister tell him to be here around one. Naomi is pretty as hell. He ain't gone blow off some pretty pussy. It'd be a different story if she was ugly as fuck."

"I feel you, but we ain't got shit to kill these hungry mutha-fuckas! I got the shit to do the lick—the least you could a did was bring some mosquito spray! I'm bit so bad nigga—you could a brought some roach spray!"

"We'll give him twenty more minutes and then we gone call it one because these the only bushes we can pop out of without him seein' us. I can't believe I'm even doin' this. This was yo brilliant idea, remember. You actin' like you ain't down to do this shit now."

"Look bro, I'm bein' eaten alive by a thousand fuckin' mos-quitoes! You right about this bein' my plan, but you wrong as hell about me not bein' down to do this though. All I'm sayin' is that we need some fuckin' RAID or something to—" SQUEAK was explain-ing before he was cut off by BONE who whispered, "Shh, somebody comin' up the alley."

A new modeled blue diamond metallic colored Lincoln Navigator slowly drove near them and parked behind the garage. Arriving a little later than he expected, CASPER was busy explaining why to Naomi on his smartphone. Never going anywhere without his chrome Desert Eagle, he placed it in the small of his back before he opened the door to get out. Feeling good and dressed to impress, he sprayed a little extra cologne on himself to finish the final touch.

But as soon as he got out and was in the process of closing the door, he was accosted by two gunmen with their faces covered. Not wanting to be shot or worse, instead of complying with his armed aggressors, he bolted through a yard and sprinted as fast as his legs could move to escape, leaving BONE and SQUEAK caught off guard and with no choice but to chase after him.

CASPER ran through yards, jumping over ornaments and furniture to avoid being captured, but his attackers were hot on his trail. They didn't let anything he tried to do deter them or slow down their pursuit. BONE and SQUEAK jumped on and off backyard patios, leaped over flipped garbage cans and yard furniture to keep up with him. But as they were closing in, CASPER pulled out his Desert Eagle and fired off five rounds in their direction. When he heard shots fire back, there was no doubt in his mind about being killed if they catch him.

"He got a gun!" BONE exclaimed and fired two rounds back at him.

"Don't kill him BONE, we need him alive!" SQUEAK shouted to remind him of the ransom money they were after.

"If I gotta choose between him and me: I'm choosing me!" BONE yelled and fired another round at him.

CASPER ran through gangway after gangway trying to escape his unseen assailants. His heart was pounding like a kick drum in his chest, and it was beating so rapidly—he thought it was going to overwork itself and stop. He wondered how many masked men were chasing after him and imagined a number so high—it only frightened him to run more. He ran and ran—until he reached a bridged creek with a twenty-feet drop that prevented him from going any further. The walkway to cross it was a block and a half away and he was too exhausted to take another step—but he had no choice but to try and reach it.

Sweating profusely and panting heavily from being overheated and in desperate need of water, CASPER took some time to take in large breaths of air before he cautiously headed to the bridge. He looked around with extreme paranoia and tried to speed up his pace twice, but each time, he had to slow back down or risk passing out. When he was about halfway there, he thought he heard someone behind him, so he quickly turned around and scarily shot off three more rounds from his handgun. After realizing it was only a figment of his imagination, he breathed a sigh of relief and tiredly continued onward to the walkway.

Every car he heard go by spooked him and even the noise he kept hearing from crickets sent him looking in every direction as his anxiety steadily progressed into panic. Making matters worse, CASPER lost his phone while he was being foot-chased, making him feel alone and helpless. He needed a safe place to hide and a way to call for help, but he didn't know anyone where he was. At almost two in the morning, he knew no one would help him anyway, even if he did spot someone to ask.

When he finally reached the small bridge, he thanked God for giving him the strength to accomplish it, even with painful spasms in both his legs. After giving his aches some time to go away, he slowly walked onto the iron-fenced walkway and sorely began a light jog across it. When he was almost midway, a masked gunman stepped onto it to block his exit. Frantically, he turned around to get back off, but another masked gunman was waiting for him. With only two rounds left in the ten-round magazine inside his gun and outnumbered, he began to weigh what options he had left.

As both gunmen approached him with their weapons drawn, he knew he'd lose his life instantly if he tried to shoot his way out of it, so CASPER chose to give up and try to negotiate his release. To show his surrender, he dropped his gun on the ground and kicked it away from him, then he stood silently with both hands in the air as he nervously watched them menacingly approach him. Now disarmed and at their mercy, he hoped his violent past wasn't coming back to haunt him.

"That's the smartest thing you did tonight! Get on yo knees!" SQUEAK shouted with his voice disguised.

Doing as he was instructed, CASPER sorely got down on his knees and panted, "I don't know what this is all about, but I'm sure we can work it out without me being murdered. I don't know who hired you to come at me, but there's gotta be some room fa negotiations."

Deciding to play on his fears, BONE walked up to him and smacked him in his face with his handgun and angrily shouted, "Do you think we can be bought off so easily? We were hired to do a job and that's what we're here to do!"

"How much did they offer y'all to kill me? I'll double it—triple that shit to kill they ass. Better yet, tell me how much it would cost me fa y'all to walk away and forget about me," CASPER pleaded in a desperate attempt to broker a deal.

"Two hundred G's," BONE declared without hesitation.

"Bet. Give me an hour and you got it. You got a phone?" CASPER asked as if things were now worked out and his life was no longer in danger.

"Fool, you gone stay with us and have somebody bring us the money! We'll let you go when we get it," BONE replied and pointed his gun at CASPER's head.

"OK, OK. I thought we was good now. You don't have to put yo strap up all in my face—you could shoot me by mistake. Ain't no payment if I'm dead," CASPER joked, but the gunmen didn't laugh.

"I don't have to hear you talk anymore either if you dead," BONE replied seriously.

"Cool, I'll shut the fuck up then. Y'all gone let me know who hired y'all after I hit y'all hand, right? I just wanted to thank y'all fa not—"

But before he could finish his sentence, SQUEAK walked over with a black pillowcase and put it over CASPER's still talking head. He then pulled out some long black tie wraps from the pocket of his jeans, put two together and tightened the pillowcase around his neck. Afterwards, he tie-wrapped his hands tightly behind his back. Once they were certain he couldn't see or move his hands freely, they walked him off the bridge and led him to BONE's new modeled green Camaro with volt colored racing stripes.

The entire time CASPER tried unsuccessfully to convince the armed duo that his restraints weren't necessary. So, rather than risk angering anyone, he felt it was in his best interest to be quiet and do what they say. As far as he was concerned, there was no amount of money he had that was worth more than his life. And fortunate for him, he had a lot more than a couple hundred grand saved up—a whole lot more.

When they got there, BONE popped the small trunk open with his car remote and made CASPER lay down inside it. Not fighting or resisting in any way, he sorely climbed inside, and BONE closed it shut. Afterwards, he waved for SQUEAK to meet him in front of his car.

"He barely fit. We need somewhere to take him fast," BONE told him as he looked back at the trunk of his car.

"I got that covered. We gone take him by Sheila's crib," SQUEAK replied coolly.

"That crackhead gone want a least seven grams of hard to keep her big fat mouth shut! You sure we should take him over there?"

"We ain't got a lot of options fam. At least niggas mind they business over there and she got a basement we can chill in until we get paid."

"Fuck it, we take him there then, but you gone pay her."

"Cool, I'll hit her hand. Who cares because we gone have the bread to pay her, LOUIE-V, and anybody else we owe cause we bout to get paid!"

"That part. I want this to go quick and flawless. OK, it's time to roll out."

"Bro, yo trunk *is* little as hell. I hope he don't die before we get there. Fuck! What if he needs to take a shit?" SQUEAK asked because it was his first time thinking about it.

"I told you I heard he made a nigga eat his own shit before—leave a teaspoon!" BONE laughed while he got in his ride.

"Damn, that's cold. I'll leave his ass a tablespoon!" SQUEAK joked back as he got in too and they headed to Shelia's house with their $200,000 meal ticket wiggling in the trunk.

Chapter Six
FLOW HOTTA

"Wat up? Wat up? This ya boy BIG MONEY MIKE and we back live in the studio of ya favorite morning show with the BOOTH of TRUTH on 103.6 FM fa Hip-Hop and R&B on ya radio and we have a special guest here today! LOUIE-Vs in the house! Let me hear all my dogs' woof to that! (Woof-Woof! Woof-Woof!)

So, tell the BOOTH of TRUTH: Is it true about the beef you got with MACK DADDY? There's a lot of crazy rumors circulating about you wanting to spar with the heavyweight in the ring! Is it legit or not?" the veteran DJ excitedly asked the recording artist with his two co-hosts MARGARITA MAY and TANG-TANG eagerly waiting to join in the discussion.

"That's not true. People start these rumors to get subscriptions on their YouTube channels. I grew up listening to MACK DADDY like everybody else. Let me be clear: MACK DADDY is a legend in this game, and he should be respected. There's no beef," LOUIE-V declared in the microphone in front of him.

"No-no-no, uh-uh, don't you even come up in the BOOTH of TRUTH and try to tell a lie to TANG-TANG! I personally read your deleted Tweet and saw the video you made with LADY SHAY when you said Mack Daddy was as old as the damn dinosaurs and then you called him a caveman! I will make you 'Taste the Tang' up in here if you even think about playing me!" TANG-TANG boisterously rebutted in the microphone in front of him.

"Don't make him 'Taste the Tang' TANG-TANG. But people across the world do want to know: What made you make those comments if you don't have beef with him? Is it to create hype for a new single release?" MARGARITA MAY asked as she tried to probe the rapper for more exclusive details.

"I voiced my opinion about the new trends in rap music—that's all. I didn't mean for it to be misconstrued and completely blown out of context. All I tried to do was talk about today's culture," LOUIE-V expressed passively, trying not to put himself in the hotbox with the radio show hosts.

Taking his cue to speak again, BIG MONEY MIKE chimed in and stated, "You know, there's a lot of talk nowadays about 'The Culture' and I need to know: Which culture are we talking about? Is it the Black culture, the rap culture, the street culture? I want you to tell all the misled listeners out there who's asking this question: What culture is LOUIE-V talking about specifically?"

Making sure he chose his words carefully, LOUIE-V told his fans: The culture of our own artistic evolution. Like all evolution—it must outdo the old."

"Bam! There he goes again, MARGARITA MAY! He just told the world he's more evolved than MACK DADDY! Evolution takes thousands of years boo—not a generation or two!" TANG-TANG countered with some science of his own.

"I see TANG-TANG has the Science Channel recorded on his DVR. I wonder what else he records?" MARGARITA MAY hinted to their listening audience.

"I'm not sure I wanna know," BIG MONEY MIKE joked.

"Well honey pie, let me break it all the way down to you and all the listeners like this: What TANG-TANG records in the privacy of my beautifully and tastefully styled condo loft would have everybody up in here wanting to Taste the Tang!" TANG-TANG retorted and snapped his fingers around in the air.

"Well, I'll tell you right now, I'm not gone Taste the Tang. I'm perfectly fine with my coffee," BIG MONEY MIKE responded with a chuckle and took a sip of some out his favorite coffee mug.

"Me either. I like strong drinks—not tangy ones," MARGARITA MAY added for good measure.

"Then don't be up in here asking me about my personal video choices because there ain't no shame in my game and to Taste the Tang—all you got to do is add water baby! I only have one question to ask you LOUIE-V: What makes you think you're more lyrically evolved than MACK DADDY?" TANG-TANG broke away from conversing with his coworkers and asked LOUIE-V in a pessimistic way.

"Tell me if you heard a flow hotta. I'm not some new rapper who plans to be here fa two or three years and then I'm out. I'm not gone give my fans only one good hit every album I make. My goal is to spit that fire until the rap game expires," LOUIE-V answered him honestly.

"You do flow hot LOUIE-V and your over 40 million followers think so too! Is that why I hear you're creating a rap contest? Is it to see whose flow is hotter?" BIG MONEY MIKE asked excitedly.

"That's right BIG MONEY MIKE! A few weeks from today, the RAP or DIE contest will be live at the Riverside Theater! This is a no-holds-barred event so submit yo best mastered songs if you wanna have yo chance to win $100,000 and be signed to one of the hottest labels in the industry! All you gotta do is beat everyone else and you can enjoy the wealth of an extra hundred grand! Beat me and you win a record deal! You and yo crew can host it BIG MONEY MIKE!" LOUIE-V shouted to hype up the many, many listeners tuned in to him.

"Well, if I won the money, I'd take a nice trip to an island and flaunt my sexy bikini at the beach! Aye!" MARGARITA MAY hyped it up like it would be a party.

"Uh-huh, me too child!" TANG-TANG agreed.

"I'm not gone even elaborate on that, but winning cash and a recording contract is lit! You heard it here first! The BOOTH of TRUTH will be hosting the rap battle royale of all time right here in Milwaukee so make sure you're dialed in to win free tickets and other cool swag on the station that reps the nation 103.6 FM! Now chill and listen to a few commercials so we can pay our bills!" BIG MONEY MIKE shouted in his microphone before he paused his show for several paid advertisers.

LOUIE-V's ride home after his guest appearance on the early-morning radio talk show was not a happy one. Yeah, he got to promote the upcoming contest he was directed to do, but he wondered if he'd lost some of his street credibility with his following for back-peddling on what he said about MACK DADDY. To him, there was no question about being better than the veteran rapper and he should be able to say that without being labeled a hater. As far as he was concerned, he was introducing a new, improved style to the rap game, not insult every established MC in the business.

When his phone started ringing and he saw it was STACKS, his mood didn't get any better. As soon as he picked it up, his CEO stated, "The prize money was $50,000—not $100,000. At least you didn't change the name of the contest. I still don't appreciate you increasing the prize amount without any approval or consultation. When I signed you, I told you then how loyalty means everything to me and then you turn around and pull this. What's up?"

"Look, I thought $50,000 was a small amount fa such a big event. I mean, these contestants gone be rappin' they asses off to win, so I made the purse a little fatter. I wanna make sure my name is represented with respect to the fullest when they mention this event. Don't worry, I'll pay the extra money out my own pocket if it's that much of a problem. As for the name of the contest—I like it. I'd never change somethin' I like," LOUIE-V said in a way that hinted to his boss he shouldn't try to change him.

"The point isn't whether you like it or not. We selected that name from dozens of names that cost many work hours to create. The approval for it wasn't finalized until the conceptual stages were complete and then surveyed by a panel. Only then do print reach our legal, marketing, and sales divisions. Had you changed the name of the contest—you'd be in deep shit. Listen up LOUIE-V because I'm only saying this one time: Stick to the script—anything less can nullify your contractual agreement with BIG DOE RECORDS. I hope you understand the potential problems you could've caused the company," STACKS told him as professionally as he could, even though he felt the young rap artist overstepped his ground by doubling the prize money without his consent.

"I understand and I apologize fa makin' changes without any OKs first. I was feelin' pressured by the whole MACK DADDY situation and wanted to create a bigger buzz fa myself. But don't worry, it won't happen again, STACKS. From now on, I do it the way you want me to."

"We good homie. The only other issue I had was that you didn't give MACK DADDY enough props on the show. I wanted you to make sure he understood you weren't dissing him."

"Look STACKS, I did everything I could to get that point across. What you want me to do—kiss the nigga ass?"

"I would never ask you to do that. Our artists aren't ass kissers—they're soldiers. You're a soldier—and that means I expect you to successfully complete the missions that are assigned to you. You might have to do things you don't agree with, but you must complete each mission. You feel me?"

"I feel you. We good?"

"We good."

"That's what's up! Don't trip STACKS, we gone get this money bro! This RAP or DIE contest is gone open the doors to even more! We can't lose with the forty-city tour we got set up, the single's still toppin' the chart, and with our media promotion team on they shit! I need you to believe in me the same way I believe in you!" LOUIE-V expressed excitedly to inspire his boss and made the CEO feel better about the prize increase.

"I do believe in you. Look, I'll be in touch. Don't forget the studio session you got scheduled tomorrow in New York. Your flight takes off early, so don't party too hard. Later." STACKS told him and then ended the call before LOUIE-V could respond back.

"I hope it ain't coach." he vented out loud while driving to several of his weed houses scattered across the city to pick up his money and meet the man who supplies him.

Laying back in his bedroom, FRICTION was up early and looking over the list of job contacts he had with the radio playing.

An avid listener of the BOOTH of TRUTH morning radio talk show since they came out a few years ago, he had listened to today's show with their special guest LOUIE-V when he announced the RAP or DIE contest. After wishing he had fully recorded songs so he could be in it, FRICTION sighed in disappointment and gave his list a long stare before preparing for the tedious task of trying to convince White people to hire him. Call, fill out the application, do the interview and then wait ... wait ... wait to see if they call you was something he knew took mental preparation to endure.

After making a few calls and being told to come in and fill out an application by several companies, he was in good spirits when C-DOG surprised him with an early-morning phone ring. He wanted to share his job-hunting progress with his friend, but he still had a lot of calls to make so he chose to ignore him and continue to see which ones on his list was still hiring. But his friend was persistent, C-DOG called again and again until FRICTION felt he had no choice but to answer it, even if it was only to explain to him why he couldn't talk right now. After all, C-DOG did give him the phone.

"Yeah. What up?" FRICTION answered it like he was busy doing something important.

"G, the radio had LOUIE-V on talkin' bout a $100,000 RAP or DIE contest at the Riverside in a couple weeks! This is yo chance bro! I know we gone enter that bitch!" C-DOG shouted excitedly.

"I heard it too. I would, but I only got some lyrics I wrote—no music. I couldn't pay the recording costs even if I did luck up and find a good producer."

"Who's the man with the master plan?"

"What?"

"Who's the man with the master plan in the palm of his hand—ya understand?

"I guess you are. What's the masterplan though?"

"I know somebody who makes music and he owe me. I can tell him to produce you some music you can perform with. I mean a fully mixed, engineered, and mastered song with yo vocals and a performance version too."

"They did say they want you to submit mastered music. I don't know—that shit's expensive bro."

"Don't trip about the cost," C-DOG assured him.

"What do we need to do to get accepted?" FRICTION asked, not fully understanding the rules.

"We'll check out LOUIE-V and the BOOTH OF TRUTH's websites to do it right. Just make sure you got the best lyrics you ever wrote when we link up later. That's all you gotta do," C-DOG reassured him.

"So, we really gone do this?" FRICTION asked with his anticipation slowly beginning to build.

"To the fullest. I'll hit you up around six so you can meet him."

"Cool. Hey, where's MOOCH? I haven't heard from him yet."

"MOOCH still MOOCH. I'm on my way to his crib now."

"Bring him with you when you come and snatch me up. That's my dog."

"I'll ask him."

"Aye, much love on the music plug fam. See you round six," FRICTION told him with much appreciation.

"No thang, love bro," C-DOG replied.

"Love," FRICTION said feeling good and ended the call.

As soon as he hung up, he quickly sprung up out of his bed and went to get his clear property bag from prison. Pouring out nine large envelopes on his bed, he opened one up and inside it was dozens of rap songs he'd written. Sifting through them as if he was looking for something specifically, he didn't see it in the first enve-lope, so he tossed it aside and picked up another one. After searching through six altogether, he found the song he was looking for, pulled it out and placed the folders back inside his property bag.

As he recited the lyrics to his song, he knew it was the perfect one to use for the contest. His two main concerns were: picking a song he felt had a unique flow style and a widely accepted message that stood out. He knew he didn't want to rap about being rich and spending money he didn't have so he chose a song that he thought was entertaining and felt good.

While he was in the middle of rehearsing his song, FRICTION's mother knocked on his door. Feeling good about his new opportu-nity, he told her to come in before he realized his room wasn't clean. As soon as she came in, she looked around and shook her head with a frown. Then, she took in a big whiff of how it smelled in there and frowned even more.

"Ugh, it smells like funky asses and sweaty balls in here! You need to do something about it—now! Go grab the disinfectant spray out the cabinet in the hall! Spray everything! Then you need to take off your old clothes and burn 'em!" she shouted while she used her right hand to fan away the musty smell from her face.

"Do it stink that bad in here?" FRICTION asked while he sniffed around and didn't smell anything.

"Enough to cuss in church! Enough to melt your nose hairs! Enough to look for whatever died up in here!"

"OK Mama, I get it! It's stinks enough to make you go off on me! You don't have to get all worked up over it. I'll get the disinfec-tant spray and take care of it. Is there anything else you wanted?"

"Yes, there is. I wanted to make sure you were doing what you're supposed to be doing with your job search."

"I'm callin', but it's Friday. I did get in touch with a few who told me to come in and fill out an application on Monday. I still got a few more to ring up though, but I should probably wait until Monday."

"Well, make sure you call. Don't put off Monday what you can do today."

"OK, Mama."

"Oh yeah, I need you to go to the corner store and get some maple syrup. I'm cooking pancakes, bacon, and eggs for breakfast and we don't have any pancake syrup," his mother told him while she continued to fan around her.

"Mama, do it stink that bad?" FRICTION asked while he sniffed the air.

"Yes, it does! It stinks so bad it stank!" she teased as she left.

The walk to the store was a dangerous one now that he had beef with a young hoodlum and the older crew he ran with. With no gun or any other weapon to help protect him, he had to rely only on his alertness and street smarts to peep any drama. It wouldn't be the first time he had to do it; in fact, he did his entire stint in prison using his wits to avoid conflicts. When you don't have the option to grab a gun, you better have other ways to handle your business or the ability to see danger and avoid it.

The entire time he walked, FRICTION hoped it would remain a peaceful one. His intention wasn't to get out of jail and start a war with anybody in his own neighborhood. He just wanted to enjoy being free and around family—instead of being locked up with strangers. A small part of him wished he could've handled things differently between him and the young thug, but a bigger part of him felt justified reacting the way he did. Had it been prison, the youngster's flippant mouth would've been swollen and bloody from being punched in it.

As he approached the busy-looking store, FRICTION didn't see the youngster. When he went in and got the small bottle of maple syrup, he wasn't inside either. While he waited in the long line ahead of him, he began to think maybe the little tyrant didn't hang around the store as much as Ki-Ki thought he did. Relaxing his alertness some, by the time he made it to Abdul at the register, FRICTION wanted to know if he knew more about the strapped teen and his crew.

"What up Abdul? Have you seen that young dude I got into it with in here today?" FRICTION asked nonchalantly.

"He was here earlier. Wait a minute, I don't have to worry about any shootouts around my business, do I? There's a lot of good people who come here to get the things they need. Bullets always hit the wrong people—always," Abdul uttered gravely.

"No, I don't even own a gun. I was curious, that's all. Do you know anything about him?"

"Yeah, he's a troublemaker. All he does is harass folks and loiter around my store. I've seen him with some real bad people as of late—they ride around in a red car. Have you seen it?"

"Yeah."

"Look, I know where you were. I want you to be careful with those guys. The last thing you need to do is put yourself right back there."

"How do you know where I've been?" FRICTION asked very curiously.

"Me and your mother talked about you often. Not only do I provide great service—I also provide great listening too," Abdul joked as he took FRICTION's money for the maple syrup.

"She grown and she gone speak her mind. But check it, I gotta go. Thanks," FRICTION told him as he grabbed his bagged item and left the store to head back home.

With his alertness risen back up, he looked around for the red car that had stopped him and his little sister. Not seeing a sole car that resembled it driving around, he cautiously took his normal route. He knew he couldn't continue to live this way—fearing he would be ambushed, or surprise attacked every time he walked around his neighborhood. FRICTION concluded, one way or another, he would regain his peace of mind back again.

While he was walking home, a new modeled metallic white Porsche Panamera Turbo pulled up beside him and blew its horn to get his attention. Unable to see inside because of its dark-tinted windows, FRICTION was still apprehensive about walking over to it—even if it was a $160,000 automobile. After blowing it off as someone possibly needing directions, he walked over to see what the driver wanted. When the passenger window rolled down, he was shocked to see MANIAC's female cousin driving it with him relaxing in the passenger seat.

After nodding hello to the lovely driver, FRICTION walked to his window and MANIAC greeted him by saying, "I heard someone upped a chopper on you and your little sister the other day."

"Yeah, but how do you know about that?" FRICTION asked suspiciously and began to wonder if the man had spies lurking in the shadows.

"Word travels."

"I'm a deal with it."

"It's already dealt with."

"What you mean?"

"What you think?"

"Oh."

"I can't have fools shoot up a real nigga. Remember what I told you about your rarity? You don't have to worry about anyone inside that red Maxima ever again. I want you to know that I take care of my crew even better than that, FRICTION. The job offer is still on the table—fa now. I'll be in touch," MANIAC told him coolly as he sipped his glass of cognac—then the tinted window rolled back up and the car slowly cruised off.

A few minutes had passed since the expensive Porsche drove off and FRICTION was still standing in the same spot absorbing in everything MANIAC had told him. Several questions had formed inside his head: "Did MANIAC really kill everyone in the red car? Was the trouble-making teenager inside it? Did he kill 'em to help me? Should I be worried about MANIAC?"

Chapter Seven
AN EYE FOR
AN EYE

When C-DOG ended his call with FRICTION, he was only a couple of blocks away from where MOOCH was. Driving a black GMC Yukon with five additional armed men with him, the intimidating expression he had on his face meant someone was in serious trouble. When he stopped in front of the small ranch-style home, everyone got out and began to surround it's front and back doors so no one could escape. Armed with either an assault rifle or automatic shotgun, all of them were carrying firearms that were designed to do extensive amounts of brutal damage.

Once they were positioned, both men armed with black and chrome Daewoo USAS-12 shotguns with 20 cartridge drums shot off the doorknobs and locks that were on the front and back security doors; afterwards, they did the same to the front and back doors of the house. When C-DOG and his crew stormed inside, no one was expecting it or was prepared to defend themselves against his surprise attack. Dozens of AK-47 rounds were fired from him and the other three gunmen's assault rifles while the other two with shotguns exploded 12-gauge slugs at whoever they saw.

Two men in the kitchen tried to get up and run, but they had both of their backs blown out by an automatic shotgun. Before they fell to the floor, several assault rifle rounds ripped through the back of their shoulders and heads. Another group in the living room met a similar fate, only the two men and a woman were shot multiple times with assault rifles and shotguns in their chests when they stood up from a couch. One man tried to escape out a bedroom window, but he was shot to death with half of his body hanging outside it.

When C-DOG went to the other bedroom and kicked the door open, it was just as MOOCH was going for a gun under one of the pillows on his bed. Looking like a kid caught with his hands in a cookie jar, he immediately stopped and motioned for his longtime friend not to shoot him. Two armed men with C-DOG went in the room to assist him, but he waved his left hand for them to leave. Now with only him and MOOCH in the room, C-DOG wanted answers.

"You had to keep it up MOOCH," C-DOG told him disappointingly.

"I don't answer to nobody. I'm my own boss," MOOCH stated defiantly.

"You were warned to shut it down."

"So, he sent you."

"He sent me."

"You used to be a nigga who didn't take orders from nobody. Now look at you, he points at it, and you kill it."

"You not the only one who need to eat," C-DOG declared coldly.

"I hope you feel good about killin' a bunch of high mutha-fuckas! I was the only person in here with a gun!" MOOCH shouted at his comrade.

"It doesn't matter. No witnesses."

"What the fuck happened to you? We used to be boys."

"I got smart, and you stayed dumb."

"I'm smart enough to do me!"

"It wasn't smart."

"This my neighborhood—not MANIAC's! I dumped boy over here since a shorty! Now, out of nowhere, this rich ass nigga come around with ultimatums about hustlin' fa him or leave the game! I do what I wanna do!" MOOCH stressed to C-DOG as he attempted to get his friend to see his logic.

"Why was you stupid enough to think you'd still be able to sell dope here after you was told that? Why didn't you stop?" C-DOG asked MOOCH with a disappointed expression on his face that read he really messed up bad by his decision.

"Because this is my neighborhood! I grew up here—not him! I got my stripes in this hood! I can't believe you even asked me that! He owns you now, don't he?"

"I do what I'm paid to do—there's no ownership. You could've been right next to me if you wanted to."

Seeing C-DOG lower his assault rifle, MOOCH began to feel comfortable enough to lower his hands; after all, they were friends since they were little kids. But for more than a year, he saw his friend become more and more estranged from the things they always did together. No more smoking weed and drinking liquor together or meeting females to sleep with. As a matter of fact, he hadn't heard from him in over a month before today.

While thinking about the length of time that had gone by since he'd last seen C-DOG, he sighed heavily and stated, "So, this is how you greet ya homie after not fuckin' with me fa over a month. I thought yo new boss got you killed or some shit."

"As you can see—I'm still here. I tried to warn you to get down or get ghost, but you too damn stubborn fa yo own good," C-DOG told him regrettably.

"No man tells me what the fuck I can and can't do—period!"

"That's how this whole country was built! Somebody's gone always tell you what you can and can't do—you chose to ignore that shit!"

"Only God has that type of power."

"Then MANIAC is God—if you believe that."

"Fuck MANIAC!"

"The way you feel about him don't matter. We're here, in this room together because you didn't believe it would ever come to this moment. You could've avoided all of this, MOOCH, if you would've made the right choice."

"Choice! Ain't no choice! MANIAC don't give choices! I see the choice you made though! You chose money over yo bros!" MOOCH stated disgustedly.

"I chose to see when change has come. You thought you could ignore an unstoppable force when it come yo way, but now you see it can't be ignored," C-DOG replied disappointingly to his old friend.

"Why does he even care so much about my hustle? I don't even make a lot of money! Shit, I barely make enough to pay the bills around this bitch!"

"He controls the things around him. He destroys what he can't control."

"He will never control me! I'm a man before I'm anything!"

"Men are controlled all the time, MOOCH—that's what you fail to grasp homie. Everyone on the planet is controlled by someone or something. The real question you should ask yo self is: How much of you do you control?"

"I'm in complete control of myself homie! I make my own way in these streets, and I don't let outsiders dictate which direction I should take!" MOOCH began to shout as he became more emotional.

"You not in complete control—I wouldn't be here if that was true. You lost control the minute you ignored all the signs it was gone. You don't have control, MOOCH—any control at all," C-DOG revealed dismally to his old friend.

MOOCH began to sense C-DOG was feeling conflicted about things so he attempted to reach the humane side of him, hoping it would bring his friend back from his cold-hearted detachment. He knew C-DOG had been through a lot himself—losing his mother to an overdose when he was young and never knowing his father. Being in and out of foster homes until he chose the streets to raise him, he understood C-DOG had a rough life surrounded by poverty and sadness. Now, when MOOCH looked at his homie from way back, all he saw was a man who was all about his money and nothing else.

"I'm not gone beg fa my life," MOOCH told him firmly as he stood on the opposite side of his bed from C-DOG.

"I know—you a man before you anything," C-DOG told him with a tear in his eye and shot his childhood friend several times in his head and chest with his assault rifle—killing him.

Hearing the gunshots, a couple of his armed entourage rushed in the room to check on things and still overwrought with raw emotion, C-DOG yelled, "Get the fuck out his house! I'll be out soon!"

After seeing what he'd done, they left without saying a word. It was as if they knew he was someone close to C-DOG and he needed a moment of silence to mourn him. So, knowing there were time constraints, his crew focused on making sure there was no one left alive to identify them and removing any potential evidence that would link them to their surprise visit. Since they were very thorough in their planning of the murderous home invasion, there wasn't much for them to discard. There wasn't any fingerprints, blood, or traceable ammunition for the disposable weapons they carried. They made certain the homicides they committed would go unsolved.

While C-DOG sat in his dead friend's room with him in silence, his burnout phone began to ring in his pants pocket. When he looked and saw it was MANIAC calling, he shook off his somber mood and went back to it being one more job out of many. Disregarding the bloody carnage throughout the house, he answered the call of his employer and didn't show any sign of weakness.

"Is it done?" MANIAC asked.

"Yeah, it's done," C-DOG answered.

"Good. Meet me around the way."

"I'll be there as soon as it's clean."

"Cleanliness is next to Godliness."

Silence...

"Any problems?" MANIAC asked curiously.

"None at all," C-DOG responded coldly as he looked over at the deceased remains of one of his best friends.

Around the same time, on the south side of town, MEAN-MUG and TRIGGAH G were parked several cars behind Pedro's custom candy-coated burnt-orange colored Chrysler 300. With a completely customized orange interior and sporting large 30-inch chrome rims, it stood out as the most eye-catching car on the block. While they waited for their target to come out and leave, they indulged in tooting cocaine and smoking cigarettes to help time pass by. Using darkly tinted windows to conceal their presence, they both agreed it would be best to leave the engine off to prevent drawing any unwanted attention.

After taking a long snort of cocaine off a contest flier he was handed on the north side of town, MEAN-MUG passed it to his homie and told him, "We ain't gone be here long. I bet a hundred it'll be one hour or two at the most."

"I hope you right cause its daytime and we over here strapped in a parked car. The police sweat Hispanics on the south side just as bad as they do our Black asses on the north," TRIGGAH G remarked a bit paranoid as he sniffed up a thick line of blow.

"Fuck the police. That little bitch better hope I don't kill his ass fa that garbage powder. It's a 'Eye for an Eye' with me and that nigga in violation."

"Bro, we need his ass alive so we can snatch his cousin. We only get one chance to do this. We stay broke if he dead."

As pedestrians walked by the car, none of them saw the two thugs inside it snorting cocaine and plotting an abduction. When a woman casually strolled up to MEAN-MUG's window to briefly check her hair in its reflection, he held the cocaine filled flier up to her unsuspecting face as if to offer her some and snorted it himself. Not noticing or seeing any of his actions inside, she continued up the block. They both laughed and continued getting high.

They sat out there for almost two hours before Pedro came out of his house and jumped inside his car. When TRIGGAH G looked at the clock on his smartphone, he didn't even argue about it; instead, he passed his homie the hundred-dollar bill he won and left it at that. Feeling satisfied about winning, MEAN-MUG thanked him and wrapped it on top of his bankroll. As soon as Pedro pulled off, he started his car and began to follow him.

In the early-morning weekday hours, there's always a high number of children either waiting for a yellow school bus to get on or walking to their nearby neighborhood schools. They were everywhere as MEAN-MUG stayed only a vehicle or two behind Pedro. During a red traffic light, a small group of teenagers ran in front of him to cross the street just as the orange car they were following turned a corner. The teens were almost hit because he drove right through them! MEAN-MUG didn't care one bit when he looked back and saw the kids giving his car the middle finger for accelerating on them.

When he turned the corner and spotted Pedro's car merely a half block away, his anger at the children subsided and he was back focused on his task of not losing sight of him. Following Pedro went on for blocks and blocks, with MEAN-MUG and TRIGGA G not seeing one opportunity to make their move. They both knew it had to be discreet with near-perfect timing; otherwise, they wouldn't be able to pull off their plan successfully. So, they continued to tail him, waiting for the right moment to strike.

Becoming fed up with the length of time spent tailing him, MEAN-MUG frustratingly said, "Damn, where this fool goin'? I thought he was goin' to the gas station fa some squares or some shit."

"I don't have a clue fam. Maybe he got a run to make," TRIGGAH G guessed.

"With what? We took all his shit!"

"I know. Why you yellin' at me bro?"

"My bad. I'm geeked up."

"It's cool. Watch, he gone stop in a minute."

After fifteen more additional minutes of driving, Pedro parked at a large chain grocery store and went inside. Thirty minutes later, he came out with several full bags of groceries in a plastic shopping cart and used his car alarm to open his trunk. When he was done and got inside his car to leave, his front passenger door flung open and an armed man wearing a "BATMAN" mask abruptly entered his vehicle pointing a large black semi-automatic handgun at his face. With a look of sheer terror and the fear of being killed by bullets to his face, Pedro instantly began sweating and trembling.

Without any delay, the armed masked man jumped in next to him and said with the low-toned grimness of the "Dark Crusader" himself, "Drive."

Not wanting to ask any questions that would agitate the armed aggressor, Pedro became emotionally distraught at the mere thought of not being around anymore to care for the three people he loved more than anything else on the planet: his beautiful girlfriend and his two lovely little girls. So, with no clue which way to turn, he pulled out of the grocery store without saying a word and drove down the main street it was located on. Not knowing if his silent captor was there because of what he did for a living, or because he was a deranged lunatic, he felt the only option he had was to comply with him and silently pray to God for a way out the madness.

After fifteen minutes of driving in silence, Pedro was approaching a set of red traffic lights when the BATMAN masked man told him in the same baritone voice, "Turn right."

Doing as he was instructed, Pedro turned right at the corner and proceeded to drive, waiting for his next command. The way he figured, he'd do whatever the man wanted to make it back to his family safe and sound. After twenty more minutes of driving, the masked gunman directed him to turn left into a residential area. Ten minutes later, he ordered him to park.

"I don't want any problems. All I want to do is make it back home to the ones I love," Pedro stared at him and spoke sincerely.

Not relaying anything to ease his mind about him being able to do so, the gunman remained silent with his weapon aimed at the driver's head. Inside the "Caped Crusader" mask, MEAN-MUG stared intensely at Pedro, making him uncomfortably face forward to avoid eye contact. While he looked out the front windshield, he thought being robbed by one of his favorite superheroes was too surreal to comprehend. To Pedro, it was wrong on so many different levels.

"BATMAN. Out of all the people in the world, I'm about to be killed by BATMAN," Pedro muttered in sad disbelief.

Responding, the masked man checked an incoming text on his phone and stated with a deadly tone, "You put poison in the cocaine you sell. You deserve to die."

The entire time he spoke, his gun remained aimed at him. When he saw a look of guilt on Pedro's face, it wasn't what he was expecting at all. He was certain there was going to be all types of denying and lying to paint a better picture of himself, but that wasn't the case. He looked like someone who allowed somebody to put a bad idea in his head and he ran with it.

"Shit."

"Now shut up."

Doing as he was told, Pedro sunk back in his seat like a sick man who learned he only had a few weeks left to live and have now come to terms accepting his terminal fate. He knew he couldn't charm or finesse his way out of what he was being blamed for. He had no excuses to validate his reasons for mixing powdered household cleaner in his cocaine. The truth was: he wanted to stretch his package as far as it could go—so he cut it with the poisonous substance to make as much money as he could off it.

After being parked for several minutes, the rear passenger door was opened, and another gunman got in wearing a "SUPERMAN" costume mask. Pedro couldn't believe what he was seeing—not one, but two of his favorite crime-fighters were inside his car at the same time. The only bad thing about it was that they were both there to punish him for *his* injustice.

"Call your cousin and order your usual. Tell him to meet you in the alley behind your house. You fuck up—you die. He plays you—you die," SUPERMAN commanded while he aimed his gun at the back of his head.

Wishing neither superhero was there with him, Pedro reluctantly replied, "OK. I don't know how you know about him, but OK. Hey, I'm glad you're friends again."

"We made up to beat yo ass," the SUPERMAN masked robber stated and nudged the back of Pedro's head for him to start calling.

Not wanting to irk the armed man behind him anymore than he felt he already had, Pedro reached for his smartphone to call his cousin and drug plug Carlos up. But before he dialed, the gunman with the BATMAN mask sternly stated, "Turn the speaker on."

Complying, he put the call on the speaker option of his phone so everyone could listen in on the conversation he was about to have. He could tell from the way the masked men carried themselves, this wasn't their first-time doing dirt and he didn't want things to go to another level. What got to him the most was their nonchalant attitude about it all. They had absolutely no remorse—like it was personal. Pedro then thought about the robbery at his house and knew they were the ones who did it.

The phone rang several times before Carlos answered it and said, "What's up?"

"I need you," Pedro told him with the two guns now pressed against his head.

"Damn, you get it in! I told you it's the best in the city, didn't I?"

"Hell yeah."

"That's all I'm saying. All you gotta do is keep listening to your big cousin and you'll be gravy homes. Where you wanna meet up at?

"The back of the house is cool. I want the same thing."

"Give me the same number—only because you family," Carlos told his younger cousin with love.

"Thanks for looking out," Pedro told him with appreciation and deep regret as he felt the guns ease up.

"Give me thirty minutes. Adios," Carlos replied before he hung up.

"Adios," Pedro spoke in Spanish to the dead phone, feeling lower than the belly of the snake he was forced to become.

Then instantly the guns were removed from his head and the overwhelmingly dreadful feeling of having his brains splattered across the windshield inside his car began to slowly go away. Now, he wished they'd go away.

It was during his wishful thought that the abductor wearing the SUPERMAN mask interrupted it by yelling at him, "Gimme the phone! What the fuck you in a daze fa? Drive!"

Chapter Eight
THAT'S THE WAY IT GOES

The drug addict's house that BONE and SQUEAK took CASPER to was filthy and smelled like the many cats they saw overrunning the place. With the tie-wrapped pillowcase still over his head, they had ushered CASPER out of the trunk of BONE's car and into Sheila's house without anyone seeing. Exactly the way SQUEAK told him, her house was secluded in the rundown neighborhood she lived in, making it the perfect place to keep their captive. Already knowing they were coming over from a phone call she had with SQUEAK, she eagerly opened the door, hoping to quickly get her payment of rock cocaine.

They thought the living area reeked, but the foul stench was even worse going into the basement of her dilapidated home. While taking the stairs down, their nostrils was hit with increased pungent smells of feline urine, feces, and the animals not being washed. At first, the cats' funky odors made it unbearable for BONE and

SQUEAK to even breathe properly, not until they eventually got used to it. Neither of them had ever smelled anything that bad before. As for CASPER, he made his displeasure known for all to hear.

"Do y'all smell that? It smells like somebody pissed and shitted all over the floors in this muthafucka!" CASPER complained as he went down the dimly lit stairwell that led to her musty basement.

"You can smell all the flowers you want after we get our money. Until then, it is what it is," BONE stated sternly.

Not wanting CASPER to recognize his voice, SQUEAK altered it to a lower tone and added, "Now shut the fuck up."

"This some real bogus shit right here! I need a phone so I can get this over with!" CASPER yelled out between the gasps of air he tried to hold in.

"First, you gone sit on this chair and wait fa us to come back," BONE ordered.

After they finished making sure he couldn't escape his bondage of tie-wraps and duct-tape, they left him to go upstairs and talk in private. BONE had a few questions he needed answered and he didn't want CASPER hearing any of it. Leaving all the "particulars" of their kidnapping up to SQUEAK, he wondered if he'd handled everything to complete the job. So, with no television or radio, they left CASPER alone in a stinking, dimly lit, bug-infested basement with a tie-wrapped pillowcase over his head, subdued by his arms and legs, and bound to a table chair while they discussed their plan to collect a ransom for him.

Once they were upstairs and out of earshot, BONE asked SQUEAK, "Did you get a burnout?"

"Yeah, it's in my pocket. I told you I thought of everything," SQUEAK said cockily.

"Cool. We know where we want the drop off to be, but I think we should make sure none of his goons do it. We don't need no problems."

"What you think we should do?"

"We'll tell him to make sure it's a female."

"But what if he calls my sister? She'll know it's us and then it's a wrap!" SQUEAK exclaimed nervously while he motioned his arms expressively as he talked.

"It's only a drop off. We won't have shit to worry about," BONE assured him.

"Me, you, and our families are dead if he links this back to us! My sister is too risky!"

"What else should we do? Do you want one of his boys to bring the bread? We need someone who'll do what they're told and that's it."

"Do you really wanna take that chance though?" SQUEAK asked his homie worriedly.

"I don't see a better option," BONE replied flatly.

Not thrilled at all with the idea BONE came up with, SQUEAK reluctantly agreed to it because it was the best option they had. But if things backfired and they don't get the money, he planned on making sure LOUIE-V knew who had created a clever caper to pay him back and who screwed it all up. So, after they shook hands to show they were both committed to the plan, they headed back downstairs to tell CASPER what to do next. By the time they made it back to him, he was more than ready to get things underway.

"Yo, all I need is a phone and a place to drop the money off! I'm gone throw the fuck up if I stay in this funky-ass room any longer!" CASPER exclaimed from underneath the pillowcase.

"We got you a phone to use and we want it dropped off in the trash can at the gas station on the corner of 35th and Mt. Vernon Ave," BONE told him.

"Done. All I need is this thing off my head so I can see the numbers I dial. Believe me, I want this to be over faster than y'all think.

"Oh yeah, make sure you have a female do it. We don't want nobody else."

"To get out of here, I'll have a one-legged mentally retarded lesbian bitch bring the shit!"

"We gotta keep your head covered too so you'll have to tell us the number to call. Don't play—"

"It's y'all show. Call this number…," CASPER quickly intervened and gave them a phone number to call.

While SQUEAK dialed, BONE looked like a man who was only minutes away from having a $200,000 payday. He knew people who lived and died without ever seeing that much money at once before. And now, while he was still young, he'd have it in palm of his hands. He gave his friend a smile to show things were finally looking up. After a few rings, a male voice picked up the phone and SQUEAK placed the untraceable cellphone by CASPER's ear.

"Who dis?" the unknown male voice asked.

"This CASPER. MOE, I need you to get two hundred bands together and take it by my bitch crib."

"OK. You cool."

"I'm cool."

"On my way."

"Later," CASPER remarked.

"One," MOE responded and hung up.

AJ THE GRINDA

After he hung up from his call, CASPER told them from underneath the pillowcase over his head, "I need y'all to make one more call fa me, call…"

When SQUEAK heard the number, he dropped the phone on the floor and then quickly picked it back up. An ominous feeling swept over him as he began to dial his own sister's smartphone number! It was like a nightmarish dream coming to real life while he waited for Naomi to pick up. He never wanted to involve her and now she's about to answer a call to drop off a large sum of money to pay a ransom for a kidnapping. While in the middle of trying to mull over the situation, his sister answered the phone and he almost inadvertently answered her in his real voice, but he caught himself before he did it.

Placing the phone back by CASPER's face, he calmly told his girlfriend, "Baby, I got a homie on his way over there to bring you some shit I need."

Before he could finish telling her what he wanted her to do, BONE interrupted him by saying, "Tell her to put it in the garbage can by pump 6 in one hour from now."

Doing as he was instructed, he then told her, "Look baby, I need you to go to the gas station on 35th and Mt. Vernon and put it in the garbage can by pump number 6 in one hour.

"Alright. Are you OK? Why didn't you answer any of my calls? I thought you said you were on your way over here."

"I was, but some shit came up and now I need you to do this fa me. I'll be finished up here in a couple more hours and then we gone kick it fa real," CASPER reassured her from underneath the pillowcase.

"I like the sound of that. How you gone make it up to me?" Naomi naughtily asked.

"I got a few ideas," CASPER replied sexually.

Disgusted at his hints of having sex, BONE said, "Nigga, I don't wanna hear all that shit. End the call."

Not wanting to cause any problems with his kidnappers, CASPER reluctantly told her, "I'll call you back as soon as I'm able. Thank you and I love you baby. One."

"I love you too. Bye," Naomi replied puzzled by his call and hung up.

The panic building up inside SQUEAK left as soon as his sister hung up the phone. He knew she was going to do it for CASPER before he even called her because the manipulator had her wrapped around his little finger. She made drug runs for him in the past so he knew his sister wouldn't think twice about it. He only hoped she would do as she was instructed and go back home.

With only an hour to go before they were literally paid a king's ransom, BONE and SQUEAK gave each other a hood handshake expressing how happy they were with each other's part in pulling their caper off. Although, there was doubt on both sides about the other backing out of it, neither did and very soon they were going to be well compensated for their loyalty to one another. The only part of the plan left was also the riskiest: SQUEAK was going to take BONE's car to get the money because he sure as hell didn't want to stay there alone with CASPER.

As LOUIE-V drove around picking up all the money from his weed houses and had no more premium marijuana to restock them with, he assured his workers that the wait wouldn't be long. To keep his word, he called and got the green light for a house visit to his weed plug "G-MAN" beforehand. He had to know if the supply would be around to keep things moving. The last thing he wanted was to be perceived as a liar to the homies who relied on him.

He always liked pulling into G-MAN's subdivision because it reminded him of how America should be—full of prosperity and people who want to grow wealth. The homes were only a few hundred thousand dollars, but they were almost three-thousand square feet of spacious living. But the most appealing thing about his neighborhood was that it was a melting pot of different ethnic groups all working with the same goal in mind: providing a better life for their families. There weren't any racist neighbors or undercover bigots, only friendly people trying to uplift their lives.

When he pulled into the driveway, the garage door opened, and he was able to pull in unhindered by onlookers admiring his sports car. As usual, G-MAN was there waiting to escort him into his home. He usually used the time to let his guests know what was going on in his house, so they'd act accordingly. When he met LOUIE-V, he informed him that his twelve-year-old son had a few of his friends over and to expect them to be excited to see a rap artist up close and personal. Not wanting to disappoint his plug or his young fans, the rapper shrugged it off to show talking to the kids didn't bother him.

Once they entered the kitchen from the garage, they were bombarded by G-MAN's son "Q" and several of his young friends. When his company saw LOUIE-V standing there in the flesh, they all looked at their coolest friend like he was a demigod. They knew they'd have a great time eating endless slices of delicious pizza and playing the best video games if they spent the night, but they never thought they'd meet a rapper whose song was playing nonstop on the radio. With Q leading the way, they brushed his dad aside and encircled the rap artist.

"What's up, LOUIE-V?" Q asked him as if they were good friends and not fazed by his widespread popularity.

"My bro, Q. How you been? I didn't see you the last time I came through. You good?" LOUIE-V inquired like they hung out all the time.

"Joined a new basketball league. I spend a lot of my time there and over at my tutor's house. I know my dad told you about my report card, didn't he?"

"I heard it could be better. I also heard you chill with slackers at school. Let me tell you right now, those low grades ain't cool. Stay focused on the A's bro."

"I know, I know. These some of my buddies that go to my school. Except him, that's my cousin, Percy. I usually be on top of it, but I got this hater at school now."

"All y'all need to step up more. Y'all think y'all parents gone always be there to hold y'all hand through life? You gotta put yourselves in a position to go to college. A good education can make your adult life a lot easier. And Q, I know you not gone let some little dudes hate on you."

"It's not a dude," one of his classmates revealed.

"What?" LOUIE-V had to ask because he didn't know if he heard him correctly.

"It's not a dude—it's a girl with really big titties," Q's other friend clarified, and the rest of his friends agreed with nods. Now confused by what he was hearing, LOUIE-V peeped over and saw G-MAN shaking his head in shame like he knew about it already and then turned back to Q and asked, "Is they fa real? Why you let a girl bully you?"

Feeling defensive now, Q quickly shot back, "She don't bully me. She says crazy things."

"What crazy things?"

"Bogus things sometimes, but mostly things about bosses."

"What you mean?"

Q told him she says: "A boss don't worry about school because a boss doesn't need school to make money. A boss hangs out with cool friends. A boss is supposed to have a girlfriend."

Understanding a lot better, LOUIE-V looked over at G-MAN to see if it was cool to give his kid some friendly advice, and after he nodded for him to school him, he looked at all of them and stated, "The majority of the bosses that run the world have a college education. It's damn there impossible fa a Black man to get rich without a degree in America so don't believe none of that crap unless you wanna end up in jail. All the bosses I know have years of education under they belt. I mean master's degrees too. Don't let little misled girls confuse you about what a boss is. You better not make her yo girlfriend either! Find a smart girl who wants to go to college and make real money one day."

"I told you Rochelle likes you." One of Q's friends teased.

"Is she pretty?" LOUIE-V asked him curiously.

"Yeah, I guess," Q responded a little embarrassed that he was talking about Rochelle around everybody.

"Well, you make sure you don't ever, ever like her back. Those kinds of girls grow up and ruin a lot of good men lives. Stay away from that type. You feel me?"

"I feel you. You think she gone grow up and be a THOT. Me and my crew don't mess with THOTs. I watch the Maury reruns."

Everyone laughed.

Tickled by what he was hearing from the youngster, LOUIE-V remarked, "Now Q, what do you know about the Maury show?"

"I know … that baby don't look like me … that baby don't look like me!" he sang over and over with his goofy little homies while they danced and acted a fool.

Everyone laughed even harder.

When the children finished clowning around, G-MAN caught LOUIE-V's attention and nodded for him to wrap things up with his son so they could talk business in private. The kids were enjoying talking to him very much, but he knew the rapper was pressed for time and had to leave soon. He, himself, wanted to know why he was back so quickly. G-MAN knew it usually took LOUIE-V almost a month to move all the premium marijuana he purchased but he's back in almost two weeks.

Reading between the lines, LOUIE-V nodded to his supplier, then looked at the children and told them, "I know y'all look at me and think I got it good. Truthfully, I'm out here earnin' my percentages. I try day and night to fulfill the obligations I'm contracted to. I make mistakes and upset people all the time. Rap's one hustle … but there's thousands out there. Pick one and learn it. I gotta go, but first I need to speak to your dad. I'll take some selfies with y'all if somebody got a phone."

Almost simultaneously, all the kids standing around pulled out their smartphones to take their own snapshot with him. Surprised everyone had one, he chalked it up to their never-ending advancement of modern technology and their cheapness. He decided in the end to only allow Q to use his phone. That way, he would "Share" them to their phones as the head honcho of his crew. The other kids didn't put up a fuss about it either; LOUIE-V figured they knew Q was going to hook everyone up. Using Q's camera option, the rapper took individual pictures with the youngsters and then held it out far enough to include everyone in some nice group pictures posing and smiling together.

When he finished, he gave Q his phone back and made sure everyone saw him show love with a handshake and a hug while everyone else only got a handshake. Then, not wanting to waste any more time, LOUIE-V followed G-MAN throughout his home until they reached the den. Once they were inside and out of everyone's earshot, his plug closed the door behind them. Before they sat down to talk business, G-MAN walked over to his small refrigerator and opened it up.

"You want anything?" he asked as he pulled out a bottle of beer.

"Got a lemon-lime in there?" LOUIE-V replied, feeling a little thirsty.

"You know it. Here," G-MAN responded and tossed him a cold can of soda.

"Thanks," the rapper told him appreciatively—then opened it up and drank almost half of it.

"Damn, yo throat was dry as camel pussy."

"Good one."

"But fa real, you didn't sound cool when you called. What's up?"

"Somebody … some bitches stole most of my package a few days ago from my main stash house," LOUIE-V expressed angrily.

"How the fuck did they manage that?" G-MAN asked as his intrigue began to grow.

"A couple homies slipped and got played."

"Fa how much?"

"A bale."

"Damn!"

"I know bro."

"You know where they chill?"

"No clue."

"Yeah, you took a serious loss," G-MAN acknowledged as he shook his head to show he felt his homie's pain.

"At the worst time too," LOUIE-V agreed.

"That's the way it goes."

"That's the way it goes when ya hustlin'. It still hurt."

"You gone bounce back."

"That's why I'm here. I gotta gig lined up in a couple days, but I need you to throw me anything you can stand before my customers dip somewhere else.

"It'll be two weeks before the new pack comes in. You know what, I got eighteen left, and you can hit my hand later. Cool?"

"Hell yeah, we cool! Thanks G fa havin' my back when a nigga down and out."

"That's what real fam do fa each other. I hope you recover quick bro."

"Yeah, I gave the two fools who lost my shit three days to square it. They only got one more day left."

"They deaths ain't gone bring yo money back. All you gone bring is unnecessary heat. They work fa you so it should slowly come out they pockets until the debt is paid in full. The main problem with street niggas nowadays is we too quick to kill and too slow to build," G-MAN told him while shaking his head.

"They do look up to me. How am I supposed to keep my niggas in line by givin' passes fa major mistakes like that?" LOUIE-V wanted to know.

"Mistakes happen. Loyal brothers pay they dues."

"I'll try it yo way. But I swear, they better be loyal."

"Murders murder money in these streets," G-MAN pointed out.

"You right," LOUIE-V replied with very little optimism for BONE and SQUEAK.

Chapter Nine
THE TIME IS RIGHT

While FRICTION was in his bedroom rehearsing what he wanted to record with the music producer C-DOG was linking him up with, his mother knocked on his bedroom door to get his attention before she came in. With a faithful look all mothers give their sons, she still saw the potential in him to live a prosperous life outside of prison. As a single parent who often worked doubles to provide for her two children, she often felt guilty for not being more actively involved in his life. More so, she wished she'd chose a real man to impregnate her than his nonexistent biological father.

Looking at his face and still seeing the beautiful child she'd nurtured since he painfully came out her womb, his mother said, "I know the weekend's over and you're back to calling the job leads I gave you, but you don't have to stay in here all day and exclude yourself from the world. You haven't even sat in the living room with us yet. I remember when I couldn't get you to come in the house when you were little."

"Honestly Mama, I'm still takin' it all in. I spent a lot of years in a room half this size so it's easy to stay in here and chill. I'm sorry if you thought I wanted to avoid y'all. I gotta memorize my lyrics to make a song. C-DOG plugged me with a music producer," FRICTION told her in good spirits while he sat on his bed reading the lyrics to the song he was going to record.

"C-DOG, huh? I heard you call yourself 'Fusion' or something."

"It's 'FRICTION', Mama."

"Oh, FRICTION, but you always gone be Malik Thompson—the only son of Monique Thompson and don't you forget that when you leave me and become a famous rapper."

"I won't forget because you gone make sure I don't. Just like you won't let me forget you carried, birthed, and nurtured me."

"You damn Skippy I won't—I'm your mama. Your only mama."

"Yes, you are."

"I know I am, that's why I'm in here. I want you to put on some clothes and come with us to the mall. I'm getting you a few things you need while I'm getting Ki-Ki some more school clothes," his mother told him in a way that left very little wiggle room for debate.

"Mama, I can't let you do that. I don't want you to spend yo hard-earned money on me. I'm a man. I'll get what I need." FRICTION tried to debate anyway, fully expecting the wrath that was going to come.

"Let me tell you something, I never said you wasn't a man! I know you're a strong Black man because you did all that time for that no-good ass friend of yours, so I don't need to be reminded about how much of a man you are! You still my son! I don't care if you sold crack to the judge who sentenced your ass—you are still *my* son! Don't you ever think you can't ask me for help! You came out of me! I don't care how old you get—don't you ever forget that!

"OK, Mama. Breathe."

"I'm breathing—I'd be dead if I wasn't breathing! Now gone put some clothes on so we can go to the mall. I ain't got no more time for your foolishness."

"OK."

"I know you're a grown man now and you gone make your own decisions about how you want to carry your manhood—but listen to your mama when I say: Trust is earned," she stated wisely.

"What?" FRICTION asked, hoping she wasn't about to bring up his conviction again.

"You trusted someone who left you in there to rot for over three long years! He didn't come by with no money for you—I scrounged up all the money that was in your account! He was over here every day before you went to jail; so much, I got sick of seeing his ass. But as soon as you get locked up for his crime, you couldn't find him! Your trust should be earned!"

"I know what you mean Mama, but I did what I did because I thought it was the best choice to make at the time. Don't be mad at C-DOG, he didn't make me do it."

"I wish you didn't do it."

"I wanted to prove to myself that I'm as loyal as it comes when it comes to my friends. I got out in three and a half, C-DOG would've been gone fa twenty-five."

"At the end of the day, what's done is done and you a grown-ass man. You have the right to feel how you want to about things, but C-DOG's not welcome in my house. Ever."

"He gone respect that too. When he come and get me later, he gone stay in the car. Don't worry, Mama, you won't even see him."

"Good. He doesn't deserve you as a friend. You better keep your eyes wide open around him. Now gone get up and put on some clothes," she told him, a bit peeved because of his continuing friendship with C-DOG.

As she was about to leave out his room, she turned back around and sniffed the air inside it. He gave her a puzzled look as she tried to track down the rancid scent that made her frown her face. After a full minute of sniffing around like a bloodhound, she gave up her search of where it originated from and told him with her top lip and nose scrunched very closely together, "I hope you take a shower first because it smells like wet farts up in here!"

Not knowing what she might be smelling, his alarm for what it could be turned instantly into a laugh once he realized it was just his mama's raunchy sense of humor. Ever since he was little, her comedic personality resembled many of the great profanity-laced Black male and female comedians he grew up watching with her. It was her good-humored persona that made everybody in the neighborhood like her and speak whenever they saw her.

"I'm on it, Mama," FRICTION chuckled as he smelled himself.

When FRICTION walked into Mayfair Mall with his family, it appeared as if it went on and on for blocks. He also couldn't help but notice how clean and sanitized it was throughout it. There weren't any litter or old dried-up soda spills on the floors, which by the way, shined like it had been recently buffed. Out of all the things he saw, what intrigued him the most was how packed it was full of shoppers.

They were everywhere. Shoppers of all colors and ages, walking in and out of the countless storefronts that leased space there. The satisfaction of purchasing items you want to buy shone on most of their faces. While he was checking everyone out, a philosophical thought came into his mind. It was then, he philosophized with a rhyme: The world should be like shopping mall places—full of all races with smiles on their faces.

"Here, take this money. Me and your sister is going to look at some makeup and buy some panties. You can come if you want to," his mama teased, already knowing his answer.

"Thank you, Mama. I'm good on the makeup and pantie run though. Man, they changed a lot of stores in here. When and where is we gone meet up at?" FRICTION asked and then thought about the last time he hung out there as a young teenager.

"We'll meet up at the food court on the second floor in one hour. That'll give you enough time to walk around and go in some stores. I'm sure you'll find something."

"My first stop is the shoe store. There's some Jordans inside with my name on 'em. Thanks again Mama fa the help, I love you."

"Make sure you get a couple pairs of pants and a few shirts too. I don't want you running all around looking homeless with some new basketball shoes on," she told him in a tone that meant it.

"You blessed me with more than enough to do that. I'll see y'all in one hour," FRICTION told his mother and little sister, then he headed off to the popular shoe store he'd seen at the mall's entrance.

That's when he saw her. The most beautiful woman he ever seen was checking out some running shoes all by herself. Not dressed to impress anyone, FRICTION decided to brush aside the minor setback with his attire and let his charming character win her over. He knew one thing quite well about himself: he was never short on confidence.

"That shoe over there compliment you better than those do. I mean, you already have stop and stare beauty, people might as well stop and stare at yo kicks too," FRICTION walked over and told her in his smooth voice.

"Thank you, but I don't know. Those cost more than these," the lovely young woman replied as she looked at FRICTION's choice and weighed out her options.

"True, they a little pricey, but you're the kind of woman who deserves the best. Yeah, those will feel good on yo feet, but these right here will feel great on yo feet," he remarked coolly and held it up to show her the large air bubble to support the soles of her feet and the comfortable looking sock-like material for the top portion of the running shoe.

"You're right, these are nice. Do you work here or something? I mean, your sales talk is very persuasive."

"Naw, I'm here to grab a pair of kicks too. But don't get me wrong, I'd work here though. I mean, I don't think I'm too good to work a nine-to-five."

"OK."

"Check this out, since I helped you with yo selection, maybe you could give me a woman's point of view about mine. I believe men buy things to impress women. So how about it?"

"I guess I could. I don't even know your name," she said a little hesitant about socializing with him.

"My name is FRICTION, but you can call me 'a friend with benefits' if you want to," FRICTION told her with a flirtatious smile afterwards and then asked, "What's yours?"

"My name is Celestia."

"That's a unique name."

"My mother is mixed with French and African. She named me from her French heritage. She came to America as an immigrant and fell in love with my father," Celestia went on further to explain.

"The story of a captivating woman who travels thousands of miles across the vast ocean in search of adventure and love in the great unknown. She sounds very brave. What does your name mean?" FRICTION really wanted to know.

"Heavenly."

"That name fits you."

"Thank you. You're a sweetheart. You know what? I'll help you. I feel weird about doing it though because I really don't know you."

"This will give you all the time you need to know me. It also gives me time to know more about you."

And from there, a mutual attraction began to form. Taking his advice, she ended up buying the pair of running shoes he'd recommended. And because he was feeling her, he chose the basketball shoes she picked for him—even after he saw two different pairs that looked cooler. Since she was there alone, he asked her to accompany him while he tried to find a store to purchase the rest of his clothes and she agreed to go only on one condition: when they were done, they would stop at the food court to eat a salted pretzel with cheese dipping sauce because it was her favorite mall food to eat when she felt hungry.

Feeling like meeting her must be fate because the food court was where he was regrouping back up with his mom and sister, FRICTION happily accepted her condition and even volunteered to pay for her snack, but she politely declined. He could tell from his first encounter with her she was the independent type, so he chose to leave it alone and enjoy each other's company—and they did. They went inside almost every store in the mall, making each other laugh as if they'd been friends for years. By the time they wound up at a table in the food court to eat their pretzels, the feeling of friendship was strong enough for her to talk openly with him.

As they sat across from each other, Celestia asked him while in the middle of dipping a broken piece of her pretzel into her cheese sauce, "So, when did you get out of jail?"

Her question made him stop chewing. He began to panic, and his heartbeat accelerated because he felt exposed. He never told her about the time he spent in prison—that his introduction to adult life had been overseen by correction officers. Knowing the only way to end the uneasiness developing inside him was to confront it head on, he decided to be open and honest about the things he felt comfortable divulging to her.

"Only a couple days. How did you know?" FRICTION asked curiously and nervously, hoping his honesty about everything would be acknowledged and accepted.

"Those sweatpants and that white T-shirt. The way you stared at everything in the stores like it was your first time seeing it. I've got family who acted the same way when they first got out."

"It's that obvious, huh? I've been away from my family for almost four long years. I could've been home sooner, but you know how it is. I'm lucky to be out on my feet, you feel me. It easily could a been in a box."

"The inmates were that bad in there?"

"Hell naw, the medical treatment is that bad in there. You can have a bug bite and end up with a staph infection."

"You funny." Celestia smiled as he made humor out of his bad situation.

"It's true. When I first went to prison, I thought I'd have to worry about all the gang bangers locked up, but it's the mentally ill people in there you gotta worry about."

"They have mentally insane people in prison with normal people?"

"Yes. All over America."

"Wow. That's news to me. I didn't know that."

"A lot don't. Eventually they snap because they nuts and then the officers take it out on everybody. Room raids, no day room, no calls ... all because of a crazy person," FRICTION replied as he thought back angrily while eating another portion of his pretzel.

"What did you do?"

"What was I convicted of?"

"That's what I asked."

"No, you didn't. You asked what I did to go to prison. I personally didn't do shit, but I was convicted of manslaughter."

"You went to jail for something you didn't do?" Celestia asked, wanting to know more.

"It's a long story. The short side of it is that I saved a good person a life sentence, but it cost me over three years of my free life and now I'm a felon forever with a violent crime attached to it. There you go—that's pretty much all of me in a nutshell. What about you?" FRICTION asked, turning the table on her to tell him more about herself.

"I've never been locked up in a jail cell before if that's what you mean."

"That's good to know. It's hard as hell for two felons to raise a family together, but I would still try with you."

"I got a man, FRICTION. Well, I mean, I have an off and on man—and we're off right now. I don't want you to be in the dark about that. The time is wrong," Celestia told him sadly with visible pain from her tumultuous ordeals with her unstable relationship.

"The time is right," FRICTION replied with a caring smile and gently held her hand.

"It's complicated," she insisted while staring deeply in his eyes.

"It always is," he assured her.

It was while their eyes were locked in a heartfelt stare when he heard his mother yell out his government name. It affected him like the snap of a hypnotist's fingers, awakening his conscious mind back to reality because he was completely transfixed by Celestia's cool personality and beauty—she had a face you could gaze at all day. A photograph of her could easily become a cherished memento or an often-viewed work of art.

"Malik, why are you all the way over here? Hello young lady, I'm Malik's mother—Ms. Thompson," she said cordially and reached out to shake her hand.

Subtly, Celestia put the food in her right hand on a napkin and pulled her left hand free from Friction's grasp. Then with a warm smile and a polite handshake, she introduced herself to Ms. Thompson and her daughter. She spoke of how she met her son and how helpful he was in the shoe store. She then complimented the way his mother raised him when she called him "courteous" and "respectful" during the time they've spent together. By the time she was saying, "Goodbye, it was nice meeting you all." and got up to leave, Celestia had left a positive impression on all three of them.

While she was walking away, FRICTION caught up to her and stated with raw emotion, "I wanna see you again."

Feeling the same way, she told him, "You need my number to do that?"

After they exchanged numbers, FRICTION leaned in for a hug and she gave him one. He'd never held a woman before. Sure, he hugged girls when he was a kid, but he'd never felt the touch of a beautiful woman and it was absolutely electrifying! He felt the energy inside him quadruple while he embraced her.

When he finished saying his farewell and went back to the table where his family was, Ki-Ki was the first one to say something to him. While giving her big brother a studious, long stare, she stated with almost certainty, "You look mad. Are you mad?"

"No Ki-Ki, I'm not mad."

"You look mad. Your friend is pretty."

"She is, ain't she?"

"She's nice too."

"She *is*."

"Are you going to invite her over to our house? I bet *she'll* play with me and my dolls," Ki-Ki suggested with an upset look at her brother since FRICTION hadn't done it with her yet.

Quickly looking at his mother, he wisely answered, "Only with Mama's permission."

And with only three words to say before leaving the subject alone completely, FRICTION's mother looked at him like she could still take a belt to his butt and told him, "You damn Skippy."

Chapter Ten
YEARS OF YESTERDAY

Back on the south side of town, in the alley behind his house, Pedro patiently sat in his car and waited for his cousin Carlos to pull up. Already an hour late, he nervously began to wonder if he was even going to show up. He kept imagining crude images of himself being tortured, or worse, by the masked gunman as time slowly passed. When his impatience had reached its limit and he was about to call him, Carlos's vehicle pulled into the alley.

He was overcome with a huge sense of relief as soon as he saw his cousin's pickup truck. It also revitalized his optimism about surviving the insanity he was unwillingly being subjected to. To him, that vehicle represented a beacon of hope—a small shimmer of light through a dark, desolate tunnel. Even though he knew setting his cousin up was wrong, he justified it by seeing the loss of a few dollars and drugs paling in comparison to the loss of his life.

When Carlos parked his Ingot silver-colored Ford F150 in front of his car, Pedro thought about all the times his older cousin aided and assisted him. Whether he was having beef with someone or needed help making a few bucks, Pedro could always count on Carlos to lend him a helping hand. He couldn't remember a time when his big cousin ever turned him down and he loved him dearly for it. He only hoped there would be room in Carlos's heart to forgive him for what he was about to do.

When Carlos aka "LOS" got out of his pickup truck, he quickly scanned the area for any police cars and hurried over to Pedro's still running automobile. He was proud to help his younger cousin hustle cocaine and held a brown paper bag with the next package he was fronting him. Feeling good to see his protégé coming up financially, a large smile was stretched across his tattooed face when he jumped inside the front passenger seat. Reaching the bag out to Pedro, LOS told him in a mixture of Spanish and English, "Que pasa con la familia? I see you making it happen. I knew you had it in you to come up. Here."

But his cousin didn't move. Instead, he only stared at his good-natured cousin with the look of a thousand apologies. As soon as LOS was about to question Pedro's appearance of deep shame, the answer was soon realized when a 9mm emerged from the back seat in the hand of a person disguised in a BATMAN mask. With the firearm aimed at his head, LOS stared vehemently at his cousin for being a good-for-nothing snake.

"You set me up! You fucking puta!" LOS yelled at his cousin, who was too overwrought with guilt to refute his accusation.

The only words his cousin kept repeating over and over was, "Lo siento, LOS."

"You're not sorry! Rato!" LOS shouted at Pedro with disgust, wishing he could reach over and punch him in his face.

Then the masked man, tired of their verbal exchange, interrupted him by saying, "Yo cousin had to call you or die. What would you do in his shoes?"

Seeing water form in his younger cousin's eyes like he wanted to cry, LOS realized the gunman behind him was telling the truth. Feeling trapped and not wanting to be shot, he concluded the only option was stay cool, calm, and collected. As far as he knew, the robber only wanted some drugs to get high with and a few dollars. What else could he want?

"Listen. I don't know who you are, and I don't care. I got about a grand on me and you can have the package I brought him. This don't have to turn into bloodshed," LOS told him without turning in his direction.

"First, gimme yo phone. Now I'll take the money and the dope. I really want the dope you got stashed in yo storage space more—ya feel me," the masked gunman revealed.

Not knowing how the masked man had any clue about where he stashed his kilos of cocaine, the first thing that came to mind was that his cousin Pedro had divulged this information. He frowned at his cousin with a gaze that wanted to hurt him very badly, but Pedro appeared just as shocked as he did about it. He continuously shook his head to signal to LOS that he had nothing whatsoever to do with the robber knowing where he stored his drugs. He saw the truth in Pedro's eyes, but he also saw the guilt and shame for his deceitful role in getting him robbed.

"Right now, you got it good. Nobody knows how you look. You got cash and a nice amount of cocaine. Nobody's hurt and everyone can go back to their lives," LOS told the robber without looking at him.

"You right, amigo, I could take this and go about my merry way, but I can't. You wanna know why? Cause I'm greedy. I'm a greedy muthafucka. Now you gone take us to the stash spot or both of you gone die right now in this car!" the BATMAN masked gunman began to yell with his finger on the trigger.

"Us?" LOS asked and before he could hear a response, the rear door swung open, and another gun was positioned only a few inches from the back of his skull.

Not wanting to make eye contact with this robber either, LOS began to stone-face his cousin and sent off a vibe that he was a dead man if they survive their ordeal. Where there was once a small hope for an escape—now there was none. He had no other choice but to concede and give them what they want, or risk being murdered. He'd never felt this helpless before and he didn't care for it one bit.

"Yeah. Us," the other gunman in the back seat stated.

"OK, you win. I'll take you there, but you must let us live. That's the deal."

"We don't do deals."

"Then nobody wins, and all of this is for nothing."

"All I do is win."

"Then give me your word as men."

"You gone take us."

"Life is worth more than money homes. The value of a man is determined by his value of others. Our lives have value."

"Where was the value of life when yo cousin cut his dope with Ajax? I bet you was the one who put that dumb-ass idea in his head, didn't you? Where the fuck was the value of life in that move?"

"I don't have nothing to do with that. I believe you should sell it the way you get it. I don't know who told him to violate the game that way."

"His punk ass deserves to die. How long y'all go back?"

"Many years. I've known him since he was six weeks old. I held him when he was a baby," LOS reminisced as he looked at his younger cousin with deep disappointment.

"The years of yesterday. Life was easy back then. None of us knew any of this, right? It was only kid shit," the gunman remarked as he thought back to those more carefree childhood years.

"Those the years we should cherish the most. I'm the one who give him his package, so I apologize for the stupid way he hustles."

"Apologies ain't gone fix this."

"He sees now how seriously he fucked up. As compensation, I'll give you what you want. All I want is your real word as men that our lives will be spared. Do I have your word?" LOS asked.

The second gunman didn't have anything else to say, but the one disguised as BATMAN promised, "We'll let you go if you don't play games. You have my word."

LOS was relieved to hear his deal would allow him and his cousin to see another day, he concluded it by saying, "OK, the only question I have to ask is: Which ride do we take—this one or that one?" and pointed to his new pickup truck.

"We'll take yo shit," the BATMAN masked robber in the back seat answered.

The ride to the storage facility was tense. With both handguns aimed at the cousins and ready to shoot if provoked, the BATMAN masked robber sat up front with LOS while he drove, and the SUPERMAN masked one sat next to Pedro in the back seat. With no music playing—there was a deadly silence in the air. Wanting to lighten the heaviness of the serious atmosphere some, LOS decided to say something humorous.

"Hey homes, I thought the Justice League was supposed to save people and fight evil super-villains and shit," he stated loud enough for everyone to hear him.

With SUPERMAN choosing not to respond, BATMAN answered, "Blame Marvel."

"Damn, that's fucked up bro. I hate to think what the other Super Friends is doing," LOS chuckled.

Seeing his effort to make them more relaxed didn't work, LOS drove his pickup truck the rest of the way there without saying another word. While driving, he wondered why BATMAN was more talkative than SUPERMAN? Did he know Pedro or hold a personal grudge against him? Were their lives still in danger?

When they pulled up to the facility's locked gates, LOS had to use a special entry code to gain access onto the grounds. Since it was around 10:30 am, there were different groups of people scattered throughout the area. Some were standing outside their rented storage units with moving trucks to remove their belongings and others were coming to add a few things. Through the business's window, LOS could see the same two stressed-out employees who serviced him scrambling to tend to the needs of their moody customers.

Bypassing the office building, LOS drove directly to storage unit D-409 on the far end of the storage facility. Located where there were few renters, he parked his pickup truck near it and was about to get out when the SUPERMAN masked robber told him threateningly, "Don't get goofy and get yo cousin murked."

"We're here. No need for smoke," LOS expressed calmly as he slowly got out and walked over to the front of the unit to unlock it.

From inside the truck, BATMAN (MEAN-MUG) watched as he lifted the metal storage door up and coldly declared, "I don't trust his ass or his ass. They both gotta go."

Pedro's eyes grew large with shock from what he'd heard and immediately defended their lives by exclaiming, "You gave your word, BATMAN! My cousin is doing everything you asked him to do! Why do you want to kill us?"

"Because you muthafuckas ain't gone let this shit ride. You gone try to find us. You gone try and try until either you give up or you luck up."

"I don't want to look for you! I don't ever want to see you again!"

"I don't believe you."

"It's the truth! Why turn a robbery into a double murder? Why kill people when they are cooperating?"

"Because I'm not gone be the one who get crept on in the end—it's that simple," the gunman replied with his mind made up.

"Is that how you feel too, SUPERMAN?" Pedro asked the gunman next to him.

"When we get the shit, we'll let you out a few blocks from here and give you the phones back. He gave y'all his word," SUPERMAN (TRIGGA G) proclaimed as he watched LOS enter the unit and turn on the light.

"No, we not! These muthafuckas gone want revenge! This bitch tried to kill us!" MEAN-MUG turned around and shouted at TRIGGA G while reminding him about their terrible sickness from the bad cocaine.

"Because they right. This is supposed to be a lick—that's it. I'd want a chance to live if we had straps on us," TRIGGAH G explained while he watched LOS lock the storage unit back up and return with a large black shopping bag.

When LOS got in and sat down in his driver's seat, he passed MEAN-MUG the bag and told him, "This all I got. You can get out and check if you don't believe me."

"Naw, I believe you. We good. Drive," MEAN-MUG ordered and briefly looked inside the bag to check out its contents.

What it contained gave MEAN-MUG one of the biggest smiles he'd ever made before. With no one else able to see his joy behind the mask, there were no signs of him being nothing less than a fearful presence. But in his mind, he danced and celebrated for accomplishing one of the biggest hustles of his life. With their last-minute decision to snatch up Pedro to rob his cousin, they got four kilograms of pure powdered cocaine out of it!

TRIGGA G was trying not to lose his temper because he wanted to look inside the bag too. As far as he was concerned, anything they got was thanks to him and he didn't appreciate the way MEAN-MUG was acting like he ran the show. He didn't enjoy feeling left out either so when he spoke to his homie, it wasn't with a lot of love.

"Gimme the bag. I can't believe I gotta ask fa it," TRIGGA G complained angrily.

"It ain't much to brag about," MEAN-MUG lied as he handed the bag of drugs to his upset partner.

When TRIGGA G saw how much it was, all he wanted to do was get back to their side of town and enjoy the spoils. Since he wasn't into killing people, keeping their word was his main concern. So, when they exited the storage facility and were a few blocks away, he ordered LOS to stop his pickup truck. When Pedro and LOS both got out, they stood helplessly on the sidewalk while he opened the back door and jumped in the driver's seat to drive.

Having pity for the stranded pair, he tossed both of their phones in some grass nearby as they sped off in LOS's pickup truck. Besides the drugs, they added an extra five grand to their total come up because the new truck they were in was easily worth that much at the chop shop. When they finally took their masks off, they both had looks of great triumph spread across their happy faces. As they fled the scene, LOS and Pedro quickly shrank until they disappeared completely in the stolen pickup truck's rear-view window.

MEAN-MUG and TRIGGAH G didn't hold anything in as they headed back to the north side of town. They bragged and boasted while pumping up each other's self-esteem with compliments. They also continuously gave each other hood handshakes for a job well done. By far, the large amount of cocaine they possessed exceeded both of their expectations, making it the largest amount they ever stole.

"What now bro?" TRIGGAH G asked, still feeling on top of the world about their score.

"You gone hop in my whip and follow me to the chop shop. As soon as we get paid, we gone have the party of all parties, bro! I mean music, freaky-ass strippers, liquor, pills, weed and blow— plenty fuckin' blow! We earned this shit! Look at what we pulled off today nigga!" MEAN-MUG exclaimed with elatedness.

"We made enough to never look back," TRIGGAH G replied happily as he opened the nine-ounce bag of coke that LOS brought for Pedro and placed an outdated plastic gas card in it to toot some of it up his nose.

"Only forward fa us my G. Fa real, we just took our game to the next level. We not gone never be broke again—ever. All we gotta do is hustle the hell out these bricks and we caked. No more petty licks fa us," MEAN-MUG toned down and spoke seriously to his homie.

"I'm down. We gone be the D-boys on the block now."

"We gone run the whole hood."

"Time to get rich," TRIGGAH G remarked with a gangster's frown and held out his hand to get some love.

"Time to get rich," MEAN-MUG repeated with an equally dangerous facial expression and shook it firmly.

When FRICTION made it back home from the mall with his family it couldn't have been sooner because when they pulled up in his mother's tan colored Chevy Traverse, C-DOG was parked outside his house in a fully restored powder blue and white drop top 1964 Chevy Impala. The chrome and gold hundred-spoked Dayton rims sparkled from the rays of sunlight as it brought a rare glimpse of coolness mainly seen in Southern California. Respecting his homie mother's house, C-DOG was playing his stereo system very low and was on his phone. And not wanting to agitate his mama about his presence in front of her home, FRICTION got out of her car as soon as she parked and went to see what was going on with him.

"Why you over here bro?" FRICTION asked puzzled by his sudden appearance.

"Damn fam, I left you with a phone and you don't even answer it. I hit you up plenty times," C-DOG expressed, a bit peeved while he sat on his customized white ostrich-patterned leather seats.

"I must've had it on silent while I was at the mall with my family. I thought I wasn't gone hear from you until later."

"Yeah, I know. Plans changed. That's why I'm here. I talked to that producer I told you about and he got some time right now to work with us. We up."

"OK, first I need to run in the house and get all my stuff. Damn, I can't believe I'm about to record my first single!" FRICTION replied excitedly.

"Believe it G. But like I told you, dude got shit to do so we better get ghost. I'll wait fa you out here because I already know yo moms don't want me in her crib," C-DOG divulged from his gut feeling.

Not seeing it as the right time to explain to him why his mom didn't want him in her house, FRICTION agreed with C-DOG's good idea and hurried through the front door. While inside, he scrambled to get everything he needed to make his song. Just in case the producer wanted to hear more, he even brought along a few extra songs he wrote. Words couldn't express how happy he was to be doing something he loved to do.

As he was about to leave back out the front door, his mother made sure she added a few parting words of wisdom she felt compelled to say before he left by saying, "I see that good-for-nothing Curtis is out front waiting for you. You better not get yourself caught up in no more of his foolishness. You gone mess around and spend your whole life behind bars if you're not careful."

Not wanting to get into a big, heated argument over his homie, FRICTION looked at her with compassion and told her, "I love you too, Mama. I'll be back a little later."

When he walked out the front door of his mother's rented single-family home and stood on the small concrete area in front of it, he took in the sunshine with a renewed lease on life. For the first time ever, he was about to partake in something he had control of.

The words were his. The emotions—his. He was on top of the world with no plans of coming down.

As FRICTION jovially strutted over to C-DOG's car and got in, his homie could tell he was in good spirits and stated, "Damn fam, I wish I felt like you. You look like you could outdance Michael Jackson in this bitch."

"I ain't ashamed to say it: I'm geeked up! I'm about to record my first song, bro! You don't know how much this mean to me! Thank you, again, C-DOG, fa doing this fa me—I mean it bro," FRICTION told him sincerely and gave his homie a strong hood handshake.

"I wish I could do more than this fa you. You sat down fa me bro. You saved my free life. You as real as they come," C-DOG acknowledged to him while he shook hands.

"That's what real homies do," FRICTION declared and then leaned back in the old-school Chevy and enjoyed the ride.

The ride to the producer's house took about forty minutes on the highway. Not really paying much attention to the street names or any of that because of his deep thoughts about the recording session, FRICTION did notice the producer's home was in a decent neighborhood. He was glad too because he truly felt the better the living conditions, the better the music recording equipment. The last thing he wanted to do was make his first song on shabby recording equipment that'll make his rap music sound weak.

"Yo, these some nice-ass cribs over here. I put 'em at about five or six easy," FRICTION deduced as he checked out the properties in the subdivision.

"Yeah, it's nice over here. I bet the only police they see is the ones who live here." C-DOG added as he maneuvered through the curvy, well-paved streets until he pulled into the driveway of one of the many lovely homes.

When they got out, FRICTION realized he'd been so caught up in his own excitement that he didn't even know the producer's name. So, before C-DOG called the producer on his smartphone, FRICTION asked, "What the homie go by?"

"KRINGLE."

"KRINGLE?"

"Yeah, KRINGLE."

"Whatever fam."

Leaving it alone, FRICTION didn't object when C-DOG motioned if it was now OK for him to make the phone call. It didn't take long at all for KRINGLE to come to the door. And when he did, FRICTION was completely caught off guard by what he saw. Because KRINGLE, true to his nickname, looked exactly like the many images seen around the world of Santa Claus, aka Kris Kringle.

From his overweight belly to his snow-white long hair and beard, he resembled the lovable Christmas character. He even wore small black-framed glasses and a red T-shirt. Had it not been for the warm August weather, FRICTION would've sworn he was meeting Saint Nicholas of the North Pole in person. He wondered if his appearance was the reason why he felt so comfortable with him before they even spoke.

Wasting no time to go inside, C-DOG said with nothing but love for him, "KRINGLE, my man. What up?" and gave him a brotherly handshake as he went in.

"What up, KRINGLE? It's nice to meet you," FRICTION told him as he entered behind his homie.

"I'm good. I'll be better once I hit some of that good ass weed you got for me. Y'all want something to drink? Pick your poison: Hennessy, bottled water—or both.

After C-DOG and FRICTION chose a shot of cognac and a bottle of water, respectively, KRINGLE left the pair standing in the living room while he went in the kitchen to get their drinks. Using the time to get a better understanding of the much older White man, FRICTION looked around at all the pictures he took over the years that were hanging in frames on the walls. A few showed KRINGLE in his youth looking fit and strong—his hair was still long, but jet black and he was with a group of guys that resembled a Funk band. There were even some with him hugging a variety of beautiful women and celebrities, showing he'd been to a lot of different places and had met a lot of different people during his music career.

In a low voice that KRINGLE couldn't hear, FRICTION murmured quite impressed, "Damn, I was a little worried I was gone have only Rock and Roll samples in my music until I saw all these pictures of KRINGLE with Black people. My mama still listen to some of these singers on his wall. Dude know everybody from back in the days."

"Bro, KRINGLE is one of the rawest producers around. He does it all: producing, mixing, engineering, and mastering—whatever needs to be done to make yo shit sound professional. Trust and believe, you gone leave here with a hit," C-DOG promised him.

"I hope you right. I want this more than anything else I ever wanted in my life. All I need is a dope beat to win that contest. The other rappers there won't know what hit they ass."

"And you will. Look at all those singers and musicians KRINGLE's worked with. The man's a musical genius—and that's why we're here. Yeah, it's other producers out there, but I know you don't care about nobody color. You want a professional and that's exactly what he is."

When KRINGLE walked back in with their refreshments, there was a kindness about him that FRICTION immediately felt again, which made his prior doubts and fears begin to fade away. When he was offered his drinks, he took them and nodded his head in appreciation. Then, with an arm gesture to follow him, KRINGLE led the duo to the door that led to his basement. As they walked down the stairs behind him, FRICTION's eyes grew large with anxious anticipation when he saw the basement was converted into a recording workstation filled with recording equipment and several musical instruments.

"Your studio is dope as hell! The design and all this equipment must've cost you a small fortune," FRICTION told him in awe as he looked around.

"Yeah, this is a culmination of my life's work down here. The sound booth over there is completely soundproof."

"This is nice."

"I've got digital and analog recording capabilities, and I play five different instruments ranging from bass guitar to keyboard."

"Five? Damn."

"I do my mixing in the box and everything we create will meet the standard loudness units relative to full scale from mix to master because I also master the final mix."

"What's loudness units relative to full scale?"

"LUFS. It enables a normalization of audio levels. Radio, different streaming services, etc., all want a certain amount of LUFS to operate on their systems."

"I didn't know that."

"It's cool, I got you. You'll walk out of here with your song version for radio and streaming, and you get an instrumental version for performing."

"I never thought about my music on the radio. That would be a dream come true."

"You also get the recording data, but I keep a copy for remixes and stuff. Do you have any questions?" KRINGLE asked while he led them to a lounge area beside his workstation.

"I do. How much is this gone cost me?" FRICTION asked worriedly because he was broke.

"Don't worry about that. All you gotta think about is making a hit. I got all that other shit covered," C-DOG reassured him.

"Oh, I'm making a hit! The whole world's gone know my name when I'm done!" FRICTION exclaimed excitedly as he admired KRINGLE's setup.

The recording session went better than FRICTION and KRIN-GLE had ever imagined. The way they fed off each other's vibe made creating the song fun and enjoyable, never once letting creative differences upset the atmosphere. FRICTION rapped like his livelihood depended on it, while KRINGLE produced like his reputation was on the line. At the end of the session, he had two copies on CD and a flash drive of the best song he'd ever made.

"Yo, fa real KRINGLE, thanks a lot, bro! I'm gone have this concert lit! That first-place title is mine!" FRICTION stated ecstatically as he listened to a replay of it on the producer's studio monitors.

"What you gone say if anybody asks who made your music?" KRINGLE asked with a satisfied smile.

"KRINGLE made it!" FRICTION shouted proudly.

"We good then. Make sure you got that bag the next time you come," KRINGLE told him as he lit up what was left of a blunt in his ashtray.

"I got you," FRICTION promised and looked over at his homie like it was the best moment of his life.

Not wanting to spoil his homie's mood at such a high moment, C-DOG let him enjoy himself for a few more extra minutes before he declared, "I gotta move I need to make bro. We gotta raise up."

They bumped FRICTION's first recorded song entitled, "Jus' Boogie" the entire way home. C-DOG didn't mind since it had a hood feel to it and the hook was catchy. He even sang the chorus every time they played the song—which was possibly over fifty times. With the top dropped and the music subbing with over 5,000 watts of power, the bass could be heard several blocks away.

When they were close to FRICTION's house, he didn't want to upset his mother with the loud music, so he asked his homie to turn it down. Feeling where his friend was coming from, C-DOG respectfully lowered the volume when he drove on the block.

"Now you good fa the audition. I gotta chop it up with MANIAC about some shit and then I'll be right back to get you so we can celebrate. I might even have a surprise fa yo ass," C-DOG said cryptically as he pulled up to his house.

"Cool, I'll be at the crib. Hey, you think MOOCH gone show up to support me at the contest?" FRICTION asked his homie before getting out.

"I doubt it bro," C-DOG answered in a matter-of-fact tone as he gave FRICTION a hood handshake goodbye.

Chapter Eleven
C'MON NIGGA RIDE

While FRICTION sat in the house for over an hour waiting for C-DOG's call, his mother came to his closed door and knocked in her signature style. When he told her it was alright to enter, she came in ready to have a deeper conversation with her only son. Regardless of how he tried to convince her he wasn't getting locked back up, she wanted to be certain he wasn't going to.

"I just want you to know that I'm not putting a damn dime on your books if you go back to jail. I'm dead serious, Malik—I hope the menu's a lot better there now than what it used to be," his mom vented sarcastically while she stood in his doorway with her hands on her hips.

"I'm not goin' back to jail, Mama—that's the last place I'm tryin' to see. I recorded my first song today and I believe I can win this contest. It was C-DOG who made that happen fa me. I know how you feel about him, and I understand, but please, let me enjoy this—I deserve it," FRICTION said a bit frustrated because she was killing his great mood.

"Look, I can see right now that you're happy and I swear I don't want to steal your joy, but any friend who let another friend take the fall for something they did—isn't your damn friend. I don't care how much they portray it—they're not. When the shit hits the fan—and it will—those kinds of friends will sacrifice you faster than a pawn on a chess board."

"I wasn't sacrificed though, Mama! I made that decision on my own! Why can't you understand that?"

"Number one: Don't raise your voice to me like I'm one of these bitches in the streets—I'm your Mama! Number two: I almost died having you and I almost died when they charged you first with murder—that's right, murder! Do you have any idea how much that hurt my heart? I wouldn't be alive today if Ki-Ki wasn't here, so don't you sit your ass on that bed and talk to *me—your Mama*—like the pain I feel inside don't count! I grew you from a sperm cell all the way to the man I'm looking at today, dammit, so give me my respect!"

"I *do* respect you, Mama. I'm sorry fa raising my voice."

"You were lucky the DA lowered it to manslaughter to get you to take his plea bargain!" his mother stressed to him while the memories of the fear and helplessness she felt rekindled inside her.

"I know, Mama," FRICTION said with shame.

"How do you think it makes me feel seeing you running around with the same person who put me through all that emotional torment?" she asked and wanted him to answer her.

But before he could, his phone began to rap a ringtone he'd recently downloaded as its ringer. When he appeared hesitant to see who it was, his mother knew right away it was "the main topic of their discussion" trying to get in touch with him. A part of her wanted to physically show her rage about how she felt about him reassociating with his friend, but she knew it would be a pointless act that would only push her son further away from her and closer to the streets. So, choosing a smarter path, she decided to back off and be there when he needed her.

"We're out of toilet paper," she stated bluntly, changing the subject entirely while she ignored his ringing phone.

Sensing it would be wise to not answer it, FRICTION looked at his mother confused and asked, "What?"

"TOILET PAPER. I need you to go to the corner store and get me some, please. Women take pride in their hygiene. Here's the money. Thank you," she told him with a smile as she shot a five-dollar bill on his bed and walked out of his doorway.

To give him back his privacy, she even closed his door back as she left, which FRICTION noticed and appreciated her for it. He knew she despised his homie C-DOG more than any other person alive, which he figured was a hell of a lot considering she knew a few despicable human beings. Not wanting to miss his call, he quickly picked up his phone and answered it. From the way C-DOG sounded on the other end, he could tell right away he was going to have a good time.

"You lucky as hell, this was my last try. You almost missed me and my special gifts," C-DOG mentioned before FRICTION had a chance to say hello.

"Gifts?" FRICTION asked a bit puzzled by what he'd heard.

"Yeah … gifts. C'mon nigga ride. Since you been away, you haven't had a chance to play. I want you to come outside and meet a couple of my friends."

"Oh—gifts! OK bro, I'll be out as soon as I brush my teeth again. I don't wanna knock nobody out with my breath—ya heard me."

"Yeah, I feel you. Hurry up, we gotta lot a freaky shit to do and not enough time to do it," C-DOG hinted and coughed from a blunt of premium weed he was smoking.

"Say no more. One," FRICTION said with a huge grin as he ended his call and went into the bathroom to freshen up.

When he stepped outside and saw three long-haired White women in C-DOG's old-school Impala with him, he thanked his boy in his head about ten times. The lovely ladies were as pretty as rare, exotic flowers, and he could tell from where he was standing that they were curvy in all the right places. With a little pimp strut, he walked to the car with the confidence of a lion in heat sizing up his potential mate. Sensing one of the two females sitting in the back seat was there to meet him, FRICTION made sure he gave them a "very interested" gaze and smile before he spoke to his homie.

"I see you brought some very beautiful friends with you, fam. How are you ladies today? My name's FRICTION," he announced as he sat between the two woman and reached up front to shake his homie's hand.

"They know about you already. This is Ava, Deja, and Natalia. They from Ukraine, but they live in Vegas. They like to drink, pop pills, and party hard. I say we get a suite with a jacuzzi and kick it like some players," C-DOG suggested to him as he nodded to his music playlist and hit his blunt.

Making it even more alluring, Natalia turned to FRICTION and began to rub her right hand on his right leg to show she also approved of his friend's proposal. But she didn't stop there, the very sexually energized woman began to zip down his pants and insert her hand inside his zipper. Wearing a silk, pink flower-patterned body dress, she looked surprised by what she felt and smiled seductively as she began to massage his penis. With her left hand, she caressed his left shoulder and the back of his neck to assure him he would be in excellent care.

Seizing the moment, FRICTION began to rub his hands across her tanned body while he leaned in and smelled her perfume sprayed across her large breasts. He led his right hand gently up the inside of her smooth thighs until he was underneath her dress. Feeling the tips of his fingers blocked by her G-string panties, he slowly moved it to the side and slipped a couple of his fingers inside her. As he began to massage her inside and out, the look on her face showed she was enjoying it.

After breaking away from kissing on her neck, he looked at C-DOG and said, "Yeah, I'm down."

Saying no more, C-DOG sped off from the curb in front of FRICTION's house and headed to Sybaris Pool Suites. The suites there also came with a waterfall, a warm pool, a steam room, two massage chairs, and a few other nice amenities that fit the plans they had in mind. With over a half an hour away from reaching their destination, FRICTION and C-DOG had some kinky ideas about what their sexy female friends could do to help time pass by. Raising the top on his automobile for much-needed privacy, they headed to Mequon, WI.

FRICTION, for some reason, kept feeling like there was something he was supposed to do but he couldn't remember what it was. He tried to, but he was too preoccupied by the sexual agility of Natalia to think properly. All he could do was succumb to her sensual nature and wait in anticipation for her next sensuous act. While he enjoyed her tantalizing pleasures, in the back of his mind he knew there was something important he was supposed to do.

Midway into their route, C-DOG's phone started ringing and he answered it with his blunt in his mouth. Soon after, his demeanor went from engaged to enraged. He started cussing vehemently at the person on the other end and hung up. Next, he made another call to someone else and gave him instructions to gather a few men. He then told him to call when it was done and hung up.

Turning the music down and looking at FRICTION like a very serious issue was underway, he managed to contain his anger and stated, "Change of plans bro. I need to take care of some shit."

Sensing it was a situation that could result in gunfire, FRICTION looked at his homie with love and loyalty before he asked, "Do you need my aid and assistance?"

"I could always use a real nigga like you, but I got this fam. I appreciate it though." C-DOG told him sincerely.

"Well, I'm here fa you if you need me," FRICTION let it be known.

The three women couldn't believe what they were hearing. When they first met C-DOG online, they knew he was going to be cool to hang out with and he didn't disappoint. When they flew in from Las Vegas, he came to Mitchell Airport with an armed friend and took them to get their rental car. He even helped choose the best hotel that fit their tastes.

So, with all that had transpired, it did come as a surprise to them when they heard him say the time they were going to spend together was now over. Not the type of women who are used to being so easily dismissed by men because of their modelish looks, Ava was the first person to say something about it. And by the dumbfounded look on her face, she was not OK at all with the way her one-day vacation was about to end.

"Tell me you're joking C-DOG. I flew here because I thought we were going to spend time together and get to know each other better. You told me your friend would like to meet one of my cousins—who are both really like my sisters since we left Ukraine to escape the war together, so I brought them with me. I can tell he likes Natalia. So, tell me, why do you toss us aside like old clothes? Are we not attractive enough for you?" Ava asked with a playful pout on her gorgeous face.

"Oh, hell yeah, you are three of the loveliest foreign women I ever met! But I'm a gangster baby and some real G shit is about to go down. You didn't fly all the way over here to be involved in all that. You came here fa a quick temporary escape from the problems in yo life," C-DOG explained while he caressed her left cheek.

"You are not the first gangster I've ever dated. You are not even the first Black gangster. I'm not a weak woman, C-DOG. I've done things and I've seen things that would make some women—and men—cringe," Ava divulged to him.

"That's good to know. I need a woman with a brave heart in my corner, but this isn't one of those times. I'll make sure I hit you up when a move come around that we both can profit from," C-DOG assured her.

"So, that's it? No romantic night together after all."

"These kind of problems takes time. I'll call you when I'm done and see if you wanna link up."

Overhearing her cousin's conversation while she was busy exchanging sexual flirtations with FRICTION, she looked at her new friend with a disappointed look and asked, "Do you want my number?"

"I want your number ... your email ... Facebook/Meta ... Instagram ... Twitter ... whatever you wanna give me," FRICTION joked and held out his phone to store her contact information.

While they were busy exchanging their info, C-DOG made a U-turn in the middle of Port Washington Ave. and Hampton Ave. to drop the ladies off at their hotel in downtown Milwaukee. Along the way, he gave the women more ecstasy to party with and the rest of the vodka he had since their plans had to be postponed. There was a part of him that wished he and FRICTION could've finished their good time, but the part of him that chose to be loyal to MANIAC would never allow it. There were some rivals who needed to be dealt with and he was the one tasked with seeing to it.

After they dropped them off at their hotel, FRICTION jumped in the front passenger seat and C-DOG hurried back to the north side of town. Not candid at all about the type of lifestyle he was now living, C-DOG made a call to his crew and told them where to meet him. He figured it would save more time since where they were going wasn't too far from FRICTION's house. Fifteen minutes later, he pulled up beside a new modeled black Ford Explorer and three men got out of it and got in the back seat of C-DOG's car—then they all drove off.

FRICTION glimpsed the men checking handfuls of extended 9mm magazines and their Glock 19s for defects out the corner of his eyes. Now seeing how serious things really were, he looked at his homie and said, "Bro, you my fuckin' homie. If you need me G—I'm ridin.'"

But C-DOG didn't respond. Instead, he dropped FRICTION off at his house. As far as he was concerned, it was a mission that needed veteran killers, and he knew for a fact FRICTION wasn't one. He was a loyal friend—not a cold-blooded killer.

When FRICTION got out of C-DOG's car, he saw them still checking their guns and magazines as they drove off. He wished whoever they were going to meet—the best of luck. Even though he was in front of his house, he decided to go to the corner store. He needed a blunt for the pungent dime bag of "OG Kush" his homie gave him after they'd dropped the ladies off and a can of orange soda pop to drink while he smoked it. Since he hadn't smoked in years and would have to take a drug test to get a job, he was a little skeptical about putting the thirty-day drug in his system.

Nevertheless, when he was inside the store, he bought the blunts and pop, but there was still something he knew he was forgetting to do. It wasn't until he walked outside with his stuff that he remembered what it was: he was supposed to get some toilet paper for the house! Quickly running back in the store and purchasing a roll of toilet paper, he sighed a breath of relief for avoiding a confrontation with his mom over the matter. He only hoped no one had to use the bathroom yet.

While he was halfway home, his phone began to ring. When he looked at it to see who it was, a smile came over his face because it was Natalia calling him. Using his cool voice, he answered it and talked to her while he walked home. He had to admit, she was someone he wanted to know more about. Not only could she turn a man on, but he found her foreign nature intriguing.

"So, y'all bout to go back to Las Vegas tomorrow?" he asked while he secretly wished they'd stay longer.

"Yeah. I wish you could come and visit me sometime. I get discounts on the rooms at the casino I work at if you do decide to come," Natalia answered.

"I will. You got this swag about you that makes me wanna know you more."

"I know. I feel the same way. You're cool, FRICTION."

"I think you cool too, Natalia."

"I'm not going to hold you up any longer. Make sure you call me later because I want to see you before I leave tomorrow. My sister Deja thinks you're handsome, but I told her we already have a special bond. I could tell she was jealous when we were making out next to her. Oh well, she'll be OK. Bye-bye," she trailed off slowly and seductively before hanging up.

"OK. Bye," FRICTION replied smoothly and hung up his phone.

The way she said it made him certain she wanted to have sex with him. And to be frank, he wanted her too. But at the end of the day, it wasn't up to him because he didn't have a car. He knew his sexual escapade relied primarily on his homie C-DOG, and there was no telling what time he would be finished doing whatever the hell him and his goon squad was on. To him, all C-DOG did was dangle some prime steak in his face—and then snatched it away.

Across the north side of the city, CASPER's loyal right-hand man MOE did exactly what he was told and took $200,000 cash to his girlfriend Naomi's house. When he handed her the designer black leather backpack filled with rubber-banded cash, she did as she was told and silently took it. With no reason to talk himself, MOE walked back to his dark blue Ford Expedition and got in it to leave. Before he drove off, he sat there quietly for at least five minutes trying to figure out why his gut was saying something wasn't right.

Not long after, Naomi came out of the house with the backpack and got inside her silver Toyota Camry. With the intention of doing everything her man told her to do, she headed off to the gas station on 35th and Mt. Vernon. While she drove with it on the front passenger seat, she couldn't help looking at it a couple times. She was tempted on several occasions to look inside, but she feared she might see something she could never forget—like a human body part.

So, rather than traumatize herself by being too curious, she chose not to do it and leave it alone. While trying to stay focused on her task, she thought about how strange her boyfriend CASPER sounded to her. Usually, he would always apologize when he missed one of their dates; but this time, there wasn't a sorry or anything from him about his absence. To her, it was either: he didn't remember he was supposed to come by, or he wasn't able to speak freely.

The way he came out the blue and asked her to do some clandestine act for him made things appear even more suspicious to her. He never asked her to throw a backpack inside a trashcan before. When she thought about it more, he'd never asked her to do anything remotely similar in comparison to what she was about to do for him. The mysterious "Cloak and Dagger" nature of it all began to slowly gnaw its way deep into her consciousness, consuming her rational thinking.

So much so, by the time Naomi pulled up to the gas station she was supposed to leave the backpack at, her mind was made up to find out who was picking it up. With a continuous wave of anxiety, she could feel deep in her spirit CASPER was in trouble. But just in case, she wanted to be sure he was in danger before she involved the police. Because if he wasn't and she put the police in his business, there would be some serious physical fighting afterwards.

Seeing pump 6, she looked around the gas station to see if anyone was waiting to pick the backpack up, but she saw no one. Cautiously checking her surroundings, she drove over to the gas pump's trashcan and dropped it inside. But instead of leaving to go back home, she drove across the busy street, went up the block, made a U-turn and parked where she could easily see everyone coming in and out of the gas station. With her mind made up to see it through, she knew one way or another, the truth about everything would soon be revealed.

Naomi observed several different kinds of vehicles pull up to the pump to use it, but no one went inside the trashcan to retrieve the backpack. Five minutes of waiting soon turned into thirty, making her doubt herself about someone coming to get it. It had gotten to her so bad, in a fit of frustration, she put her car in drive and decided to leave. Taking it as a sign CASPER was fine, she pulled away from the curb as she tried to call his phone for the thirteenth time.

While his sister was dropping off their money, SQUEAK was driving BONE's Camaro and thinking about how much he always liked it. The customized car was kept in mint condition and belonged in a showroom. It rolled dominantly on 28-inch green-colored rims with 2-inch tires. With its green customized leather seats and green LED lighting, the interior was as superior as the exterior, making it a mobile emerald in the streets of Milwaukee.

He briefly thought about his black BMW—mainly the car crash he was involved in several weeks ago and wished it never happened. He wasn't at fault, and nobody was seriously injured, but the damage to his customized car was estimated to take two months to repair. So, other than pricey rental cars, cabs, and driver services, he was basically a twenty-three-year-old without a vehicle. Feeling overcome with jealousy over BONE's flawless ride, he stopped mulling over the damage to his car and began to think about the large sum of money he was on his way to pick up at the gas station.

SQUEAK knew they were playing a dangerous game, but he couldn't think of any other alternative to get the cash he owed his homie/employer LOUIE-V. He knew those females were in the wind with the weed they stole. The more he thought about it, him and BONE played themselves by bragging about their status in the weed game and showing off by letting the thieves see it. At the time, he didn't think nothing of it because they didn't look or act like they scammed and schemed for a living.

As a matter of fact, the thieves gave the impression of pretty girls from upper-middle-class families. The way they confidently walked and intelligently talked made him believe they were from a classier crowd than him and BONE. It was an assumption he knew now was the complete opposite—they were really trash in designer clothes. In fact, he declared them the most trifling, scandalous females he ever met in his life. He'd never been drugged, given wild sex, and then robbed blind before—and he knew BONE would strongly agree.

The entire incident made him regret they'd ever met. He never would've left a message in her "DM" to kick it with him had he known they "catfish" people on social media websites to commit robberies. He'd heard about females doing it, but never in a million years did he see him and BONE being a victim. He wished he knew where they were so he could show the grifters how much he despised thieves. As far as he was concerned, each one should have their pretty little faces beat up—and then shot.

He'd never felt that way about any other female before until he ran across those two. Going by the nicknames "DESIRE" and "PASSION," he honestly didn't care to know more than that—other than the females being down for whatever. There were no first names, last names, or any addresses to locate the thieves—making them virtually impossible to find. What angered SQUEAK more than anything else was that they weren't even from the hood—they got played by some bitches from the burbs.

When he drove into the gas station thirty minutes later, all the customers' eyes were glued on BONE's green sports car. He couldn't deny it—he loved the attention, especially the kind that made his money look long. Letting the intense sound system vibrate its bass throughout it, he quickly pulled up to pump 6, got out of the car, and discreetly placed his right hand into the trash bin next to it. Seconds later, his hand emerged from the filthy garbage container with a very expensive-looking designer backpack.

Feeling like he'd accomplished an impossible mission, SQUEAK hastily got back inside the car and peeped inside it. Seeing so much cash at once was the absolute happiest moment of his life and he couldn't foresee anything else that could make him any happier. He was so elated by his newfound money that he almost hit an old lady as he sped out the gas station to go back to where him and BONE had taken CASPER. Pulling out his smartphone, he eagerly called BONE to tell him they were no longer poor men.

The phone only rang once before BONE picked up the phone and asked, "We good?"

"As a bitch," SQUEAK declared with a grin while he nodded to some rap music.

"We'll talk more when you get here," BONE expressed in a way that let SQUEAK know he was near CASPER.

"On my way," SQUEAK told him and hung up.

A part of him did feel a small bit of remorse for kidnapping CASPER because he knew how hard it is out here in these streets. Trying to figure out who you can trust and who you better not trust. Hoping you can find a few good men to link up with because you always could use some dependable help if you need it. Indeed, SQUEAK knew how hard it was to make a dollar in the ghetto—$200,000 was very difficult to do.

But then he thought about the beatings CASPER gave his older sister. The most recent one left her right eye swollen shut and blueish/purple looking. It was swollen so bad, her long fake eyelash looked trapped between her eyelids because of its puffiness. SQUEAK was angry enough to kill him over it and that rage never went away. But to appease his sister, Naomi, he stayed out of it while they reconciled their differences, patiently waiting for the next time he put his hands on her so it could be his last.

Fortunately for CASPER, he hadn't struck her since. SQUEAK figured they must've had a serious talk about their relationship and CASPER didn't want to lose her to someone else. Love has a way of making a crooked man straighten up. So, SQUEAK truly felt the money was atonement for CASPER's past transgressions against him and his family.

Paying LOUIE-V back consumed him more and more as he got closer to his destination. He looked at the backpack full of cash in the backseat and thought about his life back in the good graces of his Billboard-charting homie. The stylish mansions and five-star hotels he partied at thanks to his homie's talent and his rapidly rising celebrity status introduced him and BONE to a whole new world of living. A life filled with going on tours, being at topline fashion shows, attending various galas at extravagant locations, and a lot of other things he'd never done before made him see it was the only way to live.

The lifestyle LOUIE-V introduced him to went far beyond a mere $200,000—it was millions and millions of dollars. The kind of money that have you flying to your destination in private jets, planes, and helicopters. Where you're sitting in a whole section of a gentlemen's lounge or a ritzy nightclub that's been reserved with waiting bottles of chilled champagne. It was encompassed around loyal, cheering fans and the wild excitement of hip-hop music.

He had lived the American dream and he wanted it back. By being true to his homie, his financial problems were slowly going away. His bills were being paid ahead of time and he was saving up to buy a house. It was perfect—until him and BONE's incident.

Now he believed LOUIE-V considered them the weak links in his crew. Other than the threats he made in his home, LOUIE-V hadn't called neither of them to hang out with him. Being bumped back down to lower-class income when you felt the rich and famous lifestyle of upper-class income is a cruel and unusual punishment as far as SQUEAK was concerned. He made an oath to never disappoint his homie again if him and BONE were allowed back in his clique.

After twenty-five minutes of reflecting on how he was going to handle everything with the cash while he drove, he eventually turned onto the pothole-filled driveway of the rundown house where CASPER was being kept. Before he got out, he took some time in the car to thank God for letting him and BONE's plan succeed without a hitch. The last thing he wanted was for people to get hurt. At the end of the day, SQUEAK felt a plan to make money should be precisely that—a plan to make money.

After he finished, he grabbed the backpack and got out the car. Feeling good, he was heading to the back door of the house when he heard a very familiar voice. When he looked behind him, he saw his sister's car and she'd already got out. Slamming the door and rapidly approaching him, her intense anger was evident on her face.

"I should've known this had something to do with you! SQUEAK, I'm only going to ask you once: Where's CASPER?" she fumed vehemently.

Chapter Twelve
JUS' BOOGIE

"What up?" FRICTION said quietly into his phone while he watched a movie in the living room with his family.

"I'm gone make it up to you, bro," C-DOG started off by saying, already knowing his friend wasn't happy about him ditching their dates.

"Alright fam, if you say so."

"You in fa the night?"

"I don't know. I'm chillin' with my moms and little sis. Why?"

"It's about nine now, I'll be there to get you at ten-thirty."

Now feeling more curious than disappointed, FRICTION asked C-DOG, "What fa?"

"We gone hit the club up hard. I got some clothes in my closet that still got the tags on it and I got the perfect fit for you bro. You can keep it too because I know how it is when you first get out," C-DOG stated like he wasn't taking anything less than "Yes" for an answer.

"I don't know. I ain't never been to one before. I don't wanna make myself feel uncomfortable."

"You won't know until you go. Plus, I gotta surprise fa you when we get there. Don't worry, bro, you gone have a boss night."

"OK, I'm down. I hope you right," FRICTION expressed skeptically.

"Don't trip, it's gone be lit. Look fa me around eleven," C-DOG told him before he got off the phone.

"Wait, I thought you said ten-thirty," FRICTION remarked like he doubted him.

"Cool, I'll be there at ten-thirty. I'll just take a shit over yo house then," C-DOG stated like it wasn't a big deal to him.

"You know what, on second thought, I'll be looking fa you around eleven-fifteen so you can wash yo ass," FRICTION laughed and hung up.

Observing their interaction in its entirety, his mother could only look at him and shake her head in disapproval. She sat in her recliner and began to imagine all kinds of felonious activities her son could get mixed up in if he went out with C-DOG. From fighting to shootouts, her mind pictured it all. When she'd finished creating her violent scenarios involving her only son, her mind was made up that she wasn't posting his bail if he's arrested.

Even his young sister gave him a look filled with frustration. In her young mind, he was messing up big time because he was making her mama mad, and he wasn't watching the computer-animated movie with her anymore. She was already being allowed to stay up past her bedtime to enjoy the entire film and he told her they would see it together. Now, she felt abandoned after one stinking phone call.

"I thought you were going to watch TV with me," Ki-Ki asked him, beginning to feel unimportant.

"Don't worry, little sis, I'm not leaving this livin' room until yo movie is over. The last thing I wanna miss is seein' if the purple pony can find his way back to the magical kingdom. She never will if the green ogres have somethin' to say about it," FRICTION told her, showing he was following the storyline and had watched every scene.

"She has to! The bad witch will take over Pony Land if she doesn't make it back with the gem to stop her!" Ki-Ki yelled in a panic.

"Don't worry, little sis, I got faith in the purple pony. She'll save Pony Land from the old, bad witch," he reassured her.

And true to his word, FRICTION sat with her on the couch for the duration of the movie. He didn't even get up for a bathroom break or for anything to drink. His time was dedicated to her, and he made sure she knew it too. After the movie was over, he gave her a kiss on her forehead and got up to go to his room.

Attempting to avoid his mother, he tried to stealthily sneak past her while she was preoccupied reading funny memes on her smartphone, but she stopped him before he was completely out the living room. Never taking her eyes off the phone's screen, she only told him, "Be safe. I love you."

"I love you too, Mama. I will," FRICTION replied somewhat caught off guard by what she said.

He was expecting a big lecture about how C-DOG wasn't shit, ain't shit, and was never gone be shit. It would then be followed up with a nonstop talk about the excessive cost of bail and how it wasn't getting paid if he got arrested. He even assumed she would use a fringe tactic about getting into conflicts with gang members and being in shootouts. But oddly enough, there was none of that—it felt weird to him.

Beginning to feel like he was being tricked into some sort of trap, he turned to her and asked, "That's all you had to say?"

"You a man now," she said and chuckled at a meme of a teen-age White boy punching an older White man in his face, which read:

FOR DADS WHO INTENTIONALLY CHOOSE NOT TO TAKE
CARE OF THEIR CHILDREN.

FRICTION left the living room wondering if his mother was
upset with him and went to get ready for his first time at a nightclub.
And like clockwork, C-DOG called at eleven-fifteen to tell him to
come outside and get his outfit. When he came out, his homie was
leaning on a white and chrome Jaguar. When Friction went to greet
him, C-DOG handed him an expensive designer Italian silk shirt
with the silk slacks that went with it and a shoe box with a pair of
alligator-skin Italian shoes that looked very far from cheap. Knowing
the top brand clothes and shoes he was given cost thousands of dollars, FRICTION was initially hesitant to accept them.

"I don't know if I can accept these. I saw that same Versace
shirt worn by a rapper in a video I saw in jail last week and I'm sure
it cost a few racks bro. I can't afford to pay fa this if it's damaged,"
FRICTION said apprehensively.

"I told you already on the phone bro. These yours. This my
little 'Welcome Back Home' gift to you and this is fa havin' my back
when I needed it most," C-DOG replied and handed his homie
$5,000 in cash.

"Fuck bro, you didn't have to do this. You already hooked me
up with a dope producer and a fine-ass White chick. We good."

"I owe you a lot more than that. You a felon forever because of
me. Jesus only sacrificed more G."

"I don't know what to say," FRICTION responded with deep
respect for his good friend and humbly accepted the lavish gifts.

"That you won't keep me out here forever while you get
dressed," C-DOG joked and relit his blunt.

After FRICTION assured his homie that he wouldn't be long,
he ran back inside the house to get dressed for his big night out.

But before he put his new stylish clothes on, he looked at them and shook his head in disbelief about how pricey they were—and how fly he was going to look wearing them. Once he was dressed, he had to admit the overall "rich look" did take some getting used to—but he did resemble a young Black millionaire. With the look and esteem that comes with being wealthy, he stepped back out like he owned the city.

As soon as he reentered the car and sat down next to him in the passenger seat, C-DOG gave him a hood handshake and shouted excitedly, "I see you, my nigga! Damn, now I wish I kept my shit! Naw, I'm fuckin' with you!"

"Love again fam, I do look fly as hell! We gone make muthafuckas hurt they neck up in there tryin' to see us—no cap!" FRICTION told him confidently.

"Oh yeah, this the final touch and you official as a referee's whistle. Here ya go." C-DOG said coolly and passed him several expensive pieces of diamond and platinum jewelry.

The eye-catching pieces included: four rings, a bracelet, a Swiss watch, two earrings, and a 30-inch necklace with a large Holy Cross emblem on it. Now feeling like the price of the clothes he wore shadowed in comparison to the few hundred thousand dollars' worth of jewelry he was being handed, FRICTION looked at it like it was a lost treasure.

"Are these real? Damn C-DOG, how much money you got nigga?" FRICTION asked while he examined the pieces of fine jewelry.

"Enough to not wear fake shit," C-DOG replied egotistically.

"I can't rock yo jewelry bro. What if we get into it with some fools in there who wanna hate? This drip is the lick of the year!"

"Here, put these Cartier shades on too. You need to look the part. I want you to kick it and floss yo ass off. Trust me, the haters don't won't no smoke."

"Damn—these nice as hell," FRICTION replied in awe as the accessories twinkled like the stars in the night sky whenever he moved.

"You gone shine like these diamonds," C-DOG assured him as they left.

The ride to the club for C-DOG and FRICTION was full of loud music, laughing, and smoking premium marijuana. They also shared some of their life stories from the past few years to catch up on lost time. Even though during FRICTION's stint in prison there was no contact with each other, they still shared an unwavering brotherly bond. There existed a timeless trustworthiness that was earned because they were best friends before that fatal night.

The nightclub, which is properly named the "HOT-SPOT," is a Black-owned nightclub located on the north side of Milwaukee. Having been owned and operated by Steve "Even-Steven" Hartman— an older man in his early sixties and a highly degreed member of the Prince Hall Masonic Temple for over thirty years—its doors were opened to entertain Blacks in the low-income area. Still quite a popular place to socialize within the community, it's seen its fair share of depreciation and lack of appreciation since it was founded in 1994. Due to the business catering to financially challenged Blacks, it had to deal with many of the nuisances that came with it.

C-DOG was quite familiar with some of those nuisances, having been the cause of several there over the years. He'd been in gang-related shootouts and fights with men over their girlfriends

... being looked at the wrong way ... over his shoes being stepped on ... even fights because he was drunk and just felt like fighting. Things had gotten so disruptive, Even-Steven had to invite him to his office one night to discuss it. By the time they were finished, C-DOG understood why the nightclub was there and had promised to give it more respect. To date, he hadn't fought or shot anyone there since.

When they pulled up to the HOT-SPOT, it was jam-packed with cars and people. The various crowds gave different glimpses of how separate peoples' lives were—even though their blackness was one and the same. There were the "Pretty Boy" and "Pretty Girl" groups who looked cookie-cutter perfect and came from families with money. There were also the "Party Like a Rock Star" groups who got drunk, did extremely potent drugs, and danced all night long. But no one could forget the "Gang-Gang" groups because they were tough-look- ing and gang-affiliated in the streets.

They didn't dress like Black hippies or made loud fashion statements—they wore expensive clothes and repped their gang col- ors, numbers, or names. Some wore jewelry—while others looked like they'd take yours. It didn't matter whether they were male or female, their loyalty was with their gang and no one else. Out of all the groups, which there were more, they were the most dangerous one if provoked.

And it was that group C-DOG was scouting for when he was looking for a place to park, but all he kept seeing was unrecogniz- able partygoers who came to have fun and didn't appear to pose a threat. Nevertheless, he tucked his gun on him when they got out and began to talk on his phone while they walked up to the club. Wearing completely different diamond and platinum jewelry than what he gave FRICTION, C-DOG wore more rings, bracelets, and necklaces than him.

"Damn fam, I was so into the jewelry I got on that I didn't even peep yo drip! How much money do you make with MANIAC?" FRICTION asked impressed as they walked past the long line of waiting patrons and went directly to the large muscular bouncer.

"I'm able to get the shit I want—instead of just the shit I need," C-DOG explained and gave the bouncer a firm handshake before he let them in.

Curious about how they were able to go right in without waiting, FRICTION joked, "You a movie star now?"

"I wish. I gave BRUISER a hundred-dollar bill when we shook hands. We don't have time to sit in a long-ass line. We gotta get this to the DJ before he start playin' slow jams," C-DOG said with a sense of urgency as they walked through the overcrowded club to the disc jockey booth.

In his hand, he held a flash drive.

Seeing it for the first time, FRICTION was amused and curious simultaneously, so he asked with a smile, "What the fuck is that?"

"This is the first day of the rest of yo rappin' ass life! This—my nigga—is yo chance to shine!" C-DOG yelled over the loud party rap music.

Leaving FRICTION still quite a bit confused by what he meant, C-DOG walked off to talk to the disc jockey—who was busy entertaining the crowd with his great music picks and energetic personality. First, FRICTION saw his homie give the DJ some cash and the flash drive. Then they talked a little bit longer. The next thing he knew the DJ was placing it in his computer for a few minutes and then gave it back to him. Then there was a handshake and C-DOG came back with a grin on his face.

"I hope you ready!" C-DOG shouted anxiously.

"Ready fa what?" FRICTION asked more confused than ever.

"To go on that stage right there and perform yo hit after he play four more songs!"

"What hit?"

"JUS' BOOGIE!"

"How?"

"I brought my flash drive with yo music! You gone slay bro!"

Feeling a subtle sense of anxiety come over him, FRICTION stared at his homie uncomfortably and asked, "In only four more songs?"

"Three now! Look fam, you got this! You just as raw as the rappers I listen to! To be real, you better than a lot of 'em! No cap!" C-DOG looked at him seriously and punched his homie in his chest to remind him he had a lot of heart.

"Is the mic on?" FRICTION asked while he looked over at the performance stage.

"The microphone and the stage lights work! Aye don't worry about props and special effects! This is about you seein' if any of these people like yo song!" C-DOG yelled emphatically to his nervous homie.

It took a minute or two for what he was being told to sink in, but when it did, he was resurged by the reality that this *was* his chance to showcase his skills. He knew a real rapper doesn't need gadgets and lasers to speak their message. It helps to get people's attention, but all a rapper need is a microphone, a speaker, their music, and some folks who don't mind listening.

So, FRICTION gathered himself and shouted to this homie, "Let's do this!"

To reach the stage, they had to walk by a couple dozen cocktail tables. The patrons were drinking alcohol and enjoying themselves when C-DOG and FRICTION casually passed by. A female at one of the tables noticed the duo and shouted, "Y'all must be some celebrities!"

One of the guys—who happened to dress like he was in the "Broke Goon" group—was sitting at the table and waited for the two to be in earshot before he rudely shouted, "I bet they jewelry ain't real! Them niggas fake as hell!"

At first, C-DOG stared angrily at the drunk man, making a few people who heard the disrespectful comment think he was going to hit him in his face, but he didn't. Instead, he shook his head like the belligerent man was beneath him on every level and continued to walk. He didn't even look angry anymore afterwards.

FRICTION thought his homie was going to shoot the man the entire time it was happening. So, to see him not even bothered by it threw him in a loop. He'd never once known C-DOG to be the passive type. He was glad his friend was cool about it, but he'd never seen him react that way before.

As they approached the stage, FRICTION turned to his homie and shouted, "At first, I thought the performance was about to be canceled due to a beat ass!"

"It almost was, but I promised the owner I would show his place more respect! Did you know this was the first nightclub in the hood that held 300 people?"

"Naw, I didn't!"

"It was only supposed to hold 250, but they didn't have all these shootings and murders on the property to upset the community all the time! People used to be able to go out and not worry about all that shit!" C-DOG let him know before he walked up the six stairs that led to the performance stage.

Then, from the back of the stage, they were greeted by the owner himself—Even-Steven. C-DOG and FRICTION each met him at the top stair with a "brotherly love" handshake before they stood next to him. From the height and position of the stage, they could see everybody in the nightclub.

"It's a beautiful sight, ain't it? Up here, the people down there is together. They gone jam with you—as long as they feel you. Ya feel me?" Even-Steven told FRICTION, hoping his advice helped.

"Yeah, I feel you a thousand percent. Thanks," FRICTION expressed to him with appreciation and walked over to the microphone.

It was the first time he held one on a stage before. He thought about how many people were there and how all the attention would soon be focused on him—his music and performance. He knew one thing for certain: he wanted to give the crowd the best show he had to offer.

As soon as the final song finished playing, the DJ grabbed his microphone and yelled to the crowd in the club, "Yo, yo, yo! It's ya favorite HOT SPOT DJ—DJ TURN UP and I'm bout to turn up! Get up out ya seats! This one is fa my rap lovers out there! Comin' to y'all live in da hive! He's here to rep the Mil and keep it real! I got my homie FRICTION in the house—and he want all y'all to JUS' BOOGIE!"

As soon as he heard his music, a different side of him took over. FRICTION rapped his lyrics with deep passion and moved with an energy that couldn't be ignored. He didn't do a dance routine, but the way he boogied showed how much he enjoyed grooving to his song. The overall feel he gave energized enough people that they got out of their seats and joined the ones who were already enjoying themselves on the dancefloor.

With C-DOG by his side as his hype man, they both sparkled and shined as they treated the stage like it was theirs. The swag they showed was so strong, a few drunk women—with exceptionally nice figures—ran on stage and began to "twerk" next to them. Those five minutes was the best time FRICTION ever had in his life! But even better than that, the people in the club loved his music!

After the performance, there was some applause and then everybody went back to doing their own thing. But this time when the two walked by the filled cocktail tables, they were stopped and spoken to.

"Where can I download it?" one man asked curiously.

"Y'all was lit!" one woman exclaimed, hyped up.

"Play another song!" another woman demanded excitedly.

"My girl loved y'all song! I felt it too! Rep the city!" shouted another man over the club music as he showed them some love with a handshake.

There were others with positive compliments too. FRICTION and C-DOG were honestly expecting way more "haters" than there were "congratulators," but that wasn't the case. In fact, there were more folks who liked the music than disliked it—some even wanted to purchase it or download it to their music playlist. FRICTION was left speechless by the positive feedback.

"WHAT YOU SITTIN' FOE? JUS' BOOGIE! WHAT YOU FIDGETIN' FOE? JUS' BOOGIE!" C-DOG rapped some of the chorus with FRICTION while he "Gangster-Boogied" and shook his homie's hand several times with excitement.

"I know bro! This means I gotta legitimate chance to win the competition! Things gone be better fa all of us if I do!" FRICTION promised his homie before two cute females came over and spoke.

"I like your music. Are you promoting your album?" one of the lovely ladies asked.

Taking the opportunity to speak on FRICTION's behalf, C-DOG said, "Today was a test run to get our target market's feedback and determine if any further invested promotion would be feasible."

FRICTION was surprised to hear his homie sound so smart. After hearing his response, he decided not to say anything and let C-DOG finish."

"Oh OK. Well, my name is PEACHES, and this is my friend COCOA. We do all sorts of modeling—mainly adult films and music videos. We've got a lot of photos and videos on our "OnlyFans" pages if you want to see a preview," PEACHES told C-DOG since he was the one talking.

"We bout to head outside to my whip and smoke a blunt. Y'all can come and show us if y'all want to—if FRICTION think y'all good. Is they good?" C-DOG asked his homie, making him appear important to the women.

"They good. Let's see what they got to show us," FRICTION responded coolly as he looked over their gorgeous figures.

Letting the ladies lead the way out the club, C-DOG looked over at his friend with a devilish grin and then looked at the two thick-hipped women wearing short, clingy mini-dresses in front of them. Picking the one he was sexually interested in, he walked behind PEACHES and began to touch her shapely hips from behind while they walked. To show C-DOG she was down for whatever, she rubbed her butt against him to the music that was playing.

FRICTION sensed COCOA was also cool with being touched, so he grabbed her slender waist with both of his hands and made his way to her large round hips. To show she was about that action, she dropped to the floor and twerked very seductively in front of him. As far as he was concerned, him and C-DOG wasn't coming back—not tonight anyway.

Chapter Thirteen
FLOSS THIS GAME

Naomi stood in front of her brother SQUEAK like she was going to punch him in his face. Beating him up often when they were young, there was a strong possibility she was going to do it too, so SQUEAK frowned at her frustratingly for trying to ruin everything and sighed, "Damn Nay, chill out."

"Where the fuck is my man?" she asked sternly while she held her right fist up at him.

"Why the hell should you care? He treats you like trash every single day! All you is to dude is a punchin' bag and some late-night pussy!" SQUEAK shouted at her angrily as he thought about the mental and physical abuse she constantly endured by CASPER.

"You're right, SQUEAK, he's far from perfect. He's done a lot of mean things to me over the years, and I know you hated every minute of it. But please think deeply about what you're doing right now. This is kidnapping, little bro. That's years and years of your life in jail."

"Yeah, only if I get caught."

"How do you know you won't?"

"Is you gone tell?"

"Are you seriously gone ask me that?"

Becoming frustrated by her meddling in his affairs, SQUEAK began to pace back and forth in front of her while he clung on to the backpack and told his sister disdainfully, "You changed. I remember when you would stab a dude before you'd ever let a nigga hit you. Now look at you—you just a 'do-girl' fa a fuckboy who punch on females. You goofy as fuck."

Feeling as if he was attacking her character and what she stood for, Naomi became defensive and stated, "Yes, I do let CASPER get away with a lot of shit—shit I know I shouldn't let him do, but you must forgive if you truly love someone. I love CASPER. I've loved him for almost eight years of my life."

"The nigga don't love you. He treats you bogus."

"He's getting better—it takes time. But make no mistake, I'll go to prison for the right reasons. My respect and my dignity are two of them."

"Go home, sis. I won't hurt him if that's what you're worried about. He gone live because I never wanted him to die."

"Then take me to him."

"Look, I know I can't point a pistol at you and make you stop lovin' a piece of shit like CASPER. I wish I could, but I know I can't. But this money right here is what he owes us fa all the pain he put our family through."

"I'm not leaving until I can see for myself how he's doing. I'm still trying to process in my head that you're the one who's responsible for this. I hope it's worth it," she stated with deep disappointment in him.

"Look, all I gotta do is take him somewhere secluded and drop his snake ass off—that's it! Why involve yo self any further?" SQUEAK asked her because she was acting dense in the head to him.

"Because you chose to kidnap the man I love, for drugs or money—probably both," Naomi retorted.

"Go ahead, let the whole block know. Wait a minute, you didn't look in the bag?" SQUEAK stopped berating her and had to ask.

"No, I didn't. I wasn't asked to do that. He wanted it took somewhere and I did it. I could care less what's inside it," Naomi told him truthfully.

"You're his loyal lap dog, huh?"

"Fuck you, SQUEAK!"

"I'm serious. You cussed mama out at the hospital when she told you to leave him alone, remember? You thought he broke one of yo ribs when he threw you down and kicked you outside that bar."

"Shut up, SQUEAK!"

"Oh, what did you do to deserve it? I remember. You smiled when a dude complimented your dress."

"Shut up!"

"Yeah, he took you outside and stomped the shit out you. After that, he tried to punt a field goal with your rib cage. Then to top it all off, he dropped you off at the hospital all by yo lonely. But it doesn't stop there. When we went to check on you at the hospital, you called the woman who gave birth to you a 'nosey bitch' because she was concerned and loved you." SQUEAK told her in a way that suggested she was a complete and utter fool for her boyfriend.

"Shut the hell up!" she shouted angrily and pushed her younger brother hard in his chest as the memory of her tragic event made her eyes fill with water.

"Not until you go home."

"I'm not leaving."

"OK. I'll take you to see him and then you go. Deal?" SQUEAK eventually gave in and suggested, hoping she'd agree.

"Deal—as long as you promise not to hurt him," Naomi agreed, only after making her stance clear because she couldn't fathom the thought of her brother killing her boyfriend.

After nodding his head to acknowledge things were now cool between them, SQUEAK led her to the back of the rundown house they were parked at. Once they were there, he went to the back door and knocked six times. When the door opened, Naomi saw a thin-looking older woman and concluded it was her house. SQUEAK led his older sister through a disgusting maze of trash and cat feces until they arrived at the door that led downstairs to the basement.

"Don't talk. You gotta go as soon as you see he's not hurt," SQUEAK whispered to her before he opened the door.

After she nodded in agreement, she followed him down the creaky stairs and into the dimly lit musty-smelling area they had her man held captive. The intense odor of cat urine and feces made her gag a few times in her mouth, but she fought hard not to puke. It was a level of disgusting that she wasn't used to and wondered if the woman she saw open the door suffered from some sort of mental illness. She couldn't comprehend how anybody would willingly live in such filth.

Naomi was beginning to feel upset about him being detained against his will in a shithole when she saw a hooded figure bound with cable ties and duct tape on a torn pleather chair underneath a lit light bulb near the back of the basement. As she got closer, she realized it was a black pillowcase covering his head and CASPER couldn't see anything. Not too far from him, she saw SQUEAK's best friend BONE leaning against a wall playing a game on his smartphone. From what she could tell, he didn't appear to be in pain or suffering too badly.

She wanted to abandon the arrangement she made with her brother and let CASPER know she was there for him, but she not only gave her word—it would reveal who kidnapped him and make matters much worse than they already were. It wasn't an easy choice, but she had to keep her end of the deal. She watched as he fidgeted uncomfortably on his seat and wished the terrible ordeal would be over soon.

When BONE saw Naomi with SQUEAK, he almost spoke out his disbelief in his real voice. Besides being livid about him not being informed about any of it, he also felt she could jeopardize everything because CASPER was her boyfriend. Not saying a word, he scowled and waved for them to follow him. Once they were out of CASPER's earshot, he looked angrily at SQUEAK before he spoke.

"What is she doing here? How come I'm the last one to know about this!" he whispered at SQUEAK with a frown on his face.

"Fam, she just showed up. I can't tell you what I don't know. She ain't gone snitch. All she wanna do is make sure he ain't beat up—and then you ghost. Right?" he looked over at her and asked.

Seeing she was not welcomed there at all, she whispered back, "Right."

BONE intensely studied Naomi's face for any sign of weakness. He knew she could put him and SQUEAK in prison for a very long time if she decided to give them up to the authorities. A part of him wanted to back out of their scheme since she compromised it, but the other part of him knew they were too close now to walk away. Not wanting to risk his freedom or the ransom, BONE weighed it all in.

With no choice but to trust Naomi, BONE looked back over at his homie SQUEAK and asked, "Did you get the money?"

"Every single cent," SQUEAK answered and then showed him the designer backpack.

When he unzipped it and held it open for everyone to see—it was filled with rubber banded stacks of cash. Everyone looked at the money like it was a holy gift from God to behold before he zipped it back up again.

"Hey, I hear y'all over there! Did you get the money yet? Hey!" CASPER yelled out from underneath the pillowcase.

Not perturbed at all by his outburst, BONE looked at Naomi and told her, "We gone let him go in ten minutes. I wanna count the money first."

She knew BONE and SQUEAK were going to see their caper through and there wasn't any point trying to talk them out of it. So, she nodded "OK" and hoped her man would be released quickly.

As BONE was about to walk over to an old kitchen table and count the cash, the silence in the house was interrupted by a loud pound and then two gunshots upstairs. Quickly grabbing his handgun, he looked over at his homie to see if he heard it too, but SQUEAK already had his gun pointed at the stairway leading upstairs. Fearing it was the police, they all rushed by CASPER and hoped no one would come down. Knowing if someone did, there wouldn't be no good ending in sight.

Hearing the commotion upstairs from underneath the pillowcase, CASPER yelled anxiously, "What y'all up to? I did my part! Let me go!"

Naomi was tempted to respond, but BONE frowned at her and put his finger over his lips to signal her to hush. He then told CASPER in a low indescribable voice, "Don't you say another word. I will kill you right now if you do. We'll let you go soon. Be quiet."

Complying with his captor, CASPER didn't say another word. He just sat there and rocked his legs. He knew something out of their control was going on but didn't know what it was. He hoped whatever it was wouldn't hinder his release.

Then from the silence, he heard a familiar voice yell out his name. *Was that MOE?* he wondered to himself.

Hearing someone yell CASPER's name made SQUEAK and BONE look at Naomi like she was the reason their hideout was exposed. Reaching for his smaller Smith and Wesson Bodyguard .380 handgun and handing it to his sister to protect herself, SQUEAK then motioned for BONE to follow him to the stairway. Moments later, they saw the basement door that led down to them slowly open and CASPER's name was yelled again. Then they watched from the shadows as MOE slowly walked down the stairs with his Draco assault rifle aimed to shoot while three other armed men followed closely behind him.

Outgunned and outnumbered, BONE hid on one side of the basement behind a nonworking icebox while SQUEAK scrunched down on the other side beside an old washer. The plan was simple: shoot once they were all down the stairs and close enough to hit accurately. If things went accordingly, they knew CASPER's crew couldn't withstand being flanked on both sides—regardless of how many there were or what type of artillery they were armed with.

They silently waited in the dimly lit corners of the basement until the last armed man was standing on the basement's concrete floor. SQUEAK, who was only feet away from the room where CASPER and his sister Naomi were, signaled for her to unscrew the light bulb above their heads. When the four-man crew divided themselves into two groups to look around, the light to the room went out only seconds before MOE and his underling turned to head in their direction. With drawn guns leading the way, CASPER's long-time friend of many years called out to him.

"CASPER! Yell if you down here, dog! It's MOE fam! CASPER!" his homie yelled out as he slowly approached SQUEAK and the room.

On the other side of the basement, the other two thugs were nervously jumpy and ready to shoot at anything that moved in the dark, so BONE took a flattened aluminum can and hit an opposite wall with it. Following the shocking sound, the two nervous thugs began to shoot blindly in the direction the noise came from. Fearing for their lives, they shot in a panicked frenzy, sending round after round into the concrete wall. When they finished shooting the ammo in their guns, BONE snuck up on the oblivious pair while they were reloading and shot several rounds throughout their chests. The two men then fell lifelessly to the cold cement floor.

Using the diversion to his own advantage, SQUEAK attacked with a barrage of gunfire as soon as MOE and his henchman turned their heads to see what all the commotion was about. One round tore through the back and out the front of the henchman's right shoulder and another one entered the lower back of his cranium before it exited out his left cheek—killing him instantly. MOE tried to turn back around and shoot at anybody, but he was hit with two bullets in his lower abdomen and once in the right upper arm he held his gun with. The round's impact swung his arm outward as it pierced his nerves, causing it to instantly open his hand and release his weapon.

Watching his gun fly unwillingly out of his hand as he fell backwards to the floor, MOE screamed out in excruciating pain. He desperately wanted to search for it, but his heavily bleeding wounds took precedent. He could only cradle himself and try to cover the bloody bullet holes in his stomach with his hands—unaware that he was also bleeding badly from the exit wounds in his back.

Needing to ensure he would die, SQUEAK ran from his hiding spot to fire his gun up close in his face, but he hesitated. He remembered when MOE used to come over his house with CASPER. It was years ago, and he usually stayed in the car, but he always rolled down his passenger window and spoke to him. He hesitated because he knew deep down in his heart—he wished it didn't have to be this way.

But because of that hesitation, MOE caught a glimpse of his face and vehemently yelled with blood coming out of his mouth, "SQUEAK! You bitch-ass nigga!"

Threw into a frightening tailspin by hearing his name shouted loud enough to be heard outside, SQUEAK emptied three more rounds into MOE's face—silencing him for good. Unfortunately for SQUEAK though, the damage from MOE's final outburst was already done. CASPER, who'd been passively silent until that point, began to hurl death threats at him as he tried with all his strength to unsuccessfully free himself from his bondage. Unknown to him, Naomi was standing right by his side.

"I should a known this was you SQUEAK! You gone pray fa a quick death when I get my hands on you! I hope you fuckin' hear me SQUEAK! You a dead man! Nobody can save you nigga—not even Naomi! You gone wish you was aborted muthafucka! You'll never be safe in this city again! I'm gone kill—", but before he was able to finish making his threat against SQUEAK, Naomi cut his tirade short with two gunshots in the top of the black pillowcase that was covering his head—ending the life of the man she loved.

"You ain't gone do shit to my brother! Why did you have to threaten his life? Why?" she cried as the gun shook in her trembling hands.

Walking over to his still highly emotional sister, SQUEAK gently took the handgun away from her and gave her a long hug for support. He felt her head fall into his chest as she cried. He didn't say anything. The only thing SQUEAK wanted to do was show his sister that he was just as loyal to her as she was to him.

He patiently held her until she gathered herself and no longer wanted his sympathy. Wiping away her tears, Naomi knew there wasn't any other option. CASPER would've killed her brother now that he knew who kidnapped him—there wasn't any doubt in her mind about it.

When BONE ran over and saw the aftermath in the room, Naomi and SQUEAK looked at him like neither of them wanted to talk about it. Leaving it alone entirely, he was more concerned about what their next move was. The way he saw it, there were three living people in a house with five dead bodies—possibly six if MOE and his crew killed Sheila upstairs. It was time to go.

"We need to bounce! The Po-Po gone be here soon!" BONE shouted frantically.

"What about—him?" Naomi asked as she tried not to look at CASPER.

"C'mon sis! We gotta go!" SQUEAK yelled at her, snapping her out of her depression.

A few days later, LOUIE-V's private jet flight back home to Milwaukee was courtesy of the very pleased concert promoter who'd booked his London show. As if his headliner placement wasn't gratifying enough, the promoter also provided him with a stretched Rolls Royce limo to drive him wherever he wanted to go and a penthouse luxury suite at a five-star hotel for the two nights he was in town. Not to mention, he was the guest of honor at an after-party event at one of London's most popular nightclubs. The rap artist was treated like royalty, and he enjoyed every minute of it. As the jet proceeded to land on the airport runway, he finished sipping the white Sangria in his wine glass and checked the time on his Royal Oak Audemars Piguet watch. Wearing Gucci apparel from head to toe, he looked like a walking commercial for the brand. Seeing he made it back home on schedule, the first thing he wanted to do was make sure his business affairs were in order. Primarily, he wanted to make sure there weren't any issues with his weed houses.

After placing a few calls on his phone, he was pleased to hear the pounds of premium marijuana at each location was almost sold out. With over $80,000 to pick up from his trap houses and a take-home pay of $100,000 for his overseas show, he was feeling pretty good about his life in general. There was a point early on in his youth when he didn't even know where his next meal was coming from.

It was those struggling years of poverty that made him determined to achieve success. He looked down at the diamond and platinum jewelry that hung majestically from his neck and felt proud about everything he'd accomplished in such a short time. He recalled, not that long ago, when he first started building up his music followers online and trying to sign with a viable record label. He had no support back then—only his own determination and motivation to make his dream a reality. Now he wears over $2,000,000 worth of jewelry on his ears, fingers, neck, and wrists to show the world it's merely the beginning of much more to come.

The fact that some of his money came from the streets didn't bother LOUIE-V one bit because it still was money he earned. He didn't rob people or steal from anybody to get it. He made his money play by play in a hands-on kind of way. He only enlisted some of his friends when he saw his product was growing more than he was able to handle alone.

When he stepped off the jet with a several members of his entourage and a few beautiful women, three new modeled white Cadillac Escalades were parked waiting for them. A loyal comrade he put on payroll as his personal driver gave him a hood handshake and opened the second vehicle's door for LOUIE-V to get in. Then the first SUV led the trio out of the airport and to his mansion.

During the drive, LOUIE-V took some time to think about the fiasco he created with the executives at the record label he signed with. He didn't foresee starting a rivalry with rapper MACK DADDY was going to generate so much negative press about him. Usually, any press would be considered good press, but the mountains of criticism he'd been receiving on all his social media platforms and by paparazzi wherever he made public appearances was a bit overwhelming. Even before and after his show and after-party appearance, he was accosted by reporters who wanted to know more about his beef with the iconic rap artist.

He felt partly the blame about it all, but he faulted the media more for taking his comments and twisting his words for their own agenda. Which was, to him, done to create a bigger feud than it really was. All he wanted to do was let the world know there was a young rap artist in the game who was ready to take on some of the bigger names—not create beef in the hip-hop industry. LOUIE-V wished he could go back in time and reword a few things he'd said but it was too late.

Since a lot of things weighed heavily on his mind, he bitterly began to quip about the rap music business loud enough for everyone inside the SUV to hear him. He didn't expect a direct reply from anyone, but he did expect every single one of them to listen and feel his pain. He started off by hollering, "It's like they wanna nigga to jump off a mountain top just to get recognized in this game! Then, when you say fuck it and jump off, they say you didn't jump off fantastic enough! I gotta die in a blaze of bullets just to shine in this bitch!

The game got people who ain't never been in the hood tellin' you to only talk about the shit they think the hood wanna hear—like they know the shit the hood wanna hear! How can our music evolve when you can't say the shit you really wanna say? *We* floss this game! *We* boss this game! *We* out here every day puttin' our lives on the line! *We* out the trenches!

I give my heart and soul to this game because I love it! The media is the real blame! They know people read and watch 'em when rappers beef with each other, so they spark up shit with their critics and opinion writers! They created all this drama!"

And he left it at that.

He knew no one around him understood what the hell he was talking about, but he didn't let that stop him from venting his frustration with the business he was in. From the outside looking in, he saw how it could easily appear there wasn't a downside to his line of work. To many, it's all fun in the sun, but that's not true. You constantly think about streams and album sales.

The way you're able to maneuver in the game depends on it. The type of gigs you get depends on it. The level of publicity you have depends on it. Even the certain people you hire as your business team depends on it. And if you don't have a lot of streams and sales— you sure as hell better have a horde of online followers somewhere to entice a record label enough to believe you're salable.

After all, it is still a business, and he knew firsthand how the profit justifies the means. It doesn't matter how many sacrifices you made to reach the stage. No one cares about the losses you had to endure to gain a few fans. If the product you made doesn't create a profit—you're dropped from the label because your option won't be renewed.

Those were the thoughts that were running around in his head when his phone rang. Looking at the number and frowning because of who it was, LOUIE-V reluctantly answered with the expectation of having his mood made worse. He thought about going on vacation somewhere beautiful and never returning. Then reality sunk back in with one sobering question: How long could paradise last once the money was gone?

Wanting to get the call over with, he dryly answered, "Yeah."

"We got that fa you—all of it," BONE stated emotionless.

"All of it?"

"Yep. What now?"

"Now you two can come by my crib and we can talk more about it. I see y'all fixed our problem," LOUIE-V said very pleased about being paid the money he was owed.

"We always got yo back, fam. We had to sort some things out first," BONE let it be known—without revealing to him everything they had to go through to get the cash.

"See you in one hour. I needed to hear some good news," LOUIE-V expressed to him kindly, revealing he was pleased by the call.

"Fa sho. See you soon," BONE stated relieved and hung up.

LOUIE-V ended his call and instantly felt better. He'd let some of the negativities of the music business make him forget one important fact that he'd overlooked about himself and that was he's a Super-Nigga! He could survive in the business world or in the streets if he had to. He knew there were a lot of people in the world who have other people hovering over them to make their cash every day, but he didn't have to live with that sort of stress.

Not to say risking your freedom doesn't come with its own form of stress, but he'd rather live with that anxiety than endlessly worry about some racist or jealous supervisor costing him his livelihood. The idea of placing your complete reliance of survival on some imperfect human's mood swing was something LOUIE-V could never fully wrap his head around. He vowed he would never put himself in that position—signed to a record label or not.

With things finally getting back on track, he began to think about the upcoming rap battle contest he was hosting in a few more days. He really had mixed feelings about it because he felt like it was created more as a tool to deflect a business conflict rather than to truly highlight and promote the best local talent. The way he saw it, you shouldn't get somebody's hopes up like their life's going to change with riches galore if they win. There would be some taxable prize money—but there wouldn't be a pot of gold at the end of a colorful rainbow.

In fact, LOUIE-V made a prediction of how it was going to go down. Someone was going to beat all the other rappers in the contest. He or she would win the prize money and get to go face-to-face against him for a record contract. If by some miracle he lost, the winner would take home the prize money, get to record a song or album, and then the label would shelf it because there's no budget money to release it—all the while you're stuck in a contract for years going nowhere. But he figured none of it would ever happen anyway because no one was going to beat him. Other than some take home money, he couldn't see how the rest benefits the contestant—it'll only make the winner feel more like a loser in the end.

When they pulled up to his gated mansion a half an hour later, he looked at his 1.5-million-dollar property with pride because he'd accomplished something only a small handful of people from the ghetto had been able to do and that's make themselves a multi-millionaire. He had a butler, a private chef, a housekeeper, and groundskeepers who were all around his home quite regularly. He also had several of his homies on payroll for his security team as well as some trained ex-military personnel to protect him. On top of that, he owned a small yacht, several expensive foreign cars, and two fully customized touring buses.

Indeed, life had been good to LOUIE-V. True enough, a few of the things he possessed had monthly payments—his mortgage, yacht, and two car loans, but those bills were always paid. No one he knew from the hood was living as good as him. He was financially able to travel anywhere around the world if he wanted to. How many people anywhere could say that?

When they pulled up to his ten-car garage that was attached to his contemporary designed home, the Billboard-charting rap artist wanted to drive one of his expensive sports cars, so he told his driver to stop and open the garage door. When the finger-proofed metal and tinted glass garage door opened—it displayed his foreign car collection like they were a part of a showcased event, with each one having their own scenic background according to their color.

For example, his metallic Blu Abu Dhabi colored Ferrari 458 Italia Spider had a wall-sized poster of a beautiful bluish starry night overlooking some of Abu Dhabi's uniquely breathtaking architecturally prized buildings—the Etihad Towers and the Aldar Headquarters in Saudi Arabia.

But that wasn't the car LOUIE-V wanted to drive, he walked over to his Canary yellow-colored Lamborghini Aventador—which had a background view of an enlarged picture of the yellow sun shining brilliantly over the vast Mojave Desert. With its clear blue skies and scenic terrain, the over $400,000 vehicular masterpiece shone like it was forged from the star. Not wanting anyone with him while he drove it, he directed his driver and security team to continue to his house without him. Minutes later, he was strapped into the vehicle's seatbelt and sped out of his garage onto the street.

As he drove by some of his wealthy White neighbors, they smiled and gave him friendly waves. Some even gave him a thumbs-up in recognition of the car brand he was driving. He had to admit it felt good being around wealthy people who were hip and trendy. The peace and safety he felt there was unlike anything he'd ever felt before.

He chalked it up to a great real estate agency because he hadn't seen anything remotely racist there. No anti-immigration posters, White supremacist rallies, or any of that kind of stuff. Now truth be told, he hadn't seen any other Black people besides him, but he held on to the possibility of there being a couple sprinkled here and there because of the acreage between properties. Besides, whether there were or weren't any didn't matter to him because he knew his way back to the hood in Milwaukee whenever he wanted to be around his race of people.

The drive was only for a short distance. There was no destination in mind, only him and a friendly road with plenty of cut green grass and large leafy trees on each side of it. He didn't play any music. All he wanted to do was enjoy his silent, peaceful drive around his wealthy neighborhood.

Chapter Fourteen
MAKE YOU GROOVE

"Yo KRINGLE, I think you just made another hit!" C-DOG exclaimed as he hit a blunt of premium marijuana and listened to one of the latest sound recordings the producer created for FRICTION.

"Cool, thanks man. Yeah, I think it's dope too! I can see FRICTION using this one. It fits him if you know what I mean," KRINGLE humbly agreed.

"I feel honored you even thought about me at all. I wish the world was only full of White people like you man. The world would be lit! Fa real, KRINGLE—this my beat?" FRICTION asked him, making sure he heard him correctly.

"I made this beat specifically for you because you're the type of rapper who enjoys seeing people having a good time. Don't worry about the money. I want you to take it home and let it marinade in your mind for a while. Then after that, write a song that complement the track. Cool?"

"Cool."

While they listened to the beat again, KRINGLE downloaded FRICTION's copy to a flash drive for him. Everyone was sharing a blunt and talking about their plans for the competition when C-DOG heard his phone ring and left the area to talk freely on it. Using the time to bond with his music producer, FRICTION began to talk to KRINGLE more about the contest.

"But seriously KRINGLE, this contest might be my ticket out the hood man. They said they gone sign the winner. My life could literally change overnight if I win," FRICTION explained.

"Yeah, I'm no stranger to the 'All Powerful' recording contract. I used to be in a band back in the days and we got signed to an indie label who saw our potential," KRINGLE told the young rapper.

"Word? Was it that funk band I saw a picture of?"

"Yeah, that's all six of us. Nine crazy years. I played the keyboard, guitar, wrote some music and lyrics too. It was cool."

"That's dope! What was the band called?"

"We were called "GROOVE" and there were only two White guys in the band—me and SLIM JIM."

"OK, SLIM JIM must've been really skinny."

"SLIM JIM wasn't skinny. Nope, he was a muscle head fuck."

"Then why did they call him SLIM JIM?" FRICTION asked a bit puzzled by his name now.

"That's because he was always eating a Slim Jim every time you didn't see him playing. He played the drums. I remember how he wished he could play the guitar—any guitar. Damn, that was a long time ago," KRINGLE reminisced.

"I know they didn't call you KRINGLE back then."

"Naw, they called me "REEFER RAY" or "RAY BEAM" because I stayed high on weed and played the grooves you need."

"You still cool as hell. Thanks again, KRINGLE, fa the love. I sound much more professional now. I wouldn't even be in the contest if it wasn't fa you," FRICTION openly admitted.

"Hey, what you gone say when they ask who made ya beat?" the older producer asked with a smile.

"Shit, KRINGLE made it!"

"Right on."

While the two were conversing, C-DOG came back into the room and gave his homie a glance that it was time to go. Picking up on that vibe himself, KRINGLE handed FRICTION the flash drive from the session and told him to download it to his computer.

"Sorry, KRINGLE, I don't have a computer yet. All I got is a boom box with a CD player. My mom got one though, maybe she'll let me use hers," FRICTION told him a bit embarrassed about his financial position.

"Did you say you have a CD player still?" Kringle asked him, not worried at all about it.

"Yeah, attached to my boom box."

"Cool. I'll burn you twenty minutes on disc too. That way, you can write where you feel the most comfortable."

"What do you get out of this?" FRICTION wanted to know.

"I shine if you shine. Give me twenty more minutes before y'all leave and you'll have what you need," KRINGLE told him coolly.

And as promised, KRINGLE recorded twenty minutes of his music on a writable CD for FRICTION to create his lyrics to. As soon as he gave it to FRICTION, him and C-DOG left with nothing but love in their hearts for KRINGLE. So much so, they talked about him a bit more once they left in C-DOG's SUV.

"KRINGLE is as real as they come man. Bro don't judge you or think he naturally better than you because he White—none of that shit," FRICTION stated after he determined what type of person his producer was.

"Facts. God broke the mold when they made KRINGLE. He truly down fa the sound," C-DOG agreed as he drove.

"Word. Real talk, I like dude so much I'd beat a nigga ass if I saw him fuckin' with the homie."

"You know what G? I'd beat his ass, put a bullet in him, and then I'd run his bitch ass over in my whip," C-DOG laughed while he lit up another blunt and joked about how he'd hurt somebody over KRINGLE.

"Shit, I'd go Jason Vorhees on his ass and cut his ass up into little pieces with a long-ass machete," FRICTION joked too and laughed loudly after he used one of his favorite horror movie killers.

"Oh yeah, I'd go Freddy Kreuger on his ass!"

"I'd go Michael Myers on that bitch!"

"I'd go Mike Tyson!"

"Muhammed Ali!"

"I'm gone end this shit right now and say I would go officially Naruto on his bitch ass!" FRICTION shouted excitedly while he hit the blunt after it was passed to him.

"I can't top that shit! Naruto will beat yo ass! Hey fam, you been smokin' a lot of trees. Ain't you worried about yo piss test?" C-DOG asked a bit concerned for his homie's freedom.

"I lost years bro. Thirty days back in won't kill me. Besides, I got forty-five days before they drop me. Parole a little different than probation."

"I'd a had life with *no* parole. You made sure that didn't happen though. I'd go "John Wick 11 fa you G."

"Love. I was gone use one of those weed cleanse products if one of my interviews want me to drop."

"Hold up, you got some job interviews lined up?" C-DOG asked as if it was inconceivable.

"Moms helped me send out some resumes after I called a few places. She's smart as hell when it comes to computers. They had a few in prison, but I wasn't into 'em. I signed up to take a class, but I chilled and wrote rhymes instead," FRICTION told him honestly.

The drive was silent after that. The music was still pounding loudly, and they were both nodding, but they chose to concentrate on the places they passed by while C-DOG drove. That was, until C-DOG turned the music down to talk to him.

"I'm gone let you know where we bout to go cause you my nigga and you need to know," C-DOG stated bluntly.

"What you mean? Where we bout to go?" FRICTION asked his homie inquisitively and a little guardedly.

"MANIAC wanna talk to you."

"To who?"

"To you, nigga."

"Why?"

"I don't know."

"What he want?"

"Talk to him and find out."

"Fuck that," FRICTION told him with a frown—and a bad feeling.

"I already said we on our way." C-DOG let him know.

"Well call back and say I'm not on *my* way."

"I'd look like a liar then bro."

FRICTION knew what C-DOG insinuated was true. He would look like a liar to MANIAC, and it wasn't no telling what he'd do to his homie if he felt he wasn't trustworthy and reliable. So, instead of arguing about not going, he chose to lean back and go with the flow of things.

After about twenty-five minutes of driving, C-DOG picked up his phone and went to a typical quiet block to park his car. Not long after, FRICTION saw MANIAC pull up and park the Bentley he drove home in from prison. As they approached the vehicle, they noticed his female cousin GLOW was sitting patiently behind the wheel and unlocked the doors for them to get in. When C-DOG and FRICTION got in, MANIAC was seated the same as before with a glass of cognac he was sipping. He looked ready for business, wearing an expensively tailored black Armani suit and tie.

From behind the blue tinted transitional lens of his Cartier glasses, his eyes probed FRICTION up and down several times as if he was looking for a flaw in him—something he could feel negative about, but he didn't. He saw the same attributes he saw when he first laid eyes on him: loyal, motivated, and hungry to make a lot of cash. It was those qualities that drew MANIAC to him. Qualities too profitable to ignore.

After a taking a long slow sip of his strong alcoholic beverage, he looked at FRICTION and stated to him with wisdom, "We live in a world that's always favored the affluent and wealthy. Money has an ugly way of forcing us to bow humbly in its presence. Millions of lives are lost every year over it, and it will never leave the economic system we exist in today. Our very own Black enslaved ancestors were brought to this country to help make others rich. The color of the man making money doesn't nearly matter as much now as it did back in those not so long-ago days because we've been gifted with the same freedom to pursue it—thanks to the sacrifices of the many born free and emancipated Blacks who fought alongside some real-ass White folks who saw that we too were included in the Constitution."

"I read and learned a lot about Black history and my civil rights while I was locked up. I still don't understand why you wanted to see me though," FRICTION expressed to him respectfully, hoping it wasn't about selling drugs for him.

Continuing where he left off, MANIAC said, "There's still a lot of us who think we can't make real money. They feel the White man is gone always keep us down—but that's a lie. You can live a life you only imagined in the deepest depths of your dreams if you work with influential people who are used to dealing with other influential people. Money understand money is what I'm saying."

"Bro, I don't know why they call you MANIAC, but your name should be 'THE PROFESSOR' because I feel the knowledge you dropped. These rappers like LOUIE-V got more money than they know what to do with. I'm at the bottom of the totem pole and it's these niggas at the top. I know exactly what you mean. Connections are critical to success."

"That's why the hoods in Milwaukee gone always clack at each other instead of clique with each other. We've got all this heart and raw talent bursting out the seams in the hood, but we won't link up with each other like we should to build the things we're supposed to have in this city. White people ain't gone be the ones who bring rap here. We've got to create it here ourselves to get the majors interested."

"How do we do that?"

"We need independent rap labels with enough money to release albums internationally. They need to collaborate with other independent labels here and pay to have big-name artists included in their single releases. See, the problem with Milwaukee is every artist that signs to a big label moves to New York City, Los Angeles, or Atlanta where those major labels, agents, entertainment lawyers, PR firms, etc. are located. We don't have enough record labels in the hood with the money it takes and there isn't enough music business activity happening here to grow it the way it should. But how can it ever begin if everyone leaves? The few who stayed—stand unchallenged. That was—until you showed up."

"You know a lot about the music business," FRICTION said impressed by MANIAC's intellect.

"I was one of those people who wanted to do my part to help steer the music industry's attention Milwaukee's way. I started off reading all kinds of books at home about the music business. That led to reading even more books—schooling myself about it. That's how I know what it takes. It takes Blacks working together with their millions of dollars with one main objective: Putting Milwaukee Rap and R&B on the map," MANIAC stated.

"This city won't let Blacks make the millions they need to do it. Everywhere you go—the police wanna make you a felon. The prosecutor wanna make you a felon. The judge wanna make you a felon. No one wants you to make real money."

"Nobody likes innocent people being killed for nothing. Angry niggas shooting guns in heavily populated places leads to family, community, police, and political problems for every hood in the country. We've got to get the money with our brains—not our guns. We must build it brick by brick."

"I'm still confused. What did you wanna talk to me about?"

"You got a talent that could help accomplish one of the biggest hurdles this city has to overcome. Not only could you make a lot of money if you put yourself in the right places at the right time, but you could stay here with that fame and use it to help make others here become famous too. You could be known as the rapper who brought the mini-major record labels to Milwaukee. They have the real money to make you and others here legendary."

"I get a record deal if I win the rap battle contest," FRICTION informed him.

"Record deals are only as profitable as the record label. Don't forget that shit. Look, I called you here today because I want to be your business manager. I want to help you reach your full potential. But don't decide now—I'll be in touch," MANIAC told him as his car pulled up to where C-DOG was parked.

As they were getting out, MANIAC asked FRICTION, "Do you know why they call me MANIAC?"

"Because you kill a lot of people?" FRICTION guessed.

"No. They call me MANIAC because I'm a maniac about my money. It's an attribute that can benefit you as well. Love," MANIAC told FRICTION before him and C-DOG got out, leaving the rapper with much to think about as his fancy car drove off.

Several hours later, FRICTION was hanging out in his room with his boom box playing the CD KRINGLE made him when his phone rang. Since he was having a hard time coming up with subject material or even a title for a song, he was happy to answer it because it offered him a break from his writer's block. He had some possible ideas, but none of them stood out as a potential "Hit" to him. So, when he spoke, he had an attitude in his tone.

"Yeah, hello," FRICTION answered, his voice sounding unwelcoming.

"Maybe this isn't a good time," the female voice remarked uncomfortably, thinking he might be busy.

Hearing a female on the other end did perk him up, but he didn't want to sound overly excited to talk to her, so he replied, "I was on some dumb shit. Who's this?"

"You probably talk to so many females you already forgot about me."

"If you as lovely as yo voice—how could I?"

"It's me—Celestia. You helped me pick out my running shoes a few days ago."

"I remember you, Celestia. You were the prettiest woman in the mall. I hoped I'd hear from you again. I honestly thought my mama scared you off."

"You're funny. No, your mother doesn't scare me. I was waiting for you to call me. A man is supposed to call a woman if he's interested in her. You didn't call me."

"When you told me you had a man and saw I just got out a jail, I didn't think you was interested in me, so I didn't wanna embarrass myself," FRICTION admitted to her.

"It wasn't like that at all. Do you have any idea how many Black men are in and out of jail? I'd be stuck dating only women in this city if I ruled out men with criminal records," Celestia joked.

"Well, I'm glad you didn't go that route. It would be a whole bunch of disappointed men cryin' they ass off—me included."

"That's sweet of you to say. Hey, what are you doing in an hour?"

"Not much," he replied nicely while frowning at his wordless notepad.

Sensing something was bothering him, Celestia hoped she could perk him up a bit, so she said, "Good. I want to spend some time with you. I mean if you don't mind spending some time with me."

"This feels a little weird. I'm supposed to be the one saying that to you."

"I'm sorry. Did I make you feel like a female?"

"Yes. Yes—you did. That's exactly what happened. You made me feel like a female."

"Well personally, I think you'd make a very ugly chick. The facial hair. Ugh, the muscles—too many muscles. You're much cuter as a man."

"Well, look who got jokes. OK. Well, I think you're too pretty to be a man. You'd be the only man gettin' sexually harassed and groped by other straight men. But I don't know, I've never seen you without your makeup on."

"Wait a minute, your girl looks good with or without makeup."

"I'm sure you do. Maybe one day I'll get to find out," FRICTION slyly threw in as he began to feel a small attraction towards her.

"Maybe," Celestia replied in a way that left the possibility open.

"Hit me up then. Do you wanna chill inside my house? I mean, my mom and little sis are here too," FRICTION asked her innocently, not wanting to offend her.

"Actually, I thought I'd come by and pick you up. I figured you might like to ride around and sightsee since you've been away so long. I'll be there a little before seven. Bye FRICTION," she ended melodically and waited for him to reply before she hung up.

"OK, Celestia. See you soon," he replied with a huge smile— she was the only female he'd met since his release who had the ability to make him do it.

During the hour until her arrival, FRICTION spent most of his time thinking about the encounter he had with MANIAC earlier that day. He still didn't know what to make of it all. Why did he want to manage him? Was he even capable of it?

He had to admit MANIAC was well respected in the streets and nobody with any common sense would never ever try to cross him. There wasn't one person he could think of who ever said they had beef with him. It left him to conclude MANIAC must've killed all his enemies. The whole ordeal was confusing and a little unnerving—having someone know your business, especially someone you never told it to.

The fact that MANIAC knew so much is what led to the heated discussion he had with C-DOG once they got back to the SUV after they met with him.

"So that's why you bought the studio time? You want me nice and ready for MANIAC!" FRICTION snapped as soon as he sat down in the passenger seat.

"It ain't like that fam," C-DOG said calmly.

"That's bullshit and you know it! You pop up out the blue as soon as my Black ass is free with some Farrakhan talkin' murderous-ass nigga who now 'all-of-a-sudden' wanna be my music manager! How did he even know I make music?" FRICTION asked his guilty-looking friend.

"Look, he asked me what I've been up to. Yeah, I bragged about you. He asked me if you had what it takes—learning the business and the road work. Yeah. Definitely. I said that because it's true. He believes in you—because I do."

"You still should a told me! Everybody in that car knew why I was there—except me! That's some bullshit! Homies don't do homies like that!"

"To be straight up with you, I didn't know he was gone ask you that shit. I thought he was gone ask if you changed yo mind about that bag. I knew he still needed some real niggas on his team. That's why I thought he wanted to see you," C-DOG told him truthfully.

The way C-DOG looked when he spoke convinced FRICTION that he was being honest about not knowing what MANIAC planned to talk to him about. He knew MANIAC from the streets— not from the music game. Even though, at times, the two do intermingle—MANIAC never talked about music. He only spoke to him about the illicit business they were in—drugs.

His friend telling the truth made him feel a lot better. At first, he felt played and betrayed enough to punch C-DOG in his face for it. He was glad his anger passed. Besides MOOCH, C-DOG was the only other person he considered a true homie.

When Celestia called and told him she was outside, FRICTION quickly freshened up in the bathroom before he went outside to greet her. The long hours he'd spent trying to create a rap song didn't go without its price—at least as far as his hygiene was concerned. The last thing he wanted was her smelling his ripe armpits and passing out.

When he walked out his house, he didn't expect her to be driving a costly red Mercedes-Benz SL convertible. He naturally assumed she was in a cheap car—like a lot of females in the hood. The ride she was in was very far from that though—it was immaculate and didn't appear to have a scratch on it. Not wanting to show he felt intimidated by her unknown wealth, he imagined it was the worst hunk of junk he'd ever seen in his life—and it worked too.

FRICTION got in and only asked, "Where to next?"

Happy he didn't make a big deal about her ride, she smiled and answered, "I know the perfect spot."

They drove from the northwest side of Milwaukee to the north side; then from there, they took North Avenue down to the east side of the city. The further east they went, the pricier homes began to appear. Soon after, they were on Lake Drive, and he was able to see the beautiful bluish waters of Lake Michigan. Not having seen the lake in many years, it made him appreciate his newly regained freedom and feel grateful it hadn't been longer.

The openness and vastness of the large body of water had a tranquility to it that always made it very easy for him to soul search.

Wanting to rekindle those moments, FRICTION couldn't wait for Celestia to find a place to park. Finding the gate open where people hung out by a popular custard stand, Celestia found a parking area that didn't have so many cars around. Facing the lake, she closed her convertible top and left the car running so she could keep her music and air conditioning on.

Not wanting to sit in the car after such a long drive there, FRICTION stated, "Let's chill outside. The weather's perfect. Plus, I wanna show you where I used to spend most of my time when I came down here as a kid."

Wanting to know more about him, they both got out, and he led her to some large boulder-sized slabs of concrete that help protect the lake's shoreline from being overrun by large incoming waves. Stepping on one of the large stones first, he gently helped her up and then carefully led her across several uneven slabs until they were standing on the closest one near the water. Incoming waves rushed in and splashed against the large stone, but none of the water landed on top of it—leaving it completely dry. Choosing it as the perfect place to sit down, they silently enjoyed watching the small tides rush toward their feet.

Small flocks of white seagulls flew around in the clear blue sky, and he wondered how his life would be as a carefree bird. He imagined himself flying around all day, not having a single worry in the world. Off in the distance, he observed boats ranging from sailboats to yachts lounging around. The peacefulness of it all was sublime to him, something he wished he could bottle up and take back home to use whenever he wanted.

"Why are you so quiet?" Celestia asked while she watched someone ride by on a purple- and black-colored jet-ski.

"I'm still takin' it all in. It's a great place to enjoy nature. I can think clearer already," FRICTION responded in a way that suggested he had some heavy thoughts on his mind.

"Do you want to talk about it."

"I don't mind. I can change my life fa the better, but I gotta dance with the devil to do it. I'm gone perform in this rap contest soon and my ability to rap got dangerous people interested in me now."

"How dangerous are they?"

"As dangerous as they come."

"Is there a better way?"

"I'm still workin' on it."

"Can you rap?"

"I can make you groove."

"I'll come to the contest and support you then. Sometimes to make it, you've got to dance with the devil. Just make sure *you're* the one who's leading," Celestia wisely told him to help solve his problem.

"Cool, come check me out. It's been on the radio fa a minute now. Looks and a deep mind. What other hidden talents you got?" FRICTION asked, wanting to know more about her.

"Well, let's see. I can cook pretty good, I'm a gamer, I hate a dirty house—so I clean a lot, I love comedians—"

"Damn! Will you marry me now? I think I'm with the girl of my dreams!"

"You crazy."

"I could be fa you."

"How many girls do you tell that to?"

"None. I ain't met none like you."

Changing the subject, FRICTION said, "I should chill. I don't want no smoke with yo dude. I do remember you gotta man."

Not wanting to go too deep into it, Celestia frowned and told him, "I don't have a man anymore."

"He probably gone want his car back."

"What makes you think he bought it for me?"

"You look like a rich man would spoil you with expensive gifts."

"I spoil myself. We were a team that spoiled each other, but he forgot there's no 'I' in 'team'. Besides, he has a lot of other women available to keep him happy," she said dismissively of her ex-boyfriend.

"It must feel good to spoil yo self. I only spoil food," FRICTION joked, sensing she was still emotionally distraught by her turbulent relationship.

"I want a man who loves me for me—not for the money I make."

"The money you make? How do you make yo money?"

"I'm an event planner. I travel around the US to set up events, parties, and social gatherings."

"Do you like it?"

"I like the money. I want to start a company that creates catered events featuring male and female exotic dancers. Anyways, this is *my* car and I helped him buy a new AUDI," she admitted.

"Damn, AUDIs are nice cars," he remarked with jealousy.

"I think that's the only reason he dated me."

"Not the only reason. You a dime plus a penny."

"Thank you."

"Fa real, I believe in you. You got a dream to work with and you look like you don't give up. Not to mention, you drive a drop top Benz. You on yo shit."

"You can't start a business if all your man wants to do is spend the money for it on useless things. I could've had almost half of it by now. Love feels good when it's with someone who loves you back; love sucks when you're the only one who's stuck in it," Celestia confided in him.

"You deserve better. Where do I fit in yo life?" FRICTION asked, not knowing how she felt about him.

"I want to take it slow. I want someone who accepts me for the good and the bad. I want to be in love with someone who really loves me too. I don't want it to be only about how much money I can bring home."

"We move slow then. You can appreciate a person more if you take the time to get to know 'em. I hung out with other females since I've been out, they cool, but I wouldn't share my secrets with 'em. You give me a different vibe," FRICTION confided in her while he looked deep into her brown-colored eyes and shared how he felt about her.

"I want to know more about you too," she revealed to him as she gazed back into his brown eyes and held his hand.

And that's how they spent their time—getting to know each other while they sat on a large rock at Lake Michigan, holding hands. Time seemed to stand still in each other's company. The comfortability and unguardedness they felt was indescribable. Neither would've traded their special moment together for nothing else in the world.

Chapter Fifteen
TEASE

Several days later, MEAN-MUG and TRIGGAH G were riding around the ghetto on the north side of Milwaukee trying to find a quick hustle to make some cash. They partied like rock stars for days on powdered cocaine, crushed pain pills, and top-shelf alcohol. After many wild nights of sex and drugs, their money was almost gone. Thousands of dollars went down strippers' G-strings and up their noses.

Fortunately for them though, they only used four ounces from one of the four kilos of cocaine they stole. The rest of it was stashed in an old tire inside the trunk of a nonworking car inside TRIGGAH G auntie's garage. There weren't many options available since they didn't have stable homes. Trusting only each other, he didn't even tell her it was stashed there.

While in the middle of scouting for prey, they got a call from "SPIDER" at the chop shop explaining that they needed to come back and get the truck they brought him because it was too hot. Still high and very angry there was a problem with the vehicle, the entire ride there was spent complaining about it.

"What the fuck is SPIDER on? The only thing I can think of is the whip was already stolen. But even if that's the case, he scrapes off all the serial numbers on the parts he sale anyway," TRIGGAH G vented angrily as he scrutinized SPIDER's call.

"I hope the nigga don't expect to get his money back because he got me fucked up if he do. He could a told us this days ago," MEAN-MUG stated very seriously, not liking the call either.

"Like we got time to figure out which car is hot or not. SPIDER on some straight up bullshit."

"I swear to GOD he better not ask fa a fuckin' dollar back or we gone have a problem."

"His head got big ever since he got a bigger garage. He better be glad we need his ass. He gone get got if he come at us like this again—fa real."

"SPIDER can get it too."

"Look, we bout to pull up. Should we ask him if anybody need some blow or not?" TRIGGAH G asked his homie before he pulled into the back of the tall fenced in property.

"Yeah, we might as well. The more we tell—the sooner it sell," MEAN-MUG jingled as he parked his car and turned off the engine.

Normally closed looking from the outside, SPIDER always kept a dedicated crew of four tirelessly working on dismantling stolen vehicles and packaging the parts for resale on the inside. Sometimes, the hours working there seemed endless because of the time constraints on their deadlines, but him and his crew of auto mechanics have never missed an order. He earned himself a reputation of being a professional amongst thieves.

As usual, the door to enter was locked and somebody had to buzz you in. With several video cameras positioned at peripheral points around the property, it was very easy to see SPIDER had deep trust issues of his own. He could see everyone everywhere around his garage. You couldn't drop a cigarette on his premises without him knowing who did it and at what time it was done.

Once the door buzzed, MEAN-MUG pulled, and it opened for them. SPIDER, looking glad to see they came right away, was in the doorway greeting the duo with a big friendly smile. He held a clipboard in his right hand while he motioned the pair to follow him to where the truck was parked. When he spoke about the problem with it, there was deep regret in his voice.

"I'm sorry about this, guys. I know we've been doing business for a long time, and this has never happened," SPIDER explained disappointingly.

"Not too sorry. You still called our Black asses down here to get it. You mean to tell me, there wasn't a buyer fa this? The muthafucka look brand new!" MEAN-MUG began to yell as he became angrier about the situation.

"Hey, relax MUG. Never mind him SPIDER, he just mad because White folks still racist in America," TRIGGAH G joked, trying to ease the awkwardness that was beginning to develop.

"Yeah, I'm mad as fuck!" MEAN-MUG made sure he expressed with enough feeling to be taken seriously.

"I'm sorry guys," SPIDER apologized, like he had no control in the matter.

"I hope you don't wanna refund. That money gone already," TRIGGAH G made sure he knew ahead of time.

"You guys can keep it. You got other problems," the mechanic assured them.

"What you mean? Aye, where's the guys? Is it lunchtime?" TRIGGAH G asked after he looked around and noticed his crew wasn't working today.

"I told them not to come in. Again, I'm real sorry fellas," SPIDER told them remorsefully.

"What's up with all the apologies? We already said we gone take it back!" MEAN-MUG shouted at him as he became more perturbed the more SPIDER apologized.

"He's apologizing because he knows you two are fucked. Oh, and by the way, you two give Superheroes a bad name," LOS declared as he, Pedro, and six other armed Hispanic men came out of SPIDER's office with their guns aimed and ready to shoot them.

SPIDER quickly walked away from MEAN-MUG and TRIG-GAH G, leaving them to face the full fury of LOS and his firing squad. Now wishing they didn't leave their guns in the car, there was nothing they could do—they were helpless.

"SPIDER—you bitch-ass nigga!" MEAN-MUG screamed vehemently at his betrayer.

"They showed me a picture of my son during his recess at school! My son! I don't know what you did to this man, but my son doesn't have a damn thing to do with it! Look, I'm sorry it had to go down like this—if you really wanna know," SPIDER expressed irrationally before he calmed himself down.

"Look, I'm sure we can work something out. Your truck doesn't have a scratch on it. The coke is only light a few ounces, but we can take you to get the rest," TRIGGAH G told him as he tried to negotiate a peaceful outcome.

"Don't waste your breath on these Mexican muthafuckas! It is what it is! You not gone see none of yo precious dope again unless you let us go!" MEAN-MUG shouted angrily, attempting to assert himself from a position of leverage over LOS.

Not deterred at all by either of their comments, LOS took a few steps ahead of his crew and stood with his gold-plated AK-47 in both his hands. With one-hundred rounds of ammunition at his disposal from the banana clip inside it, his right hand gripped its pearl handle, with his index finger resting comfortably on the trigger. He didn't aim it at them, but he rubbed it while he spoke.

"I got this beautiful weapon from my 'Tio Juan' when I stayed with him in Jalisco, Mexico. These engravings make it one of a kind and to earn this you've got to prove you're worthy. To earn mine, I did whatever he instructed me to do. I proved I was a loyal soldier under him. Death became so commonplace to me it felt like I was its harbinger. It was my duty to kill whoever stood in his way."

"You a killer. We get it muthafucka. Just shut up and do it then!" MEAN-MUG yelled at LOS.

Ignoring the interruption, LOS told them, "As a reward for my unwavering loyalty, when I returned home three months later, he sent me this and 500 kilos of cocaine to sell for him. When it arrived, I didn't know where to hide so much cocaine at once, so I rented one-hundred storage units across three different states and kept only five kilos in each one. I did this in the event I slipped up and let one of them become compromised. So, you see, the kilos you took are from only one percent of the storage units I use. This isn't about the drugs—this is about my respect puta," LOS told him calmly as he continued to massage his rifle.

"OK, relax. We get it—it's about respect. This can still be fixed. Don't nobody gotta die today," TRIGGAH G remarked calmly, trying to deescalate the tension between them.

"This nigga is here to kill us! All this woo-woo fix this and fix that don't mean shit to his taco-breath-smellin' ass! He wants us to be afraid of his ass before he kill us! Well too bad cause I ain't scared to die! Death is a part of life!" MEAN-MUG shouted bravely.

Ignoring them both, LOS continued by saying, "I bet you're wondering how I found you. I used to have a cherry red-colored Corvette. It was nice. Brand new. One night I went to a strip club, and it was stolen right out the parking lot. I still got my lap dances. I even got insurance money for the car. But none of it could replace the only picture I had of my four-year-old daughter I kept on the rearview mirror. I haven't seen her since I left Mexico three years ago. That loss was more than money could replace.

I was deeply hurt back then by that cowardly act of thievery. I learned two very important things about myself after that: I feel more secure with tracking devices on all my vehicles, and I hate thieves to death.

You are the lowest type of human scum there is. You take from others because you can't make money on your own. One lick after the next, never caring who you scare or hurt."

Seeing things were heading in an ominous direction, TRIG-GAH G once again tried to lighten the heavy tension in the air by saying, "We let you both go. Nobody got hurt. Yeah, we fucked up yo day a little—maybe even a lot, but that don't mean we the shittiest people on the planet. What about pedophiles and rapists? What about racists? Everybody hates those muthafuckas."

"None of those motherfuckers robbed me and my family at gunpoint. None of them stole my shit. None of them kicked me out of my own truck and left me stranded."

"But we did leave you yo phone."

"Your friend didn't want you to. Come to think of it, your friend wanted to kill us. I know he wish he did it now."

"Nobody has to die," TRIGGAH G pleaded.

"You're right. A nobody has to die," LOS stated coldly as he aimed his assault rifle at MEAN-MUG and fired over thirty rounds into his body.

As the bullets tore through him, his blood was splattered throughout the surrounding area. A large portion of it landed on TRIGGAH G, who was near him the entire time. At first, he was too frozen with shock to move as his best friend's murder played out in slow motion in his mind. He'd just witnessed firsthand what thirty rounds from an AK-47 does to a human body at close range. It was so damaging—he barely recognized his homie afterwards.

"Fuck!" TRIGGAH G yelled frantically as he snapped out of it and began to check himself for bullet wounds, then he fell to the floor to grieve what was left of his best friend.

"I have killed many men with this rifle, and I have never once shot someone I didn't intend to shoot with it. Don't worry, you are not shot. Your homie was killed because he was a piece of shit who deserved to die. I don't feel that way about you homes. You didn't want him to kill us, so you talked him out of it. You even made sure we had our phones so we could call for help. You are a conniving thief, but not a piece of shit who deserves to die," LOS told TRIGGAH G, then looked at several of his underlings and nodded to them.

Four of his henchmen put their guns away and rushed at TRIGGAH G with punches and kicks, pummeling him to the concrete floor. His beating was painful and vicious, rendering him helpless from strikes to his head until he subsequently passed out from their attack. When he came to, almost ten minutes later, his shirt was off, and he was laying on his stomach with his arms and legs pinned down by LOS's thugs. Only able to move his head freely from side to side, he struggled futilely to use his limbs.

Afraid and hurt, TRIGGAH G fearfully yelled at his unseen aggressors, "Let me go man! You don't have to do this!"

Standing above him with an iron sledgehammer and a wood chisel in his hands, LOS began to examine TRIGGAH G's back tattoos and spoke, "I'm one of those people who believe the human body is the most complex machine created by God. Man's machines pale in comparison. The precision that it takes to keep everything running smoothly amazes me."

"C'mon man, I won't tell nobody shit!" TRIGGAH G yelled desperately as he squirmed around and tried to free himself from the firmly gripped hands of LOS's henchmen.

Ignoring his pleas, LOS continued by saying, "What's even more astonishing is how the body is wired. For example, without small electrical impulses zipping around in your brain, there's no you anymore. At least, not a 'you' anyone can understand. It's the smallest things inside us that control the largest functions we have."

"Listen to me! Please listen man!"

"Another example is our motor skills. Our ability to move our legs and arms is because of long strands of nerves that run down the middle of our backs. To protect them, they are encased within our vertebrae—which is made of little pieces of fitted bones that run from our tailbone and all the way up to the top of our neck. The thing that intrigues me is where you sever the vertebrae determines what part of the body is no longer functional. I mean paralyzed forever too because our science isn't advanced enough to fix it. If the vertebrae are severed too high—no arm and legs. Too low—no legs."

"I don't wanna die," TRIGGAH G wailed and stopped trying to fight his aggressors in one more final attempt to reach LOS's compassionate side.

"I'm not going to kill you. I'm a man of my word homes. But don't you think for one minute that you're going to talk your way out of this. You will be punished accordingly," LOS declared bitterly as he reached down and placed the sharp chisel on a section of TRIGGAH G's vertebrae. Then with one big swing downward, he hit the chisel as hard as he could. LOS stared emotionless down at TRIGGAH G's bleeding back, ignoring the painful screams and struck the sharp chisel into it again and again and again.

When FRICTION woke up at nine in the morning, all he could think about was Celestia. The time he'd spent talking to her at the lake made him feel they had a real connection between them. The way they openly and easily shared stories about their lives, along with the comfortability there was holding each other's hand, he knew he could hang out with her every day. The whole thing flowed naturally and wasn't forced at all. He truly enjoyed her company.

He wondered if she enjoyed his company too. He assumed she had a good time with him, but it could've been because of her recent breakup. A breakup that might only be temporary. After all, she did buy him a new AUDI.

Then there was the kiss on the cheek she gave him goodnight. He couldn't believe she really did it. All he remembered doing was reaching out to hug her goodbye and she leaned up and kissed him. He figured it had to mean something.

After pondering over her intentions for a while, he summed her up with one word: "Tease."

The inspiration hit him like a bolt of lightning, and he exclaimed aloud, "That's it! That's the name of my new song! TEASE!"

He decided to write another song that would make people dance and have a good time. Making people move to his music was what he primarily wanted to be known for. Talking about the struggles of the streets would also be a rapping point, but he loved club music and its ability to make people want to groove their body. That's what he wanted his brand to represent—fun and good times for all adult ages.

He wanted the song to ask women if they were a tease or not. A tease leads men on. Some entice you with their loveliness—others with lies. With Friction's song however, he would hope she wasn't a tease because the way she danced on him in the club turned him on so much, he would like to have sex with her.

Not too soon after the message of the song came into his mind, he grabbed his pen and pad of paper to write a top-tier rap song for the clubgoers. By the time he finished a few hours later, he was ready to record it.

When FRICTION called C-DOG to share his good news, C-DOG was still upset about being accused of orchestrating their meeting with MANIAC. It was apparent by the way he answered the phone with, "What?"

Already knowing the reason for receiving the cold shoulder, FRICTION didn't beat around the bush and said, "I was wrong fa snappin' about that shit with MANIAC. You had my back since I got out and I appreciate it. I apologize. I hope there's some room fa forgiveness."

"We good. It takes a real nigga to apologize after they fuck up. Love."

"Love. Now come get me so I can drop this cut fa the contest."

"Word? What's it called?"

"TEASE. It's a party song."

"What about JUS' BOOGIE?"

"I'm gone perform it at the contest too. I gotta show everyone there I'm serious bro."

"TEASE?"

"TEASE."

"Cool. I'll call KRINGLE and tell him we on the way," C-DOG replied like it wouldn't be a problem recording it.

Before C-DOG hung up, FRICTION told him emotionally, "Aye, thanks fam. You the reason I got this chance. You my nigga fa life."

"Fa life?" C-DOG asked before he hung up.

"Fa life," FRICTION reiterated before they ended the call.

About thirty minutes later, C-DOG pulled up in his SUV to take FRICTION to record his new song. During the drive, C-DOG asked his homie more about it.

"So, what made you name it TEASE?"

"I met a female."

"Did she wanna have sex with you and then change her mind?"

"Naw. I don't wanna rush her."

"Is she prettier than the two we met at the club? Now they were some stallions."

"Truthfully, she fly as hell, but that's not why I dig her. She even makes a lot of money, but that's not why either. It's because she's easy to talk to. The only problem is—she might still be in love with her man. I can't be that rebound clown who ends up with his heart broke because she was confused. I found a treasure that might be cursed," FRICTION tried to explain the best he could.

"So, she teases you with her swag. You want her because she seems into you, but you ain't sure how real she is yet. You worried she might be weak in the head and play you in the process. I ain't slow my nigga. Her uncertainty makes her a tease," C-DOG deduced.

"Exactly! Everything about her seems too good to be true. I mean, I truly believe I can come up with her. That's what makes her a tease too. This song is about a man hoping he isn't on the dance floor with a tease—someone who really don't want to dance or kick it."

"Damn, she was on your mind bro."

"Deep."

"Maybe she's done with her dude fa good."

"Maybe."

"I bet she'll forget all about him once you win Rap or Die."

FRICTION thought about how his life would change for the better if he did win. With some of the prize money, he'd use it to help his mother with a down payment on a new home. She'd been renting her whole life and never once owned her own property. Over the course of his life, the rent she paid to slumlords could've bought her six houses in their 53206-zip code.

After hooking his moms up, he wanted to learn how to drive. He was arrested and subsequently convicted before he even had an opportunity to operate a vehicle—he was still catching the city bus when he went to prison. He thought back to how embarrassed he felt when Celestia asked him if he wanted to drive her car back to his house after their lakefront rendezvous. He turned down the offer because he would've crashed it.

With the rest, he'd buy him and his little sister some extra clothes to flaunt. She had some decent gear, but he wanted to buy her a few higher-end brands to show off around her school in. A new designer backpack and several pairs of Jordan basketball shoes would make any young kid smile.

It would all come down to winning the rap competition. He knew there was going to be a hell of a lot of talented men and women of all colors and backgrounds giving it all they've got to win it too. From speed rappers to slow message ones, he imagined them all using different types of flow styles to beat each other. And out of the mass lyrical battleground, his music would have to rule supreme.

Sensing he was worried about the contest, C-DOG looked over at his doubt-feeling homie and said with encouragement, "You got this fam. Nobody knows when their destiny calls—you can only hope you see the opportunity when it come so you can rise to it. This is yo call bro."

Hearing his buddy's positive wisdom did make him shake off most of his self-doubt, but there was still a little pinch of it that lingered. Not getting called back yet for a job interview didn't help it go away either. He called everyone on the list his mother gave him. Feeling let down over and over can have a toll on even the most confident person.

"You think Celestia would wanna be my girl if I win?" FRICTION asked after clearing the negative energy of losing out his head.

"I mean, I've personally never met her, but I know women love to be around famous people with money. That's what you'll be. You get a chance to be rich and famous. How many folks do you know can say that?" C-DOG asked, already knowing the answer.

"She at her money already. That fame shit might turn her off."

"Women love celebrities fam."

"I don't think she cares about that."

"Trust me, she's all yours if you win bro."

"I'll make sure I do then," FRICTION stated confidently.

"Wait a minute, I know you wrote a song about teases. What about some G shit?" C-DOG asked with interest.

"No, I didn't write anything hard—not yet anyway. I wanna make people party first. Ever since I was a kid, I always wanted to see people move to my music. Club music is me."

"Fa sho'. But remember, I'm a G who loves to listen to G shit. I'll bump some commercial music from the radio too—but I'm into uncensored street music."

"I'll make sure I put some street songs on the album fa all the G's out there if I win a record deal," FRICTION told his homie.

"Make sure you do. I don't want nobody out there thinkin' you soft. You shouldn't wanna be seen as just a commercial rapper. You really from the 53206 and went to prison. The streets are you G," C-DOG replied, making sure his homie always rep the mean streets of Milwaukee.

Feeling a little hungry, C-DOG pulled over at the first fast food restaurant he saw. With only four cars in the drive-thru, he was sure he'd be in and out in no time at all—boy was he wrong. Almost twenty minutes had passed when he finally made it to the ordering menu. Already upset because of the time he'd spent waiting, things took an even further turn for the worse when he spoke to the employee working the speaker.

"You can go ahead with your order," the young female voice expressed with frustration on the other end.

"I shouldn't have to sit around fa twenty minutes to order some fast food! I almost left this bitch to eat somewhere else!" C-DOG vented into the menu speaker system.

"Then you should a left," the perturbed female voice rudely responded.

"What the fuck did you say to me?" C-DOG asked a bit thrown off by her negative comment.

"Shoot, I'm sick of people pullin' up and talkin' to me any kind of way like I gotta take all y'all crap and all I'm tryin' to do is my job. I said you should go somewhere else to eat if you are not happy with the service this restaurant provides."

"Damn, what the hell happened to friendly customer service?"

"It's given only to friendly customers."

"That's some bullshit."

"Can I please take your order."

After seeing the exchange between the two become overly heated, FRICTION joked and said, "Bro, leave that shit alone and order before she rub your buns between her buns. You gone have sour dough bread instead of sesame seed buns."

Choosing to put it behind him, C-DOG took a deep breath and decided to give it a fresh start. After all, he began to think it was silly of him to become emotionally agitated and yell at a machine. Even though there was someone on the other end operating it, everyone behind him only sees a whack job yelling at a drive-thru speaker. So, he chose a nicer tone to speak with.

"Yes, you can. Can I get two Goliath Burgers and two large onion rings? Could you hold the pickles on one of those burgers please? I'd also like two medium orange sodas."

"So, you want two combos?"

"No. The onion rings don't come with the combo."

"You can always exchange your fries for onion rings. It'll be extra. Would you like the combos with onion rings?"

"OK, whatever. We'll take the combos."

"There isn't any orange soda—it's down right now."

"Damn, no orange."

"Nope."

"Fuck it. I'll take a lemon-lime one then. Everybody loves orange soda. That's the flavor you should never run out of."

"Everybody must love lemon-lime too because we out."

"You fuckin' with me now. No lemon-lime?"

"No lemon-lime."

"What about tropical punch?"

"Nope."

"Grape?"

"No grape."

"Damn! What flavors do you have?" C-DOG shouted into the speaker as he felt himself backsliding into his anger once again.

"Please don't yell at me. We have root beer," the female voice stated flatly.

"I don't drink root beer."

"The only soda that we have is root beer. Would you like two bottled waters?"

"I'd rather have two orange sodas."

"Wait right here and I'll walk to the gas station across the street and get you two orange sodas. Better yet, I'll run there and back since it's fast food."

"Just great, I get a comedian drive-thru box. The joke is how long it takes to order here."

"Hold on." the female voice said frustratingly, and the communication device abruptly stopped talking to him.

"Can they tell you that?" C-DOG looked over at his amused homie and asked. FRICTION shrugged he didn't know.

C-DOG couldn't have been happier when she came back and gave him his total balance due for their food. When he drove to the window, all he wanted was his burgers so he could leave. But first, he had to wait four minutes for her to come back. When she did, the very young Black girl still had a crappy attitude.

"Why you look so salty?" C-DOG said with more sensitivity while he handed the young teenage girl his money.

"Because they must think I won't snap up in here! They better stop workin' my last nerve before I show my ass! Stop talkin' to me, Kevin! Who did you blow job to be assistant manager? You sucked somebody's dick!" she yelled to some unseen coworker as she handed C-DOG back his change. They were both left speechless by the degree of vulgarity that came out of such a small innocent-looking girl.

Then she left and returned with his food.

When C-DOG first grabbed the bag, his instinct to pull off kicked in, but something told him to check his order. Giving them the benefit of a doubt, he assured himself that they had his order right when he opened his burger wrapper. He even looked at the young female worker who gave him a hard time and smiled at her with no hard feelings. But that all drastically changed when he looked inside.

"What's this shit? I didn't order chicken sandwiches! These fries—not onion rings!" C-DOG yelled at her.

"I was gonna tell you they didn't deliver the meat patties and onion rings yet, but you started to yell and cuss me out. Chicken sandwich combos is all we got until the truck arrives in two more hours. He's late and that's not my fault either," she replied disdain-fully while she rolled her eyes at him.

"You need to check that attitude. I bet you wasn't this way when you interviewed fa this job, was you? I bet you acted all nice and spoke proper English and shit. You need to remember how you was when they first hired you before you end up fired and broke as hell," C-DOG told her wisely, knowing how the struggle is real.

"I would've quit the same day I was hired if I knew I was gone be surrounded by a bunch of dumb asses! Here, you wanna cuss somebody out—cuss out Kevin the dick sucker! Come on in and cuss out dick-sucking Kevin! Do you want your money back or is you gone stay here and cuss me out some more? I can pretend I'm your bitch if you want me to," she said with a sarcastic smile that C-DOG didn't find funny.

"Naw, I'm gone take my food and leave before I catch a felony," he replied with a frown and drove off.

"Damn fam, she was evil as hell. She reminds me of that girl you used to mess with back in the days," FRICTION reminded him jokingly as he grabbed his food from him.

"She probably was that demonic bitch's little possessed sister. Thirty minutes to get the wrong food. Aw, come on!" C-DOG yelled as if he'd reached his last straw.

"What?" FRICTION asked curiously while he ate his chicken sandwich and fries.

"My sandwich got fuckin' pickles on it. I quit. I'm done with fast food," C-DOG declared somberly, like he was losing someone close to him.

"Yeah right. You gone be right back at one tomorrow. It might even be this one again. You better take those damn pickles off and eat. This chicken sandwich tastes good as hell. The fries ain't bad either," FRICTION stated as he continued to eat his food.

Taking the dill pickle slices off his sandwich and holding all three soggy pieces with his two fingers like they were disgusting, C-DOG rolled down his window and tossed them out. Then he looked at his sandwich skeptically before he took a bite.

"I'll eat it if you don't want it," FRICTION told him with food in his mouth.

"It smells like sourdough," C-DOG muttered with a frown after he sniffed it and looked at his homie like he was eating an ass-cheek-rubbed sandwich.

"Not cool. Not cool at all bro," FRICTION told him as continued to eat his food—but now he periodically sniffed his sandwich bun while he ate.

Chapter Sixteen
WHAT U WANT

The night of the RAP or DIE Rap Battle Contest was a sellout event. Finding a place to park was next to impossible as vehicles created traffic jams trying find any available space. Over two thousand people wanting to be entertained flooded the streets around the venue, while the Milwaukee Police Department and Milwaukee Sheriff Department coordinated their efforts to maintain civility and peace for the many various groups attending the show. From the extremely large turnout, you could tell it was going to be a spectacular event.

Staying true to his word, LOUIE-V hired BIG MONEY MIKE and his BOOTH OF TRUTH crew MARGARITA MAY and TANG-TANG to host it and they didn't disappoint. Armed with a colorfully lit LED strobing microphone, BIG MONEY MIKE described the contestants in the competition like they were top-prize fighters. With his diverse team aiding him, the trio didn't plan on holding back any punches. You were either going to be commended or criticized.

With his microphone flashing a sequence of red, blue, green, and yellow, BIG MONEY MIKE waited until it was time for the contest to begin before he yelled, "Are you ready for the best rap battle of the millennium! I said are you ready for the best rap battle of the millennium! Then let me hear you make some noise! RAP or DIE! It's here baby! It's finally here!"

He stopped talking and accepted the loud cheers.

"I'm ya main man BIG MONEY MIKE and I brought the rest of the BOOTH OF TRUTH crew with me! Give it up one time fa MARGARITA MAY and TANG-TANG! Make the roof cave in fa DJ RADIO-ACTIVE! Ladies and gentlemen, this is RAP or DIE! We've got sixteen of the best rappers across the state of Wisconsin and beyond coming here tonight with only three words on their minds: WIN—WIN—WIN! Let me break it down how this contest works! All sixteen rappers will square off fa two minutes each—giving it all they've got to prove they're the best! The 'CHEER-METER' located right over there will activate during each performance and judge the crowd's excitement by a contestant! As you can see by the levels, the louder the cheers—the higher up it veers! The rapper with the highest rise on the meter wins that round! Once three rounds of eliminations are complete, only two rappers will remain for the fourth round to face the crowd and the CHEER-METER—which will then choose who is the winner of $100,000! The winner will also go to the fifth and final round to take on Milwaukee's own LOUIE-V fa their chance to land an exclusive record deal with BIG DOE RECORDS!"

He stopped talking and accepted the mass cheers and applause from the audience.

"One rapper has the chance to own the throne as the best in RAP or DIE! Are y'all ready? I wanna know right now—are y'all ready? Then give all the contestants up here a huge round of applause!"

He pointed to the contestants and the response he received was much louder cheers and claps from the crowded theater.

"Is there anything you'd like to add MARGARITA MAY? What about you TANG-TANG?" he asked his famous radio co-hosts through his microphone as he entertained the boisterous attendees. Enjoying the vibe of the full audience, MARGARITA MAY shouted to the contestants with her microphone, "I'm giving a special toast to the winner! We gone 'Get Lit – Lit' up in here!"

The excited crowd erupted with cheers and began chanting her well-known catchphrase "Get Lit – Lit! Get Lit – Lit! Get Lit – Lit! Get Lit – Lit!" over and over again.

Before TANG-TANG spoke, he looked incredulously at the contestants and then shouted out wildly to the crowd, "Who gone Taste the Tang?"

Everyone burst into hollers and screams after hearing their other favorite radio personality's trademarked catchphrase. They chanted the popular saying "Taste the Tang! Taste the Tang! Taste the Tang! Taste the Tang!" repeatedly while they waited for the contest to begin.

With a couple thousand camera apps on smartphones flashing constantly and an electrifying light show displaying an array of multi-colored lasers, strobe lights, smoke, and more, it was difficult to see in the dimly lit theater, but you could tell how much everyone was enjoying the event by how much noise they made. With the latest music playing from various rap artists, the party of the year was being held on the east side of Milwaukee at the Riverside Theater.

FRICTION couldn't believe how many people showed up. He figured it had to be a sold-out crowd judging by the rows and rows of filled seats. He didn't know how much it cost to buy a ticket, but evidently, money wasn't a problem to any of them because it was packed to capacity. For a split second, the large crowd made him feel a little nervous and unsettled. To help him get over it, he began to think about going back to having absolutely nothing as far as making money was concerned and mentally told himself he had the strength to conquer any fear.

Telling himself that in the darkest of times is how he managed to get through the sentence of his conviction. He used it whenever he was faced with a dangerous and fearful circumstance. As soon as he repeated it in his mind, the fear he felt went away. Because of his "fear nullification" technique, he was never physically or sexually assaulted—none of those things. Nobody ever dared to try.

To also help kill any anxiety he might feel, his homie C-DOG was right there with him—mainly because he convinced the contest's "Auditions" staff he was the rapper's hype man. Which was fine by FRICTION, he wanted his friend there to have his back. Other than C-DOG, he didn't know any of the over twenty-four hundred people attending the event. He felt like a glass soda bottle with a note inside it that only read "Help!" floating in a vast ocean with no land or boat in sight.

Ignoring everything that was going on around him, FRICTION looked over at C-DOG in awe and said, "I still can't believe you got me in the contest. It's packed as hell in here."

"All I did was submit yo song and they felt it. Listen, just tell yourself over and over—they all paid to see me. Do that and you'll be fine fam," C-DOG reassured his homie after sensing his nervousness.

"Fa sho'. You think MOOCH gone show up?"

"MOOCH not gone show up."

"I still haven't seen him since I got out."

"I doubt if you will fam."

"Why?" FRICTION asked him curiously.

"Because he's gone and he ain't comin' back," C-DOG answered him with finality.

Deciding to leave the matter alone for now, FRICTION looked at the digital board that displayed all the contestants' rap names and located his amongst the many. Already matched up against who he'll be facing off against, now he had the name of his rival: DRACO DRE. Located at number "13" and his rival's number "15" out of the sixteen contestants, he knew it would be a while before he performed, giving him more than enough time to rehearse the lyrics to the songs he was going to use.

By being in the contest, he had a great view from backstage of each artist who was performing. He also had a chance to see how they dealt with the mounting pressure of a heckling audience and ridiculing hosts and was surprised to see some of the rappers handle things a lot worse than him. One of the rap artists saw how many people were going to critique his rhyming skills and threw up before he went onstage to face his competitor. He even saw one rapper who was so nervous to fail run to the bathroom like he had diarrhea or something.

Seeing he wasn't the only one with the jitters made him realize he did have a legitimate shot at winning the event. Sure, he saw a few who had tons of confidence from their overinflated egos, but FRICTION didn't let that get to him. He watched the other contestants performing before him studiously, comparing his music to theirs, assuring himself he was better than them all. One after another went, rapper versus rapper, in a two-minute verbal assassination against each other.

Some rappers chose to battle one another with witty insults and humorous jokes, while others chose to express a memorable message to the audience. There weren't any restrictions about what could be said—the only focus was on saying what would make the Cheer-Meter peak the most. And from the songs he heard, from spending large sums of money to murdering rappers and rivals, he felt his "Gangster Boogie" music would stand out because of its dance appeal. He had no problem personally with the other contestant's music, especially since some of the songs he wrote had the same messages, it's just that he wanted to go beyond the mainstream sound and create unique songs that appealed to diverse groups of both sexes.

Simply put, he believed you'll mainly appeal to males if you come too hard with a song. Adversely, rapping too soft will only appeal to female listeners. That's why he chose to create certain songs that ran a fine line in the middle of both sexes. He wanted listeners to see he was versatile—someone who could write and rap about a broad number of topics within the wide spectrum of different emotions.

To FRICTION, it was the wide range of different emotions a rap artist brings along with clever rap styles and innovative sound recordings that makes a multi-dimensional rap artist with a multi-dimensional album. A rapper who basically sounds the same in every song but has different collaborations with other rappers and singers can still have a one- or two-dimensional album to him. Through his music, he wanted to bring the emotions of happiness and togetherness to the event. He hoped it would trump any artist that wanted people to feel anything less.

When it was finally his time to go onstage and show them what he was made of, he heard BIG MONEY MIKE say, "Up next, we have #13 ranked 'FRICTION' going up against #15 ranked 'DRACO DRE'! They're both from the mean streets of Milwaukee and both reside in the 53206! Aw shit, we bout to get street up in here! I hope you got your straps off safety and your head on a swivel because shit's bout to get real! In fairness to both parties, we gone flip a coin to see who goes first! Lookin' at my Rolex—it's about that time! FRICTION and DRACO DRE—come on out! It's RAP or DIE!"

Everyone in the theater began to chant, "RAP or DIE! RAP or DIE! RAP or DIE! RAP or DIE!" over and over, even when FRICTION and DRACO DRE made their way to the stage. In the middle of trying to focus his sight on anything other than the incessant flashing of camera lights coming from the audience and the brilliantly colored laser light effects for the event, an extremely bright spotlight shone down on him and his competitor, making them both squint their eyes a little. With anticipation mounting, they both stood in their designated areas and waited for the host to instruct them further.

After a few more chants and screams for the newcomers, BIG MONEY MIKE began to speak from their balcony-positioned workstation. Liking the crowd appeal for both rappers, he yelled in his color-flicking microphone, "Who's the best? They both look like they got skills, but who's the best? Who do you think is the best, MARGARITA MAY?"

"I think the one with the assault rifle name might wreck shop! Somebody's in trouble if he raps as dangerous as a Draco! Big and black! Let me take a sip of this margarita to cool off!" MARGARITA MAY exclaimed as if talking about big and powerful guns was exciting her.

BIG MONEY MIKE listened to who she predicted would win and then turned to TANG-TANG and asked, "Who do you think is the best, TANG-TANG? DRACO DRE or FRICTION?"

Studying the two like he was shopping for the freshest produce in the grocery store, there was a delayed reaction before TANG-TANG replied loudly, "I don't know off top who's gonna win! All I know is the loser's gone Taste the Tang baby!"

The crowd went wild. They chanted, "Taste the Tang! Taste the Tang!" repeatedly until BIG MONEY MIKE shouted, "Whoa! The taste of victory is much sweeter! Oh look, we have the beautiful 'BABY DOLL' on the stage! Give her a warm round of applause! Here's the coin flip! OK, who won BABY DOLL?"

"DRACO DRE called heads and won! He gets to pick who raps first and he wants to!" BABY DOLL declared in her microphone attached to her multi-colored sheer silk designer body dress.

BIG MONEY MIKE shook his head shamefully as he watched her very sexually attractive physique exit the stage. He shouted, "That took a whole lotta milk to make that body good!" and left it at that. Then he yelled, "DRACO DRE! You have two minutes to prove to the world why you belong on this stage! DJ RADIO-ACTIVE! Play his song in five … four … three … two … one!"

The young dread-headed man wearing a black T-shirt and black denim jeans closed his eyes and waited for his music to start playing. As soon as the beat began, DRACO DRE opened his eyes and shouted the chorus of his song twice before he said one of his verses by saying: "NO BODY – NO MUTHAFUCKIN' WITNESSES! WITH THIS SHOT G – I'M GONE SHOW 'EM WHAT THE BUSINESS IS! NO BODY – NO MUTHAFUCKIN' WITNESSES! HE TRIED TO ROB ME – NOW HE SLEEPIN' WHERE THE FISHES LIVE!"

When the rapper's two minutes were up, the crowd erupted into cheers and the CHEER-METER responded by peaking at six out of ten levels. Very pleased by his performance and the audience's show of support, DRACO DRE bowed when he was finished. Then he waved at his new fans and blew off his competitor like he already won.

Loving what he heard, BIG MONEY MIKE yelled, "Damn, now he's in a gang! Duck when DRACO DRE's in the house! What did you think about his performance, MARGARITA MAY?"

"I almost spilled my drink! He took drill rap to a whole new level!" MARGARITA MAY shouted into her microphone and then took a small sip of her alcoholic beverage.

"What about your thoughts, TANG-TANG?" BIG MONEY MIKE asked his other co-host.

"I thought I was gone need my gun up in here! I know one thing: it's gone take more than 48 hours to solve his crimes!" TANG-TANG yelled into his microphone while he shook his head in disbelief at the high degree of violence the song had.

"If they get solved! But it ain't over! We've got somebody up in here who feel they can beat him! It won't be easy to do! FRICTION, do you have what it takes? You've got two minutes to prove you do! DJ RADIO-ACTIVE! Play his song in five ... four ... three ... two ... one!"

When the beat to JUS' BOOGIE shot out across the loud-speakers, people began to move to the up-tempo club music. With a lot more people enjoying it than the two-hundred or so who heard it first at the HOT-SPOT, FRICTION broke off into a gangster two-step dance while he rapped: "WHAT YOU SITTING FOR? JUS' BOOGIE! WHAT YOU FIDGETING FOR? JUS' BOOGIE! BOUNCE 'EM LIKE THAT BRA ABOUT TO BREAK OFF ON YA – WHILE I DRANK THIS HEN & RUB UP ON YA! WHAT YOU STANDING FOR? JUS' BOOGIE! WHAT YOU FANNING FOR? JUS' BOOGIE! YOU KEEP DRINKING THAT X & YOU KNOW WHAT'S NEXT – WE INTERTWINING IN SOME FREAKY SEX!"

Then he rapped the first verse of his song. His delivery was playful and powerful with gritty, textured tones for his vocals. His flow style went harmoniously with the music and had a voice that demanded attention. By the time his time was up, the crowd's cheers of approval made him feel so good inside his eyes began to water a little.

The CHEER-METER rose and peaked at seven out of ten levels—beating DRACO DRE and giving FRICTION his first win in the rap contest. BIG MONEY MIKE couldn't believe how professional the song sounded. The first thing he said was, "OK, why isn't this rapper already signed? Is it me or does this guy sound signed to a label already? Good job, FRICTION! I see you came here to make a statement tonight! We've got our eyes on you, bro! Jus' Boogie baby! What do you have to say about his performance, MARGARITA MAY?"

"Aye, that's what I'm talking about! That song made me wanna twerk! Aye!" MARGARITA MAY replied hyped up and then turned around and started twerking her butt from the upper balcony.

"I feel you! Not me twerking, but I feel you about the vibe he brought! What about yo take on things, TANG-TANG?" BIG MONEY MIKE turned to him and asked.

"He's different! And TANG-TANG is with different! He raps without restraint! I hate restraints! DRACO DRE! Taste the Tang baby!" TANG-TANG responded with a sour face to DRACO DRE and the crowd cheered and loved every minute of it.

When FRICTION went backstage to meet up with C-DOG, he was riding the high of winning his battle and surviving to compete in the next round. With a huge grin on his face, he strutted over to his homie and gave him a strong hood handshake. But his feeling of triumph was replaced with concern when he saw the conflicted look on C-DOG's face.

Not understanding the reason for him not being happy for his win, FRICTION asked, "What's up?"

"I don't want you to worry, but we might have a problem. I'm already on it though," C-DOG expressed in a way that made FRICTION feel nervous.

"What kind a problem?"

"You won't have any new music if you win the next round. Playing the same song again will kill us. We need new music and new songs for each round to win this thing."

"We don't have any more songs! All we have is two! I'm fucked bro!"

"I already called KRINGLE. He told me he got a new beat fa us as soon as he gets back home."

Knowing the bad news wasn't over yet, FRICTION asked, "When will he be back home?"

"He said it'll be over an hour," C-DOG answered with disappointment.

"More than one hour! The second and third round will be over by then! Wait! I got a plan."

"I hope it's a good one."

"Check this out, it's three rounds of music, a round in front of the CHEER-METER, and then a final round of music to go against LOUIE-V, right?"

"Yeah, you need three more songs."

"So, I'll use the first verse of TEASE next. Then, if I make it to the third round, I'll have to pull a rabbit out my hat to win it. Man, I hope KRINGLE got me if I face LOUIE-V," FRICTION stated nervously, already forgetting about his recent victory.

He didn't think about creating four different songs to keep the crowd hearing new music from him. As far as he was concerned, he was lucky to have two songs to perform. But for some contestants, they were going to lose cheers because they had to perform the same song each round. To have a fair chance to defeat LOUIE-V, FRICTION knew he needed a brand-new beat from KRINGLE to do it.

Rap battle after rap battle ensued. One by one, a rapper fell in verbal combat. With his position number changing with each round, FRICTION was now number "6" out of eight contestants for the second round. He was matched up to take on number "4," a rapper named "RAZE."

He'd heard RAZE rap in the first round and knew the dyed red-headed rapper was going to beat his competitor—that's how good he performed. A part of him wished he didn't have to face him because he was a speed rapper. He knew people tended to gravitate more toward speed rappers because of their rapid rhyming ability. Yet and still, FRICTION knew the strength of his voice coupled with his clever word and rhyme play could compete with even the fastest rapper.

Arriving late intentionally, LOUIE-V and ten of his entourage/ security came in through a back entrance designated for the owner and his staff. After a brief talk with the manager over a few minor business issues, him and his crew continued up to the balcony where BIG MONEY MIKE and his co-hosts were located. Covered in platinum and diamond jewelry that sparkled and twinkled with every step they took, no one could ignore the group as they made their way to their seats. Especially, since they were all wearing the latest high-end designer fashion from Italy.

When LOUIE-V stepped past security and entered the balcony area where the hosts were, BIG MONEY MIKE stopped presenting the next match and yelled, "Ladies and gentlemen, he's here! The only Milwaukee rap artist to chart #1 on Billboard's Hot 100 for over six weeks straight with his single release 'DOLLAZ'! He's the man who put this wonderful event together and gave all you good folks in here a reason to put on ya best clothes and get out the house for a few hours! Besides cutting my check, he also keeps me in check! Give it up to the man who pays all the damn bills—LOUIE-V!"

The crowd went into a frenzy.

He smiled and waved modestly at all the attendants while flashes of lights from camera phones flickered off and on all around him. The noise was deafening, but he'd gotten used to it after months of performing with extremely loud concert equipment and thousands of fans screaming simultaneously. When BIG MONEY MIKE asked him "Is there anything you'd like to say?" LOUIE-V grabbed the microphone and shouted, "Milwaukee's finest came to kick it with me tonight and I thank all y'all fa the love! Enjoy the show!"

Then he sat down and began to take a stronger interest in the contest. He saw how energized the crowd was and wondered who had them so pumped. A female attendant brought him over a lemon-lime soda, and he slowly sipped it while the matchup announcement commenced. He figured since he was here now, he might as well see what was up with the competition.

After BIG MONEY MIKE, MARGARITA MAY, and TANG-TANG gave the crowd their celebrated opinions about FRICTION and RAZE when they walked onstage, and the lovely BABY DOLL did the coin toss that FRICTION lost, the countdown for DJ RADIO-ACTIVE to play FRICTION's song began. When it was time, the beat for TEASE blasted throughout the theater. The crowd, fully engaged with the song, began to move to the music they found so appealing.

When FRICTION led again with a chorus before his verse, this time he had well-known Milwaukee male R&B recording artist "G. Womack" singing: "I SWEAR I HOPE YOU NOT A TEASE! ARE YOU BOUT IT—BOUT IT? YOU MAKE ME WANNA FREAK YO BODY—BODY! WHEN I STEPPED ON THE FLOOR—I SAW

A HOTTIE—HOTTIE! YOU MAKE ME WANNA EXPLORE! I SWEAR I HOPE YOU NOT A TEASE!" while he shook hands with new fans and two-stepped to the song's chorus.

As soon as he finished rapping his first verse, the CHEER-METER rose 8 levels out of 10. Fans were now chanting his name and he was feeling like the round could go his way. But he couldn't put nothing past his speed-rapping adversary, not when he knew underestimating someone could easily get you killed where he was from. To him, there wasn't much difference between the contest and the streets. With either one, it's all over if you lose.

After the hosts gave FRICTION large amounts of praise for a nicely done performance—it was time for RAZE to rap. Unfortunately for him though, the all-red clothes-wearing rapper made the fatal error of using the same verse and music he used to win his first round. That costly mistake made the CHEER-METER rise only 6 levels out of 10, easily making FRICTION the winner of his second-round match. Yet and still, the emotional high he'd got from his victory was short-lived because there was still no word from KRINGLE.

From the balcony above him, LOUIE-V watched only two minutes of FRICTION's performance and knew he was the one who was responsible for the heightened energy coming from the audience. He was also creating fans who were willing to chant his name. LOUIE-V predicted it was FRICTION who was going to win the third and fourth rounds—and then face him for the finale.

With the second round concluded, there were only four rappers remaining. Each rapper who survived felt they were the best and could not be defeated. Clearly, the third round possessed the most talented out of the sixteen rap artists who participated in the contest.

When the round was about to begin, FRICTION saw he was number "2" matched up against number "3"—a female rapper named

"SILKY DREAM". She was light skinned with long, colorful hair, as lovely as they come with an hourglass figure, danced sexy like a stripper with amazing flexibility, and could rap her ass off. She was a total package performer who could easily make a living doing concerts if she had the right dancers and choreography. He felt a little intimidated having to go against a pretty female who dances, but he knew he had to defeat her or lose it all.

To kick things off, BIG MONEY MIKE yelled into his microphone, "Welcome survivors to the third round! Will the audience give the contestants a huge round of applause fa making it here!"

BIG MONEY MIKE remained silent while screaming fans clapped in appreciation for the entertaining event all the rap artists contributed to. When they were done, he exclaimed, "Now shit's about to get real! There's only four left! Soon there will be only two! Who will the final two be, MARGARITA MAY?"

"It's really hard to say because everyone here is so talented! You know what, I'm not drunk enough! Ask me after a few more drinks! Get Lit - Lit!" MARGARITA MAY shouted out her well-known catchphrase again and the audience went wild and began to repeatedly chant, "Get Lit - Lit! Get Lit - Lit! Get Lit - Lit!"

BIG MONEY MIKE then turned to his other co-host and asked, "Who do you think the final two will be, TANG-TANG?"

"I agree with MARGARITA MAY! It's hard to tell right now! But I'll say this: The men and women in this contest today are tremendously talented and we need to give them all another round of applause for a hell of a show thus far!" TANG-TANG declared with admiration for all the rap artists who performed.

The audience cheered and applauded for several minutes, letting it be known that they too admired all the contestants who performed tonight.

When the third round commenced, the other matchup went before FRICTION and SILKY DREAM, giving him a little more time to ready himself. And he needed it too because neither he or C-DOG had heard anything back from KRINGLE yet and it was weighing heavily on his mind. He knew now wasn't a good time to worry, but he couldn't help himself. The thought of making it all the way to face LOUIE-V and lose because of a minor technicality was too much to handle.

By the time BIG MONEY MIKE called FRICTION and SILKY DREAM to the stage, him and his co-hosts critiqued them, and BABY DOLL came out and did the coin toss that FRICTION won, he'd put it all out of his mind to focus on his matchup. Choosing her to perform first, FRICTION observed the crowd's reaction as BIG MONEY MIKE signaled DJ RADIO-ACTIVE to begin her countdown. They clapped and shouted her name before her music began. The positive energy they had only told him it was going to be difficult to defeat her.

When her music started playing, she immediately began to shout her chorus: "SILKY DREAM LOOK SPORTY IN A DROP TOP! CASH FAT LIKE MY ASS – MAKE YA HEART STOP! ALL THESE DIAMONDS ON ME – I'M A ICE BOX! THEY ALL WATCH WHEN I MAKE MY PUSSY POP! AYE! PUSSY POP AYE! PUSSY POP AYE! THEY ALL WATCH WHEN I MAKE MY PUSSY POP!" she rapped twice while she danced sexually across the stage in a colorful bodycon dress for her energized concert goers.

When her routine was over, BIG MONEY MIKE shouted over the screaming and clapping audience, "I would pop it too if I had one! It would pop it till I'm told to stop it! What do you think, MARGARITA MAY?"

"Aye, that's my chick doing her! Pop it while you drop it baby! Like this! Meow!" MARGARITA MAY said naughtily as she bent down and popped it from the balcony seats.

"Do you wanna pop it, TANG-TANG? What do you think?" BIG MONEY MIKE asked him as the hyped-up crowd clapped and shouted their love for the firebrand radio talk show celebrity.

"When I pop it—and I make it pop baby! When I make it pop—you better get a mop! Splash! Taste the Tang!" TANG-TANG yelled to everyone in the theater and then dropped his microphone to signal he was done talking.

The fired-up crowd loved his response. They loved SILKY DREAM's performance too. So much, the CHEER-METER rose 8 out of 10 levels, leaving only a narrow shot for FRICTION to beat her.

Not letting her great performance make him a poor sport, he clapped for her too. Besides a little jealousy he felt, he didn't have any hard feelings toward her. In fact, he thought she was a very good rapper. She knew how to move the crowd and her overdeveloped body.

So, when the introductions for him were over and his countdown began, FRICTION stopped DJ RADIO-ACTIVE before he got to "One …" by shouting into his microphone, "Stop the count!"

Respecting his wish, DJ RADIO-ACTIVE stopped his countdown and FRICTION yelled out to the crowd, "I was gone rap another verse to my song JUS' BOOGIE, but I see I got some real competition now—and she's sexy as hell to top it off! So, I'm gone show all y'all up in here my flow skills on the mic! I want DJ RADIO-ACTIVE to play any beat he chooses and switch it up as many times as he likes fa my two minutes! If y'all wanna hear it, let me hear y'all say hell yeah!"

Some of the crowd shouted, "Hell yeah!"

Seeing FRICTION was exciting the audience, BIG MONEY MIKE further intensified their mood by declaring, "What FRICTION want to do for you guys is unprecedented! Did I hear some folks say hell yeah?"

This time, a lot of the crowd yelled, "Hell yeah!"

To hype up the audience even more, BIG MONEY MIKE shouted very loudly into his microphone, "I can't hear you!"

The over-excited crowd went hysterical and began to chant, "Hell yeah! Hell yeah! Hell yeah!" repeatedly.

Once he felt they were revved up enough, BIG MONEY MIKE signaled for DJ RADIO-ACTIVE to restart the countdown. After the DJ got down to one, he began playing a popular song's instrumental and FRICTION began to freestyle—which is rapping lyrics off the top of his head while he performed across the stage. When the beat changed, so did the style of the rap flow he used. He kept his words clear and coherent, not once twisting any up. He was in a zone of his own.

When the music finished playing and he stopped rapping, he also snapped out of his deep state of concentration and noticed the crowd was in a frenzy. They cheered louder and clapped harder than ever before. They cheered so loudly—the CHEER-METER rose an impressive 9 levels out of 10. His freestyle rapping had earned him the praise of everyone in the theater—all except LOUIE-V.

When the third round was over, he was one of the remaining two contestants who the audience was going to decide was the winner of the RAP or DIE contest. Words couldn't express the happiness he felt inside, but he could've enjoyed it more if only KRINGLE would call one of them. All he could think about was winning the money round and not having the music to face LOUIE-V for the finale. When he walked offstage until the fourth round started, he couldn't think of one solution to solve his dilemma.

To introduce the fourth round, BIG MONEY MIKE shouted into his microphone, "We're finally here! I hope everyone here tonight is enjoying this spectacular show! We started off with enough talent to open three record labels, but now we're only down to two rappers! Only you—the audience—can decide who the winner is! Only your cheers will claim the victor! Only your cheers will make somebody's dream come true!"

He remained silent while the crowd cheered and clapped with elation for such a lively event. When they calmed down, he called FRICTION and "GUTTA"—the remaining two rappers to the stage. Each one came out and waved at the audience. And to show their appreciation for a such a great contest, the audience applauded each rap artist as they came out. They felt all sixteen artists poured their hearts and souls into their music, making it a unique display of creative showmanship of the art.

Standing side by side with only a couple of feet between them, BABY DOLL walked sexily back onstage and stood next to the two finalists. Each rapper was anxious and nervous. Each one had their eyes fixated on the CHEER-METER.

When BIG MONEY MIKE shouted GUTTA's name, the crowd cheered and rose the CHEER-METER 8 levels out of 10. His very pleased smile revealed a mouth full of gold teeth that sparkled from the many shining lights around him. Having beaten his competition by high marks on the CHEER-METER all three rounds, GUTTA knew he had the competition in the bag. He performed three different songs to make sure.

When BIG MONEY MIKE shouted FRICTION's name, time began to move in slow motion while he waited for the crowd's reaction to his overall performance in the contest. Small beads of sweat began to form on his forehead and his body began to perspire as his heartbeat sped up with excitement. With his adrenaline pumping in overdrive, the massive amounts of cheers and claps from the crowd made him feel on top of the world. Not knowing how high the meter's levels would light up, he nervously watched the CHEER-METER slowly rise to 9 levels out of 10!

FRICTION did it! He won $100,000 and now had the opportunity to sign a record deal with a well-known independent record company! The only person stopping him was the man who created the RAP or DIE contest—hometown favorite rapper LOUIE-V. Their rap messages were quite different from each other. LOUIE-V rapped mainly about the lavishness and luxuriousness that comes with having a lot of money. FRICTION, on the other hand, rapped about clubbing and partying with fun-loving women. Both rappers were very good, making it an unforgettable matchup.

The audience knew it as well. The screams and cheers from the fans were now deafening—it was almost louder than the music that was being played for the event. Everyone who paid and expected a good time got more than their money's worth and appreciated the truly memorable experience.

Stoked about FRICTION's win as well, BIG MONEY MIKE calmed the amped up audience down only to re-energize them by shouting into his microphone, "The winner of this year's first RAP or DIE contest is the one ... the only ... FRICTION! I want the audience to show him the love he deserves! Get up! Get up out ya seats right now and let him hear it! Yeah, that's right! Make some damn noise up in here! Did the winner deserve it, MARGARITA MAY?"

"Hell yeah! He took on everybody he had to face and won it! I thought his freestyle was dope too! His final opponent GUTTA was tough as hell to beat! He showed everybody up in here he's the real thing! Cheers to you!" MARGARITA MAY shouted into her microphone while she held up her margarita glass to toast to FRICTION and his victory.

Turning to address his other co-host, BIG MONEY MIKE asked, "TANG-TANG, do you feel FRICTION earned his spot as tonight's winner of RAP or DIE?"

TANG-TANG swiftly replied, "He sure did, BIG MONEY MIKE because he separated himself from the rest of his competition! He made each one Taste the Tang baby! Now he's got to beat LOUIE-V to take it all! With no disrespect to LOUIE-V, I believe FRICTION's gone give him a run for his money! I see you FRICTION! You making sure we all do!"

BIG MONEY MIKE was about to get the electrified audience ready for the main event of the show when he was alerted by text on his smartphone of an important message from the event coordinator. Not believing the text at first, he thought it was some sort of joke, but it wasn't a prank at all. The text read: MACK DADDY is here and is seated in the next balcony over! His people want his presence publicly acknowledged and some interview time. We've already agreed, so please engage him. MACK DADDY, here tonight! UNBELIEVABLE!!

When BIG MONEY MIKE looked over at the balcony next to him, he saw MACK DADDY and waved for him to join him and his co-hosts. Since LOUIE-V and his entourage left to go to the stage for the finale of the contest, there was more than enough available space to accommodate MACK DADDY and his group. When he informed his two co-hosts who was in the theater and was coming to talk to them, they were both shocked at first and then became very excited at the possibility of the BOOTH OF TRUTH getting a live interview with the veteran rap star icon.

Several minutes later, BIG MONEY MIKE was greeting MACK DADDY at their balcony. The famous rapper was dressed to impress from head-to-toe in all white top-of-the-line designer fashion from France. The hat, jacket, sweater, jeans, and shoes combined easily cost over $35,000—his jewelry was easily worth fifty times that amount. In the league of heavy hitters, he was the Hank Aaron of rap.

Knowing the audience was going to absolutely lose their freaking minds, BIG MONEY MIKE eagerly shouted into his microphone, "Ladies and gentlemen, we have been blessed tonight with the presence of one of the most famous and successful rappers in our modern era! Coming to us all the way from Atlanta is the multi-platinum selling, multi-Grammy winning rap recording artist MACK DADDY!"

The crowd went hysterical when one of the spotlights zeroed in and shone on him! His diamonds shimmered brilliantly from his body as he stood up to address them. Wearing designer shades to cover his eyes, he waved to all his fans, making sure each direction got equal attention. His presence tonight was unexpected yet exhilarating.

When most of the attendees calmed down, BIG MONEY MIKE curiously asked the legendary rapper, "We all wanna know MACK DADDY, what brought you all the way up here to Milwaukee? We all love you—don't get me wrong, but this is a total mind blow to everybody in here tonight! Fa real, my mind is totally blown right now!"

Taking his cue to speak, MACK DADDY addressed the pumped-up audience by shouting into his microphone, "What's up, Milwaukee! I came here tonight to support the RAP or DIE contest! This is a great event, and this wonderful city deserves more like it!

Don't mind me y'all, I'm a spectator too! Just sit back and enjoy the rest of the show—forget I'm even here!"

Laughter circulated around the audience—followed by claps and fans screaming. Everybody loved MACK DADDY because he had a swagger about him that made people genuinely want to befriend him. He'd never been chased out of music events like some of the other rappers or been known to disrespect people for no apparent reason. In fact, everyone who'd ever met him always speaks about how kind and generous he is. He was a rapper others should take notes from.

After a few more waves to his adoring fans, he humbly sat down and readied himself to watch the finale of the show. MARGARITA MAY and TANG-TANG looked at each other, then they both looked at him and slyly looked back at each other again. They grinned like their morning radio show was going to have a lot of entertaining juicy gossip about MACK DADDY and LOUIE-V. One of the main topics being: Why did a mega-rich rap artist who sells out arenas with twenty-thousand or more fans come to visit a contest all the way in Milwaukee, WI, inside a theater with only a little over two-thousand people?

As BIG MONEY MIKE proceeded with the final round of the contest, FRICTION was in the back pacing back and forth. He was visibly worried until C-DOG ran up to him smiling with his phone in his hand. Hoping it was the good news he was waiting for, he readied himself for the worst anyway. When his homie began to speak, FRICTION closed his eyes and listened.

"KRINGLE just sent me the music file! He got a female R&B vocalist named 'Ya-Ya' singing throughout it and it sounds dope! Listen to it and see if you feel it!" C-DOG exclaimed eagerly as he passed his phone to him.

After listening to three minutes of the music, FRICTION smiled like he had the perfect lyrics for it. He quickly told C-DOG to take the music to DJ RADIO-ACTIVE before the final round started. Without a word, his homie dashed off toward the DJ stand and began talking to him. When C-DOG completed his task, he sprinted back over to FRICTION and yelled, "We good! Do you have any lyrics to go with KRINGLE's new beat?"

"I got the perfect lyrics! KRINGLE plugged me! The female singer is dope too! He's a musical genius!" FRICTION shouted with true respect.

"So, what's the song called?"

"WHAT U WANT. That's the title of this song. I hope the women in the audience agree with my message."

"They gone love it, bro. You got a vibe that appeals to everybody. Yo, the finale's about to begin!" C-DOG yelled excitedly to his homie.

"I know we lied and said you was my hype man, but I really need one. You down?" FRICTION asked him with a smile.

"Fa real? Hell yeah. You sure?" C-DOG asked him.

"I need you. I know LOUIE-V's type. He gone flood the stage with his crew and make it a big-ass party. It's a wrap if I come out alone," FRICTION assured him.

"Then count me in," C-DOG said and gave FRICTION a strong hood handshake as he heard BIG MONEY MIKE start the last round announcement.

"This is it folks! We watched and listened to sixteen of the best rappers from all around come to Rap or Die! Now there's only one. One left to claim himself worthy enough to take on one of Milwaukee's best rappers! Let's give the man his well-earned respect! Coming to the stage—FRICTION!"

The crowd clapped and screamed his name excitedly when him and C-DOG walked onstage. Feeling their love and support, FRICTION waved and smiled at his newfound fans. The feeling of being accepted for being himself gave him joy beyond words. He wished the moment would never end.

Once the cheers and claps from the audience settled down a bit, BIG MONEY MIKE yelled, "I see FRICTION made a few new friends up in here! But now, coming to the stage, is one of Milwaukee's Most Wanted men! He's the rapper whose song is playing daily on all your favorite radio stations! His music video is everywhere they're televised! He's adored by millions of fans! He's the brother who put together this mother! I want all y'all to make some real noise up in here for LOUIE-V!"

There was pandemonium from the crowd!

Then suddenly, all the lights shut off in the theater for several heart-racing seconds before a lone spotlight shone on a thirty-foot tall "One-Hundred Dollar Bill" that slowly came down from the ceiling. As soon as the very large bill touched the stage's floor, the music to LOUIE-V's single release "Dollaz" started playing and a spectacular lightshow began. Once the audience was transfixed by the spectacular pyrotechnic and light show, LOUIE-V tore through the fake money rapping the chorus: "I'M A GOON ABOUT MY DOLLAZ! I'M A LOON ABOUT MY DOLLAZ! I'M COMING SOON ABOUT MY DOLLAZ! MY DOLLAZ … DOLLAZ … DOLLAZ! I'LL BUST STRAPS ABOUT MY DOLLAZ! WRITE RAPS ABOUT MY DOLLAZ! TRAVEL MAPS ABOUT MY DOLLAZ! MY DOLLAZ … DOLLAZ … DOLLAZ!" with his entourage behind him throwing dollar bills across the stage and into the crowd.

Not wanting to be overshadowed by LOUIE-V's high-budget performance, FRICTION and C-DOG nonchalantly walked backstage. They knew this was his event and now they knew who was going first. There wasn't BABY DOLL, a coin toss—nothing. Instead of feeling upset about the favoritism being shown for his opponent, FRICTION chalked it up as that's the way it goes. The man with the most money will always have the advantage.

While he was trying to come up with an idea that would give his performance a chance against one with stage props and special effects, his phone began to ring. When he looked at it and saw it was Celestia calling, he smiled and answered it. Somehow, her call made his stress level lower dramatically. She knew how to make him feel happy—even when the feeling was currently miles and miles away.

"What's up Celestia? I thought you was comin' to the show! I'm glad you didn't waste the trip because my competition is throwin' a full-blown concert fa his turn! "At least I won a nice amount of money to help me and my family get on our feet!" FRICTION shouted over LOUIE-V's music with an artificial cheerfulness, trying to not to show his deep disappointment.

Sensing his depression, Celestia said, "What are you talking about? I've been here since the show started. I don't want you to freak out or anything because I already know I'm an impulsive person and I am going to seek counseling for it one of these days."

"OK, slow down. I don't understand."

"Well, I knew I wanted front row tickets and then I realized I'd be sitting all alone, so I went over to your house to tell your mom what you were doing tonight."

"Wait a minute. What? My mom?"

"Yeah, your little sister heard me talking to your mom and wanted to come too, so I bought all of us front row tickets and we've been cheering for you since the first round! Please don't be upset with me!"

"Upset? Fa real? My mama and sister here? You don't know how good that makes me feel to hear that! I thought it was only me and C-DOG here!" FRICTION shouted happily.

"We're all here—for you! Your mother wants to speak to you! Hold on!" Celestia yelled before getting off her phone.

When Celestia gave it to his mother, the first thing she did was shout, "It's too loud in here! I can't even here myself speak! So, this is what you like to do?"

"This is what I *love* to do, Mama," he told her without hesitation.

"Then come out here and win this contest! I don't give a damn what this rapper is out here doing! Win it if this is what you love to do! I love you, Malik … I mean FRICTION! Win!" his mother told him with tremendous inspiration.

In the background, he thought he heard his little sister Ki-Ki yelling, "Win! Win! Win!" repeatedly.

"I love y'all too!" FRICTION told her before she gave the phone back to Celestia.

"I thought it would be nice if me and your family came to support what you're doing. It makes all the difference in the world," she believed sincerely.

"It does," FRICTION agreed with deep appreciation.

That's when he heard the music stop and BIG MONEY MIKE called out his name. After realizing he was being called to perform, he immediately got off the phone and walked back onstage with his best friend C-DOG by his side. They were both nervous and excited at the same time. This was the finale of the show—it was all or nothing.

As soon as they stepped on the stage, the ecstatic crowd greeted them with long claps and loud screams. Before DJ RADIO-ACTIVE played FRICTION's final song, the rapper took his microphone and shouted, "Before I begin, I want to thank y'all—this wonderful crowd! Y'all accepted and embraced me! I wouldn't have made it this far without y'all! Y'all gave a Black man who was in a prison cell a couple of weeks ago a chance to chase his dream! Somewhere in the front row is my mom, sis, and my very special friend Celestia. Can we put a spotlight on the front row please?"

Honoring his request, a spotlight turned on and slowly went across the entire front row until FRICTION shouted, "Stop, there they are! Ma, Ki-Ki, and Celestia, could you please come up here and join me fa my last song?"

The crowd cheered and applauded as the three were ushered to the stage by the theater's staff. When they reached the stage, FRICTION walked over and gave each one a hug. Celestia's was a little longer than the others because he deeply appreciated her for bringing his family to the show.

"Thank you," he told her from the bottom of his heart and kissed her cheek.

"What's wrong with my lips?" she asked playfully.

"Nothing at all," FRICTION said passionately and kissed her gently on her lips onstage in front of over 2,000 screaming fans.

After his romantic kiss, and before BIG MONEY MIKE signaled for the DJ to play his song, FRICTION looked around at the entire audience and yelled, "This song is entitled: WHAT U WANT! I dedicate it to all the women around the world! Especially, my three favorite women right here! Press play DJ RADIO-ACTIVE!"

When the song came on, the music had a party feel that the crowd began to nod and groove to. When the female vocalist began to sing the lyrics, "I KNOW JUST WHAT U WANT! I KNOW JUST WHAT U WANT! I KNOW JUST WHAT U WANT! I KNOW JUST WHAT U WANT!" FRICTION followed with some of the realest lyrics about what a woman wants from a man he'd ever wrote.

He wanted men to truly feel the message he was sending to women. This was his way of letting women everywhere know that he understood their pain and struggle when it comes to finding a good man. He wanted them to know that he appreciated them. That he knew a "woman" was God's most precious gift.

When he finished rapping, everyone inside the Riverside Theater was standing on their feet and giving FRICTION a standing ovation. The CHEER-METER went to the highest level of 10 and remained there for well over five minutes as screams and chants of "FRICTION! FRICTION! FRICTION! FRICTION!" reverberated throughout it. Not even caring if he won anymore, he hugged his favorite females again and gave his homie a grateful hood hand-shake. Then, with the pose of a champion, he raised his microphone with both of his hands in the air and held it up proudly. The crowd continued with their standing ovation.

BIG MONEY MIKE, MARGARITA MAY, and TANG-TANG were also applauding FRICTION's performance before BIG MONEY MIKE grabbed up his colorfully lit microphone and yelled into it, "Ladies and gentlemen, your cheers have said it all! FRICTION has defeated LOUIE-V and won the RAP or DIE competition! Give him a strong round of applause!"

Upset by what he heard from backstage, LOUIE-V and his entourage marched back to the stage and took it over. LOUIE-V stared at the packed crowd spitefully and yelled furiously into his micro-phone, "Is y'all fa real right now? He was better than *me*? That whack-ass song wasn't better than mine! This nigga ain't better than me!"

As members of LOUIE-V's entourage started frowning at FRICTION and C-DOG like they wanted to harm them, FRIC-TION's mother began to feel afraid and wanted to protect him, so she walked over and stood closely by him. Celestia and Ki-Ki soon followed suit by standing by his side as well. C-DOG locked eyes with his homie to silently say it was on and popping if anybody make a move. Some members of the audience began to boo the intimidation tactics by LOUIE-V.

"What? Boos? I'm the one who put this entire event together! Do any of y'all know how much this shit cost me? This my shit! How the hell y'all gone boo me!"

That's when LOUIE-V's microphone was cut off and MACK DADDY stood up to speak. Soon after, a large spotlight shone on him and he yelled into the microphone BIG MONEY MIKE handed him, "Enough! Now you gone beat the winner up because you lost! The thought never crossed your mind even once that you might lose! We all lose at some point! We lose love! We lose money! We lose years! Nigga, we lose lives! I came here today to see what type of man you are and I still ain't seen one! So, I'm standin' right here tonight to announce that I'm gone dedicate a whole new album with six single releases dissin' this goofy-ass nigga! Yo, FRICTION! Would you do a verbal agreement right now in front of all these witnesses to sign with my label ROLLS ROYCE RECORDS for a five-year contract with a million-dollar advance?"

All eyes in the theater turned to FRICTION. Stunned by the famed rapper's business proposal, he looked over at his mom and then replied in his microphone, "Yes! Yes, I would! I'd be honored to be down with yo record label!"

The crowd screamed and applauded for him. They were emotionally moved by it all. It was a night none of them would ever forget. It was a momentous occasion that undoubtedly helped immortalize the heart, soul, and love of urban rap music.

Still upset he was unable to operate his microphone, LOUIE-V threw it hard on the stage floor and stormed off it with his disgruntled entourage following behind him. He'd had enough of being upstaged by MACK DADDY and FRICTION. As far as he was concerned, he had better things to do with his time. He considered the event over.

When FRICTION saw LOUIE-V leave bitter from his defeat, his mood to fight was replaced with wanting to celebrate. DJ RADIO-ACTIVE began to play WHAT U WANT again, and everyone started dancing to it and enjoying his victory. He even waved for the audience to come onstage and party with them. People flooded onto the stage and began to congratulate him. A large crowd of people even hoisted him into the air a few times!

It was a moment he'd cherish forever.

EPILOGUE
ONE YEAR
LATER...

The hood was full of life and so was the weed house BONE and SQUEAK was hustling out of. Everybody in the area wanted the premium "Chemdawg" marijuana they were selling. It was for the lowest price money could buy. At least one-hundred people per day showed up to buy 3.5 grams for $40, making it the most popular weed house around. It was enjoyed so much by the weed smokers in the community, everybody who shopped with them had nothing but positive wishes of longevity for the prohibited business.

The fact they were in the neighborhood they were raised in and knew mostly everyone who lived there could've been the main reason people felt protective or it could've been because everyone knew it was one of LOUIE-V's spots—one of the many trap houses he had throughout the city. Either way, they made their money there without any outside problems and a lot of money was being made. Thanks to LOUIE-V, life was really good for the pair.

All he wanted was for them to pay back what they owed, and they did. That act of being responsible for their own actions catapulted the way they were viewed by him. There was now much more respect and trust. That's all he truly wanted, people around him who had his respect and trust.

LOUIE-V promised himself a long time ago that he would never forget where he came from. Maybe that could explain why he never felt dependent on the rap game to survive. For some folks, rapping is all they've got. Without it, there's nothing else to fall back on. He knew that wasn't the case with him. He always made money, ever since he was selling cups of Kool-Aid to back-alley mechanics for a quarter at seven years old.

So, when he stopped in through the back door to make sure things were running smoothly, only the amount of money being made from his weed was his primary concern. Yeah, he was still having a hard time getting over the fact that his option wasn't renewed with BIG DOE RECORDS, but he couldn't let it be the end of his life. He'd also lost his business manager and music agent when his full album release was shelfed. The label claimed it was due to budget difficulties, something he knew was total bullshit.

LOUIE-V felt the real reason he was snubbed was because MACK DADDY had launched a full assault against him like he'd promised he'd do. Six singles were released with full media and marketing campaigns behind them. Millions were spent dissing him and the label, making it one of the most expensive "diss rap" projects in rap. What really ate at LOUIE-V the most was that MACK DADDY's last single for the album was currently in satellite radio rotation and he didn't even have the financial backing to lyrically fight back.

When he walked into the living room, he noticed there were several young workers coming in and out of the house to pick up weed and drop off cash. The youths ranged from twelve to seventeen years old. He knew them all from the neighborhood, so he showed them some love with a head nod, and they all spoke back respectfully. Peeping the young group in his spot was a bit large, he became concerned about unwanted attention.

So, when LOUIE-V sat in a chair at the kitchen table with BONE and SQUEAK, he told them, "All these shorties gone make my trap hot."

Not wanting to piss off their homie and boss, BONE told him, "They not wild. They put in work on the corners and in the alleys. They steer the traffic away."

"That's cool. They still too deep in here," LOUIE-V explained as he turned on a nearby stereo player to hear some music.

"No problem, they stay outside then. I can't wait to see the look on everybody face when yo new album come out! Fuck BIG DOE RECORDS! Yo record label gone be on the next level!" SQUEAK assured him. He was grateful and honored to be allowed to help build it from the ground up.

"No cap. I'll be back with some new music fa they ass real soon," LOUIE-V promised more determined than ever.

While they were talking about the business plans for MONEY MACHINE RECORDS, FRICTION's song TEASE began to play on the radio. Reacting as if he'd heard it a hundred or more times, he frustratingly turned it off. From experience, he knew the rapper was busy promoting his second single release for his upcoming album. His first single "Jus Boogie" went all the way up to 3 on Billboard's HOT 100 and charted for eight weeks before it fell. LOUIE-V knew how the game went, so he didn't hate on FRICTION's success.

It still didn't mean he wanted to hear him playing everywhere he went though. Continuing with their discussion about when the new label will open for business, he casually detailed his strategy to do it while they smoked a blunt. LOUIE-V knew it wouldn't be long before he was back in business because of his determination to succeed. It all boiled down to being patient while making his opportunity for a comeback.

About a block from the weed house, a man in a wheelchair slowly rolled his way to it. About midway there, it was stopped by a teenager about fourteen years old. He'd been told by his employer BONE to keep the traffic away from the house and he intended on doing what he was being paid to do. As far as he was concerned, that meant the handicapped and disabled too.

"Aye! You headed to that trap right there, ain't you?" the kid asked the man.

"I heard they had the best weed," the nappy bearded man in the wheelchair answered.

"Yeah, they do. I work for 'em. What you need?" the kid asked as he fidgeted around in his jogging suit's jacket pocket and pulled out a sandwich bag full of $10 bags of premium weed."

"That's the thing little homie. I figured they might have some rocks too. I really could use a hit," the man in the wheelchair told the youngster as he shooed away a couple of flies.

"Oh, you want some drop. Sorry buddy, I only got gas fa sell. There's a crack house a few blocks down the street, but I don't know if they play niggas or not. You sure you don't wanna sack or two of this loud?" the kid asked again as he waved a couple of small bags of marijuana in the man's face, so he could smell it.

"I hope it's one over there. I'm already hot and tired. I don't wanna waste my time," he said skeptically.

"Fa real. It's a trap over there because my cousin hustle there. They got all kinds of pills, powder, hard, meth, fenny … whatever you need as long as you got the paper to buy it," the kid told him.

"I hope you ain't on some bullshit. The shit's dry as hell. Ain't nothin' but garbage floatin' around," the man explained as his craving to get high on cooked cocaine became stronger.

"My word to God. I can call and let bro know you on the way. Gimme a minute," the kid reassured him and pulled out his smartphone to contact him.

"Good lookin' out. You a cool little homie," the man expressed to him with sincere appreciation.

"Honestly bro, you don't look too much older than me. Yo beard is wild as fuck and you need a barber who ain't got shit else to do all day, but I bet $10 you in yo twenties. I see you in a Bentley. But fa real though, how long you been in that wheelchair?"

"My whole life."

"Hold on a minute. Aye cuz, what you on bro … got some bread fa you … hold on, cuz. Damn, yo whole life. Sorry to hear that dog. I'm back, cuz…," the kid said as he switched his conversation back and forth between both parties.

"Make sure you don't take yo life fa granted. The wrong choices can leave you way worse than me, little homie. Be the best you can be and leave all that dumb shit alone," the wheelchair-bound man told him wisely.

"It's all about the paper with me. Hey cuz, I got somebody who need you … some work … hold on, cuz. Like I was saying, I ain't got time to do dumb shit," the kid told him and pulled out a large knot of cash.

"I'm glad to see you at yo money. Smoke weed if you gone get high. You look too smart to have my kind a monkey on yo back," the man stated, then showed off his outdated clothes and worn-out gym shoes.

"No monkeys fa me. I want a mansion and a yacht. I don't smoke weed or squares. Gimme a second. How far away are you … oh, you close … OK. One. Aye bro, what's yo name? the kid asked him curiously while feeling pleased with his ability to hook the handicapped man up with the drugs he wanted.

"Gerald," he told him honestly.

"His name Gerald and he on his way…. Give dude a minute because he in a wheelchair…. Fam said he been in it his whole life … I know you don't need no problems cuz, bro cool," the kid replied with certainty about Gerald after talking to him.

When the kid ended his call, he looked at Gerald like he should never doubt him again. He'd done what he said—proving he was a man of his word. Ever since he was eight years old, he was always told real men live by their word. It was something that meant a lot to him—wanting to be respected as a man of his word.

"Much love fa the lookout. I guess I'll buy some of that loud you got after all. Can I get a three fa twenty play?" Gerald tried to negotiate, trying to score an extra dime bag of weed.

"I can't. I gotta go straight up the ladder with this sack. I got you on my next sack though," the kid replied apologetically, giving him his word.

"I believe you, little homie. You know what? Fuck it, I still want it. And thanks again fa the call to yo cousin fa me," Gerald told him with much appreciation while he held out a $20 bill.

"You remember the way?" the kid asked as he took the money and placed it amongst the twenties in his wad of cash, then he gave him the weed he purchased.

Once he received his product, Gerald began to slowly roll away in the direction he was told to go and answered, "I remember the way."

While Gerald rolled to the house to buy his crack to smoke, he thought about when he went by the name TRIGGAH G. That led him to reminisce about all the good times and more so, all the terrible things he used to do with his homie MEAN-MUG. Every single time he pictured his face in his mind, the image of how he normally looked was always replaced by the images of his brutal death. Often, he tried to block out how he lost his best friend and the feeling in his legs, but it would always resurface and plague his dreams at night—turning them into horrible nightmares.

No question, the incident with LOS traumatized him. They left him bleeding out on the floor of SPIDER's garage. If it wasn't for LOS instructing SPIDER to call an ambulance after they left, he surely would've died. LOS also told him he could keep the four kilos of cocaine. He figured it was so he could look at it later and ask himself if it was worth it. He did too. Every night for months after he was released from the hospital and retrieved it. His depression about it became so severe, he stopped snorting it up his nose and started cooking it to smoke. Ten months later, the cocaine was gone but his craving to smoke it remained.

"That's the way it goes." TRIGGAH G sighed with tears forming in his eyes. He slowly rolled by LOUIE-V's weed house and continued down the street until he faded away in the horizon.

Meanwhile, in Paris, France, FRICTION was in his dressing room getting ready to open for MACK DADDY. With 25,000 screaming fans wanting to experience him and the ROLLS ROYCE

RECORDS lineup perform their best music live, he felt blessed to be part of something so big. Only a year ago, he was fresh out of prison and trying to figure out how he was going to survive. Now he was socking away large sums of legitimate money in his bank accounts and life was great.

He owed a debt of gratitude to MACK DADDY for signing him with a large advance and giving him a chance to prove himself. The opportunity was paying off because he generated enough streams to earn his second "Platinum" single release. His full album entitled "ONLY UP FROM HERE" was scheduled to be released in two months and had enough push in promotion to all but guarantee its success. Altogether, it put him in a position to make a lot of money with endorsements, touring, merchandising, etc.

With only C-DOG in the dressing room with him, FRICTION told him contently, "I still think I'm gone wake up and see this is all a dream. I can't believe we in France bro. We about to do a huge show in fuckin' France?"

"It still seems unreal fam," C-DOG admitted.

"We still got seven more countries to tour after this. I never thought I'd ever leave Milwaukee—now look at us. We gone see the world."

"Thanks again fa the plug with the permanent hype man gig."

"I couldn't have done this without you."

"This is crazy bro. All the love from the fans. And the women—I won't even go there. I got more female friends than ever now."

"Yeah, all the women. I bet Celestia thinks I slept with half they ass."

"She trust you, bro. I see how you two lovebirds look at each other when y'all on video chats. I miss you. No, I miss you. I miss you more. No, I miss you more. I miss you the most. No, I miss you the most. It's pathetic bro."

"To be honest, I wish she was here. I like having her around me—she's my good luck charm," FRICTION said with a warm smile as he thought about the woman he loved.

"Is she still meeting you in Sweden?" C-DOG asked as he checked his messages on his phone.

"Yeah, but that's six days from now. Until then, it's you and me bro."

"I got a text from MANIAC. He got three more men added to your security. I gotta tell ya, you a genius fa the advice you gave him to start his own private security company and then you would pay him to provide us with armed bodyguards. You gave him a new legit revenue stream that's easily worth two-hundred thousand a year. He got much love fa you."

"I owed him. He handled a problem fa me before it got out a hand. I know he wanted to manage my business affairs, but I needed a professional business manager with years of experience in the music business. That's why I signed a contract with EBI—a top-notch entertainment management firm. They have strong connections with all the gatekeepers throughout the music and film industry."

Taking the opportunity to change the topic, C-DOG stated, "Before I had this bro, I didn't see any other option fa me besides drugs. I knew I didn't wanna worry about money my whole life. I used to see those homeless people in the street with their handwritten signs beggin' fa change and I vowed it would never be me. I saw a lot of old people ass out bro. It's a scary thought—thinkin' you gone be old and broke."

"I think about it all the time too. Old and broke ain't cool at all," FRICTION agreed while he thought about his future.

"That's why I need to tell you about MOOCH. I want you to know why I don't talk about him," C-DOG took a deep breath and sighed.

"Look C-DOG, I know these streets will make you do things you never thought you'd do in a million years. You said MOOCH wasn't comin' back and I left it at that. I don't want to know what happened between you two. I only got one real homie left and I don't wanna lose you. Ain't none of us angels and ain't none of us perfect. I only wanna know one thing."

"OK. What is it?"

"Do you regret it?" FRICTION asked his homie.

"Every single day of my life."

"I would too. That's why we homies."

"Love bro."

"Much love bro.

As they were wrapping up a sentimental moment, there was a knock on his closed door. After FRICTION gave consent to open it, a stage handler poked his head in and said, "The show begins in twenty minutes fellas."

Saying nothing else, the two stood up from their leather chairs wearing expensive designer clothing and custom-made jewelry, so they could make their way to the stage. While their six-man security detail provided by BULLETPROOF SECURITY escorted the duo there, FRICTION heard the screams of 25,000 fans and went to greet them with his microphone and a heart full of happiness from living his best life.

The End.